THE BRIEFCASE

BY ARIE HOFFMAN
erikhoffman@live.com

PREFACE

When Arie Hoffman was a young boy in the late 1950s, his father Yanek Hoffman would regale him and his childhood friends with stories from the war. The stories both fascinated and scared them, but they were captivated and came back for more each week.

The stories, of course, were just that. Stories. Fables invented by a father to keep his son and his son's friends entertained and frightened. If they'd been able to look in the attic right over Arie's head as he slept each night, they'd have found that the stories weren't fables at all. Arie's father had done everything he said he'd done. But Arie didn't find that out until 2005 when his father was dead and Arie flew from London to Israel to clear the now vacant house. He found an old box in the attic, nailed to the wooden structure. The only way to open it was to break it off.

Inside he found a rusty 0.22 revolver, a dusty album and an old leather briefcase with some nasty Nazi publications, one of which he kept for a film he produced (Breathe Deeply My Son) in 2014 .

The infamous Nazi emblem was on the outside of the briefcase. On opening it, he saw the yellow patch Jews were forced to wear during the war throughout Nazi-occupied Europe. This was exactly what Arie's father had told them about. And when he opened the album, clearing away the dust accumulated over decades, he realised that those stories he heard as a child had not been the product of his father's overactive imagination. They were true.

It took a while for the shivers down his spine to cease. When they did, he knew he would not be happy until he had got to the bottom of the story. He needed to understand the things his father had done, and the impact they must have had on him. And when he had done that, he knew he had to take it further. This was a story the world must hear. As fascinating and bizarre a story as one can ever imagine.

PROLOGUE

16 MAY 1948 – TEL AVIV, ISRAEL

Fifty-six years before the robbery

Less than forty-eight hours ago, David Ben Gurion had declared the existence of the state of Israel. For the first time in nearly 2,000 years of persecution, hatred and murder, the Jewish people had a national homeland. People had danced in the street – but the hatred and the murder were not over. The Arab countries that surrounded Israel intended the new state's first day to also be its last. Bombs had hit power stations and Tel Aviv airport. The mortar fire was constant. Jews in Palestine had been the target of random attacks for months, but now the random attacks had changed to all-out war.

The brand-new state didn't yet have an army. But it had the Haganah and the Haganah had honed their paramilitary skills in the hardest schools, first fighting the murderous German state's determination to kill every Jew, and then resisting British attempts to prevent a Jewish takeover in Palestine. It seemed every man and woman of fighting age wanted to join. And they had one priceless advantage over their enemy in this independence war. The Arab states were divided among each other. Every Jew – not only in the Haganah but also in the whole new state of Israel – was united. They knew what the result of defeat would be. They had seen it in Germany, in Poland, in Czechoslovakia, in Ukraine, in Lithuania. Men, women and children slaughtered for no crime except being Jewish. They weren't prepared to see it here. Enough was enough.

Israel came into existence at midnight on May 14. On the 15th, it seemed everyone capable of firing a rifle or throwing a Molotov cocktail was on the front line defending their new homeland. Britain's Palestine mandate had come to an end and the British were sailing away, leaving behind them not just offices and a radio station but anti-aircraft batteries, heavy artillery and fortified sites. The Arabs wanted to get their hands on what the British had left – but so did the Jews.

#

Next day, the bombing, the shelling and the attacks from the air show no sign of slackening. In Tel Aviv transportation is impossible, not least because of what the attacks have done to the roads. With every new incursion, people disappear from the streets to hide in hastily constructed shelters. But not Yanek. 22 years old, Yanek survived the death camps. When the war was over, he threw himself into working for the creation of a Jewish state. It was dangerous work – his closest friend died doing it, and Yanek himself held onto life a number of times by what seemed no more than chance. He's got this far – he isn't going to be diverted from his path by the fact that people are still trying to kill him.

He takes his pistol. Just in case, he tucks a kitchen knife into his belt. And then he sets off to walk to Tel Aviv's Allenby Street.

#

Clambering over wreckage and finding a way round buildings in which volunteers with only buckets and a well are struggling to douse the fires, the journey takes almost two hours. By the time he reaches Allenby Street, night is falling. There's something devilish – infernal – about the sight of what had been one of the city's main shopping streets now lit in the dark only by flickering fires. But something is going on in number 44. He recognises Shlomo immediately. And Shlomo recognises him. 'Yanek! Thank God. Come and help me.'

'What are you doing?'

'I need to get this stuff out of the safe and hide it at home. Who knows what's going to happen in the next few days?'

Yanek takes the pistol from his pocket and points it at the ground. 'Shlomo. How can you live with yourself?'

'Yanek...'

'Any decent Jew would kill himself, knowing what you've done.' He points the gun at Shlomo's forehead. 'Fortunately, I am here to help you.'

'Yanek. Think what you are doing. The mitzvah places on Jews an obligation not to take revenge.'

Yanek smiles. There is no comfort for Shlomo in the smile. Shlomo says, 'Let's come to an arrangement. You take some of this for yourself.'

'No, Shlomo. Let's not do that. Let's settle things the way we have learned in these last years.'

The gun's report is loud, but it arouses no attention. Anyone within hearing distance has been listening to gunfire all day long. When Yanek walks out of the shop, as well as Shlomo's body he leaves the safe open and the boxes on view. Let someone have them whose need for money is greater. Yanek's need was for vengeance, and it has been satisfied. For now, at any rate. It will recur, and slaking it will be more difficult.

Because Shlomo was not the only wrongdoer.

CHAPTER 1

BUDAPEST 1941

Sixty-two years before the robbery

'Peter. You've known Christina since you were small. From now on, you will call her Mother. Always. You will forget you ever had another mother. If anyone asks you, you don't know what they are talking about. Christina is your Mama. Imre is your father. They will look after you.' And you were never in a synagogue in your life, she murmured to herself.

Christina wrapped her arms around Ilana. 'We'll keep him safe. Till you return. Both of you.'

Ilana shook her head. 'Jacob is in Auschwitz. He won't be coming back. I'm safe as long as I keep my job. But how long will that be? I was a chef at the Astoria Hotel before war came. The Germans kept me on when they made it their headquarters. But give it time and they will have their own people.' She squeezed out a smile. 'It will be a relief to no longer have to cook pork. And then I will be with Jacob in heaven and I will know, thanks to you, my children are safe. God bless you. We should not meet again. For as long as I can, I will go on taking food from the Astoria – that's how I've kept them looking well so far. But I won't knock on your door when I bring it. Leave a box by the back gate and I will put it in there.'

Then she went to another Roman Catholic family on the other side of the city and took Yudka through the same process. There. She'd done what she could for her children. Given them at least a chance. How much would they remember? They were so young – a year from now and they would have forgotten her. They would see the previously childless couples they now lived with as their real parents. They would think it had always been this way. They would learn to worship in the Roman

Catholic Church. They would be safe. As safe as it was possible to be with these German lunatics, at any rate.

A last kiss on the foreheads of her children, a last hug, and she was gone.

Germany 1944

Yanek Hoffman is a very strong 19-year-old, knows he should be dead by now and is prepared to do whatever he has to, to make sure that doesn't happen. In Yanek's case, what he has to do is serve the Third Reich as a labour camp kapo. He doesn't kid himself – if he doesn't do what his German captors tell him to do, his dream of a life stretching into the future will never become reality. He was born in Berehove in what is still Czechoslovakia, though it won't be for much longer, so as far as the krauts are concerned he's a substandard human in the first place. He is also a Jew, which in their view makes things many times worse. But he's strong, with the street smarts that come from never going to school and running away from home at 14 to join a gang that yielded to no-one in brutality and violence.

As a Jew from the occupied lands it was inevitable he'd be sent to a concentration camp. The Nazis' plans will end in the death of everyone there, but in the meantime they need to get the maximum output from all who are capable of working. 350,000 Czech civilians were sent to Germany as forced labourers during the war and the majority have not survived. Yanek intends to be one of the few who do and when the SS offered him the job of supervising his fellows he grabbed it. What was not to like? Kapos allow the system to operate with fewer SS personnel, and they are more likely to go on living as long as they never forget who is in charge. They eat better than the other prisoners and they have better living conditions. They have even managed to have photographs not only taken but developed and they have held on to them - but the performance demanded from the teams they supervise is always close to impossible and the slightest hint of failure could lead to a bullet in the head.

One evening, the day's work over and his evening meal eaten, Yanek is taking a stroll and enjoying a cigarette. He has saved the end of a loaf of bread and a piece of sausage and now he's looking for a female prisoner prepared to trade herself in exchange for more than she's been given to eat all day. He doesn't expect to wait long – finding a willing partner will be less difficult than choosing between the many who are likely to offer themselves. But when he turns to a woman with the bright yellow Star of David emblazoned on her chest who looks less emaciated than most because she has been here for only three weeks she spits on the ground. 'You should be ashamed. I hope you disgust yourself because you certainly disgust me.' He turns away. Let the hunger take its toll for another few weeks and she'll be on her knees, begging him. And that's how he'll take her.

Later, his lust satisfied with a woman who, if she felt disgust, kept it to herself he sits outside the hut reserved for Kapos, smoking and talking to his companions. 'What does she expect us to do? Almost everyone in this place is going to die. If we have the chance not to be among them, why the hell wouldn't we take it?'

The man beside him shrugs. 'Yeah. We do what we must. But one day we'll have our chance. One day Germany will pay for what it does now. All I want is to be there to help extract the payment.'

'That would be enough for you?' asks another.

'What more should I want?'

Yanek answers for the third man. 'Israel,' he says. 'A Jewish homeland in the place it was promised to us.'

'Dreams,' says the second man. 'Hopeless dreams that will never be reality. The Jews have wandered the earth for more than two thousand years and we are second class everywhere.'

#

Yanek's fellow kapo who had wanted only to live long enough to take revenge when Germany fell did not get his wish. His hopelessly undernourished crew lacked the physical strength to do the job assigned to them, and he couldn't muster the degree of nastiness that might have forced them. When they missed their target for the second day in a row, one of the guards took out his Walther PPK pistol and shot him dead. Then he split the crew into two and put half into Yanek's team as well as giving him a half share in the target.

Yanek was not going to make the mistake his colleague had made. When one of the prisoners was too weak to lift a spade, Yanek took the spade from his hand and clubbed him to death with it. He looked around at the rest of his crew, most of whom were by now so used to horror and so resigned to death that they registered no alarm. 'I've told you what you have to do. Do it. Or die right here, right now.'

But it couldn't go on. By the end of the year, the first Allied troops had crossed the German border. Hitler had risked everything on one last throw of the dice – an attempt to burst out in the Ardennes in what the Americans came to call the Battle of the Bulge. Battle hardened German troops scored early victories against American units only recently arrived in Europe but the Americans, the Canadians and the British had reserves to throw into the battle who had all the experience of their German opponents but were also well supplied through Arnhem, which the Canadians had fought like heroes first to capture and then to keep open. It was a fight that could end only one way. After that, five months of mopping up and saturation bombing ended with Hitler's suicide and the end of the war.

Twenty-seven years earlier, the war to end wars which had so spectacularly failed to live up to its name ended without foreign soldiers on German soil. This time was different. Germany was occupied. That would go differently for people in different places, with Germans in the Soviet occupation zone suffering far more than those governed by the Americans and

British. The worst punishment suffered by those in the French occupation zone was humiliation: the gloire of which the French were so proud had been shown for what it was, and the French would not easily forgive.

When the future became clear, the SS started to flee the camps. The Volkssturm who took their place were no substitute. They were too young, or too old, or disabled. Men who had been in no danger of conscription until all was obviously lost. They were incapable of controlling men like Yanek, they were badly armed and equipped, and the rations available to them were little better than the prisoners got. Yanek saw his chance. If the SS could leave, so could he. He sought out the woman who had rejected him with loudly expressed disgust, put her face down in the dust and took her in the most callous way imaginable. Then he strangled a sixty year old guard crippled by polio, took his handgun and a MP3008 submachinegun, and simply walked out of the gate.

CHAPTER 2

POLAND 1945

Fifty-eight years before the robbery

The Irgun, or Etzel, headed by Menachem Begin had been operating in Palestine since the beginning of the nineteen thirties. The British called it a terrorist organisation and its members would admit that it carried out terrorist acts. For example, it killed British servicemen sent to Palestine to enforce the League of Nations mandate, which said that Palestine was the home of the people already there: but the Irgun would say those deeds were necessary to achieve its aims. The organisation's full name was Irgun Zvai Leumi, meaning National Military Organisation, and that's how it saw itself. The nation it had in mind didn't yet exist and the Irgun saw its role as changing that. It wanted a homeland for the Jewish people, who would become the Jewish nation. The place it had chosen was Palestine, which God had promised to the Jews. If God had promised something, what man could say it was not to be? Certainly not some British soldier, who probably could not have found Palestine on a map before his government put him on a ship and sent him there.

Yanek was a villain, and he did not deny villainous acts any more than Etzel denied terrorist atrocities. But he was also a patriot. Not for Czechoslovakia, where he happened to have been born, and not for Ukraine, to which his birthplace had been ceded. He was a patriot for the Jewish people. A patriot for Israel. And so he sought out Etzel and was enrolled as a partisan. The job assigned to Yanek and his friend Zoltan was to obtain money and hand it to Etzel leaders in Paris. The money would make it possible for members of the Jewish diaspora in Europe to make their way to Israel. Yanek was more than ready to risk his life to make that happen. Their contact was to be a man called Shlomo.

The war was not yet over, and Poland was an occupied country. It would go on being occupied for decades, by the Russians and their puppets, but no-one knew that yet. For now, though for not much longer, the occupiers were still Nazi Germany and it was German rules people lived and died by. One of those rules was that Jews must identify themselves. If Yanek and Zoltan were caught without the yellow Star of David, they would be shot out of hand. But their task was to extract money from rich Russians, and they couldn't do that wearing the symbol of Jewish oppression. The Russians would laugh at them and then tell the authorities what they were doing. So they went about their business dressed in high-fashion clothes and carrying a briefcase. The briefcase bore Nazi Germany's "party eagle" which carried a swastika in its talons and, unlike the eagle of the German Empire that had gone before it, looked to its left instead of to its right. They were, in other words, soliciting money from rich and famous Russians on behalf of Nazi Germany, though they had no intention of letting Germany have any of it.

Why would rich Russians hand over their money and jewellery? First and most obviously, because they didn't want to be killed. Some would make a fight of it, but most people given the simple choice, pay up or die, will pay. Less obvious but just as important was the answer to the question: what were they doing in Poland in the first place? Russians belong in Russia. And the fact is that a rich Russian living in Joe Stalin's Russia would soon be the same as almost everyone else in that country. A poor Russian. But he would probably also be classified as a class enemy and his time on earth brought to a sudden end. They didn't want to be arrested by the occupying Germans, but they wanted even less to be sent back to their own country. And so they saw payment as the only way to retain both their freedom and at least some of their wealth. Yanek and Zoltan's job was to form a view on just how much any target could be persuaded to part with if squeezed really hard, and then to squeeze a little bit harder. They had no more time for Russians than for Germans. Germans now were trying to remove from the world every single Jew they could find there. Russians had been carrying out pogroms for centuries.

Sometimes, the rich handed over money without argument. Like American businesses who donate to both Republican and Democrat parties on the basis that one of them is going to win and the businesses want the winner's goodwill, they couldn't yet be certain how the war was going to end. But others refused to give, and in their case Yanek and Zoltan did whatever was necessary. If they had to beat someone up, they beat him, often within an inch of his life and once or twice beyond that limit. If a man could only be persuaded to hand over money when his wife's virtue was threatened, they threatened it. If a woman would only give her jewellery when they warned they would castrate her husband, they unbuttoned his trousers and brandished a cutthroat razor they carried for the purpose. And if the only thing that worked was a bullet, the bullet was fired.

#

The city of Lublin would be imprinted on Yanek's mind as long as he lived. When he brought them into Etzel, Shlomo had briefed them. 'You do understand what the Germans are up to? Yes? You should, considering where you've just been. They call it the Final Solution. If there's a solution, there must be a problem. So what is the problem?'

'Us,' said Yanek. 'The Jews. We are the problem.'

'We are the problem. Exactly. And the solution? The solution is our death. The death of all of us. You look at wars that have been fought in the past, you can go all the way back to the ancient Greeks, the Egyptians, what were they fighting for? Loot. Territory. And slaves. Everybody had slaves. The Arabs have been taking prisoners from Africa since time began. They didn't kill them – they made them work or they sold them to other people who made them work. All those princedoms in India with their fabulous wealth that the British stole from them – excuse me, the British "discovered" those palaces, those huge gold elephants, the jewels more perfect than anything anyone had ever made on those miserable islands off the coast of Europe. Those princedoms used slaves to build that wealth, the palaces, the elephants, the jewels. And when somebody stronger than you decides to discover what you thought was yours, it becomes theirs.

'Egypt was built on slavery. And so was everywhere else. William the Bastard had been promised the English crown when his cousin Edward the Confessor died. Another cousin, Harold, promised to support William but took the throne for himself. William the Bastard was a Norman. A Norse man. A Viking. His people already kept the French King in subjection and they did whatever they needed to do to extract tribute and keep the French under. You didn't break your word to a Viking and expect him to accept it. So William invaded, Harold was killed and William announced that he was king.

'Did he kill everyone? Of course he didn't. He killed exactly the number he had to. Because that's how war has always been. When you went to war and you won and so you had discovered all that new territory and all that new wealth that some poor schmuck used to think was theirs, you didn't kill everybody. You killed a few to make sure people knew what had happened to them. Who was now in charge. And what the result would be of trying to undo that. But you kept most of them alive. As serfs, which means as slaves. And you know the funny thing? The Normans who had taken over the English throne carried out a survey. A Domesday book. A list of every single place in their new kingdom. Who owned it. Who held it from them. What was there. And the book was full of slaves. The old British people, and the Anglo-Saxons who'd settled there years before, and the Vikings who came and went, all of them owned slaves. Men and women they'd captured in battle.'

Yanek had never been to school and he was getting tired of the longest lesson he'd ever had to sit through, in history or anything else. 'Okay, already,' he said. 'We hear you. Wars in the past were not meant to kill everyone. This one is different.'

'Yes, this war is different. And Germany is going to lose it. The Poles will do everything they can to take their country back. They'll lose. They don't have enough people on their side. Churchill doesn't care about the Poles. Roosevelt doesn't care about the Poles. Stalin, now – he cares about them. He wants them for his slaves. Why not? He's already got most of the Russian people. He won't call them slaves, of course. They'll be citizens. But citizen slaves.

'And we shouldn't care about the Poles, because they haven't exactly been our friends. The Germans have built five killing centres in Poland. They have others elsewhere – in Germany, obviously, but you know it's a funny thing about Germany. I'm damn sure the German people know what's been going on, but they like to act as if they don't. Hitler can't rely on his own German people helping him to kill Jews. But he can rely on the Poles. Knowing what's happening doesn't trouble them. They helped the Nazis build killing centres at Chelmno.

At Belzec and Sobibor. At Treblinka and Auschwitz. But there's another centre. Majdanek. The other six make no bones about it. People are sent there to die. Majdanek isn't so simple. That's where they send people who may be able to work for them before they are killed. It's an assessment centre, if you like. If they decide someone won't be able to work, they kill them right there. They shoot them or they put them in a gas chamber. And if they can work, they spare them for as long as that lasts. They don't feed them enough to live on so eventually they can no longer work and they, too, are shot or gassed. You know all that. You were Kapos in a camp that worked the same way. It will be over soon. What you need to know is that the camp is just outside Lublin. And there's a little nest of Russians in and around Lublin. They've been working a protection racket. If you were Jewish and you had enough money or enough jewellery, they'd move you around and keep you out of Majdanek until all the money and the jewellery was gone. At which point...'

'Bastards,' said Yanek. 'Murdering, thieving Russian bastards.'

'Exactly. And those Russians need to be dealt with. And they will be when the war is over and Poland finds out the Allies are going to sacrifice it to the Russians. In the meantime, that money and that jewellery was Jewish. Your task is to return it to the Jewish people. Every contribution you collect means more Jews in the Jewish homeland. Palestine.'

Zoltan said, 'Forgive me. But... You talked about the British "discovering" India when there were already people who thought India was theirs. Palestine. Aren't there people who think it's theirs?'

'If there are,' said Yanek, 'they are wrong. God gave Palestine to the Jewish people.'

'Yes, He did,' said Shlomo. 'From Dan to Beersheba. From the entrance of Hamath unto the brook of Egypt. That is the land of Israel. Anyone who came after is a usurper. They will be welcome to stay as long as they stay in peace, but it is not their land. It is ours. We were there first. Zoltan, you must decide. You are with us or you are not. You are in or you are out.'

Zoltan nodded. 'I am a Jew. The time for Jews to run and hide is over. We have lived as guests in other people's countries far too long and been unwelcome guests far too often. It is time to say, "Enough." If not now, when? I am in.'

CHAPTER 3

LUBLIN, POLAND 1946

Fifty-seven years before the robbery

Time after time, on visit after visit, they stuffed large amounts of jewellery and money into the briefcase and carried it away to hand over to Etzel. Every trip was another boatload of Jewish immigrants to Palestine. A swelling of Israel's Jewish population. Surely, God could only approve of what they were doing. But things didn't always go smoothly.

They'd been watching a particular house for days. According to Etzel, it was occupied by a Russian calling himself Ivan Majeskyi and his family, though in fact he was the sole remaining heir of a noble family closely related to both the dead Russian monarchy and the living British monarchy. His real name would have given him away and disaster would have followed. Like the Tsar and his family at the time of the Russian Revolution, his British relations had wanted nothing to do with him. They feared that his presence in Britain would remind people that the House of Windsor was no more British than the Bourbons or the Habsburgs.

The house stood some distance from any other building, surrounded by a high fence with a man in a little hut who opened the gate when someone wanted to come out or go in and closed it again afterwards. Some of those wanting to go in the guard clearly recognised and he opened the gate without hesitation. Others were put through a verbal examination. Sometimes it ended with the man opening the gate. Sometimes the man disappeared into the house; when he came out, he might open the gate or he might turn the visitor away. And sometimes the visitor was rejected without even the trouble of checking with whoever was in the house.

Most of those who came out were clearly and identifiably staff. Maids. Lackeys – they probably did jobs that had titles but for Yanek and Zoltan they were simply lackeys. A woman who looked as though she might be the housekeeper was always accompanied by a boy in his early teens. He carried empty bags and baskets when they left the house; when they returned, the bags and baskets were sometimes still close to empty. Poland was as short of food as anywhere in Europe. Twice in almost a week of watching, a young woman left on horseback with a mounted groom following behind. She carried herself with the assurance of knowing that anyone she spoke to would do her bidding and that no-one she did not speak to would be so impertinent as to start a conversation. As far as they could see, no word ever passed between the young woman and the groom.

It was 9.30 in the morning and they had waited long enough. The housekeeper and the boy had gone out; past observations suggested they wouldn't be back for at least two hours. The maid they had identified as a night-time worker had left and the three daytime maids had arrived.

Etzel had issued each of them with a .22 calibre revolver. Where they came from, who had first used them and how they came into Etzel's possession, they had no idea. Neither of them was any stranger to handguns. They kept them out of sight as they approached the gate. Yanek held up the briefcase to show the Nazi eagle. 'We have business with Pan Majeskyi.'

The gatekeeper did not look impressed. 'Is that right? But does Pan Majeskyi have business with you?'

'Would we be here otherwise?'

'If he expected you, I would have been told. I haven't been told, so he doesn't expect you. Leave.'

Gates can be a problem to the person guarding them because they can give a false idea of security. If the gatekeeper had known his business, he'd have stood further back. Zoltan's hand reached through the bars, seized him by the shirt and pulled him against the gate. Zoltan's physical strength far outweighed the gatekeeper's, and he was about to shout for help when a revolver appeared in Yanek's hand. 'The gate,' said Yanek. 'Open it.'

'I can't. It would cost me my job.'

Yanek might have admired the man's courage, but there wasn't time. You never knew who might happen along the street. He reached out, grabbed the key from the gatekeeper's belt, and unlocked the gate himself. Zoltan had to let go of the gatekeeper in order to follow Yanek through the gate, but when the man tried to run Yanek hit him hard across the back of the head with the butt of his revolver. He wasn't unconscious, but he was wobbling. Yanek said, 'Leave him in the bushes.'

'We can't. If he comes to he could give the alarm.' Zoltan pushed the man to the ground, pulled his jacket over his head, pressed his revolver against it and fired through the cloth. The man twitched and lay still. Zoltan saw the way Yanek was looking at him. 'What?'

'He was just a working man, Zoltan. Earning his daily crust. He didn't need to die.' And then he turned away. What was the point? What was done was done. 'Put that gun back in your pocket.'

They pushed the dead gatekeeper into his little hut, straightened their jackets and walked up to the door. Yanek rapped hard, three times, on the door that gleamed, a model of polished cleanness in a world so often soiled beyond hope. The door was opened by a man of about sixty in a butler's uniform. Yanek held up the briefcase once again. 'We are here to see Pan Majeskyi.'

'Is he expecting you? Do you have an appointment?'

'We represent the government of the Incorporated Eastern Territories. We do not make appointments. We are here to see Pan Majeskyi.'

The butler's expression could have meant many things. It could have meant that the Russians were on their way and the Incorporated Eastern Territories would not be incorporated for much longer. Or, if they were, it would be as the Incorporated Western Territories. It could have meant that the butler's employer had thrown better men than Yanek and Zoltan out of his house. It could also have meant that the butler had seen the bulges in the men's pockets and, after so many years of war and occupation, knew exactly what they were. In any case, he opened a door and showed them into a room. 'Wait here.'

Since leaving the camp and joining Etzel the two men had visited some remarkably wealthy homes, but this room was more magnificent than any they had seen. The eye was drawn first to a five-legged console that stood against the wall, a marquetry confection of a number of woods with an ebony veneer and a white opalescent top. Against the opposite wall stood a six-legged mahogany settee upholstered in silk damask – but what announced its importance most clearly was the hand-carved decoration featuring a phoenix and a firebird. Arranged as if in homage to the settee were five armchairs similarly carved and also upholstered in silk damask. All of this spoke of Mother Russia. Ivan Majeskyi, whatever his name might really be, had been able when he left his ancestral home to bring some quite remarkable pieces of furniture with him. But the porcelain could only be Chinese – and there was a lot of it. Highly decorated pots, vases and plates in such excellent condition they could have been new, but they could also be a thousand or more years old. How, in times like these, had the man ever been able to keep this treasure intact?

Beautiful though it all was, Yanek's attention was drawn by a series of three photographs in ornate silver frames. Each showed a woman and the woman was clearly different in each case, but it was equally clear that they were related. Grandmother, mother, daughter would be Yanek's guess, the daughter being the young woman they had seen ride out twice on horseback. What held him, though, was not their appearance, not their resemblance, not their haughty attitude that said the world and everything and everyone in it were there for their convenience. He took all of that as read. It was the way of this class. No, for Yanek the most striking thing about the photographs was not the women but the jewellery they wore – the same jewellery in each photograph. A four strand necklace of cream, gold, brown, grey and green pearls from the bottom strand of which hung an emerald pendant. And ear rings in which diamonds and amethysts were set in silver and gold. As a younger man, Yanek had known nothing about jewellery and had cared even less. These items still failed to excite any aesthetic pleasure in him. But it wasn't beauty he was looking for. It was value. And these two pieces between them would be worth a colossal sum.

He was still staring at the three photographs when the door opened and the butler returned in the company of two maids carrying trays from which they transferred to a marquetry table a pot of coffee, three porcelain cups and saucers that were almost translucent, a jug of cream, a sugar bowl, three glasses and a cut glass decanter containing a fluid on the cusp between ruby and brown. The maids left, the butler stayed and into the room walked a man who would have commanded attention anywhere. He gave his two visitors what could have been a nod and could have been a bow. He said, 'Gentlemen, my name is Ivan Majeskyi. I am told you wish to see me. But first…' He turned to the butler and the butler poured coffee and handed cups to Yanek, Zoltan, and Majeskyi. Then Majeskyi said, 'The port is rather good. If you would like…?'

Yanek could see that Zoltan was about to accept, but Yanek had heard all about the strength of port and how it could lull the unaware into error. 'Thank you,' he said. 'The coffee is all we need.'

'Then, please. Sit.'

He took one of the armchairs and Yanek and Zoltan sat on the sofa. The smile on Majeskyi's face said he knew why the two men were here. And Yanek knew it was likely he did – this was by no means the first Russian home in Poland they'd visited and they weren't the only Etzel agents doing it. Word gets around. You go to one home to get money and jewellery out of the owners and when you've gone they tell their friends about you.

Yanek said, 'You have brought some remarkable treasures from Russia.'

'Indeed. And you have brought a very handsome briefcase from Germany. But I don't believe you could get any of this porcelain in there. So why don't you tell me what you want? And why I should give it to you?'

'The answer to the second question is that you are going to need help sometime soon. We are losing this war. The people in France won't mind. They'll have their freedom back. The same goes for Denmark, the Netherlands, Italy, Belgium, Norway and Finland. But Poland won't be free. Poland will exchange one set of occupiers for another. I don't suppose life will be very good after that for the Poles. But it will be appalling for anyone the Russian government sees as its natural enemy.'

'You're offering me protection? A route out of here to the West?'

'That would be difficult to guarantee. Life will be chaos. But chaos is good for some people. People who need to get from one place to another in a hurry without being noticed. People who the invaders have not been told about in advance.'

'So that's what you're offering. I give you money and you don't sell me out to the rabble who now rule my country. Is that it?'

'Almost. Money is always welcome – of course it is. But money isn't always easy. And who knows what the money you give now will be worth when the catastrophe strikes?'

'So you suggest...?'

'Those photographs. I take it the youngest woman is your daughter?'

Majeskyi's face closed up. 'If you want my daughter, the answer is no. You will have to kill me and everyone else in this house before you can take that prize with you.'

Yanek smiled. 'What kind of animals do you take us for? It isn't your daughter we want. It's the necklace and earrings. You hand those over and we leave you in peace.'

'Those jewels have been in my family for ever. They were made for us, to my great-great-grandmother's own design. They are without price.'

'Nothing is without price. Especially in times of war.'

Majeskyi's torment was clear to see. A battle was going on inside his head. But Yanek and Zoltan remained silent. They'd seen this before. If they had to, they could take out their revolvers and move to the next stage. But they didn't expect that to be necessary. It was a matter of allowing Majeskyi time to face reality. To accept that he had no choice. Minutes went by in silence and then Majeskyi said, 'Wait here.' He left the room.

When he returned a few minutes later, Yanek stood up and opened the briefcase. Majeskyi held up the necklace and earrings so that his visitors could see they were what they were and dropped them into the briefcase. Yanek said, 'Thank you. Your contribution to the German war effort is gratefully accepted. You will hear no more from us.'

When they got outside, Zoltan said, 'How much do you think they're worth?'

'I have no idea. But it's a lot. One boatload of immigrants? Two? More? Who can say?'

CHAPTER 4

1946 LUBLIN, POLAND

Fifty-seven years before the robbery

Jewellery was also their prize the following day. As soon as they had been shown into a room in a second-floor apartment and seen the expression on the face of the woman there, they knew she had heard about them. From Majeskyi? Possibly. But there had been other victims who could also have told her. She said, 'I have almost no money left. But I do have these. If they will buy me a favour from you, take them.' And she placed on the table a pendant and a necklace.

Yanek picked up the pendant. The woman said, 'The stones are both garnets, nice to look at but no great value. The gold is 18 carat. What is striking is the cannetille work.'

Yanek had never heard the expression. 'Cannetille?'

'A design inspired by the embroidery on peasant garments. Portugal produced some, but the best came from India and India is where this was made.'

'Is it worth a lot?'

'What is a lot? In an honest sale, it would probably bring more than a labourer in a Polish coal mine could earn in the whole of his working life. The man who owns the coal mine would throw away twice that in an evening at the casino and scarcely notice it. But the necklace...' When Yanek picked it up, she went on, 'The stones are pink topaz. Pink topaz is rare in nature; when they found it in one of the topaz mines in the Urals, it was reserved for the imperial family. It is called imperial topaz for that reason. How this came into my family's possession is something I was never told. None of the stones is less than five carats. You can get topaz much larger than that, but not in pink. And see the setting – silver and intricate.'

Yanek said, 'You mentioned a favour.'

'I ran from the Reds. I am too old to run again. Too old, and too sick. I have prayed for death to come before the Russian army. If it does not, I have no doubt it will come very soon afterwards. But I'd rather die here, in my own apartment. Resting in my chair. As I am now. A bullet would do the job.'

'You want us to shoot you?'

'It would be a kindness.'

Yanek and Zoltan stared at each other. They understood what the woman was asking and they understood why she asked for it. When Shlomo had given them the revolvers, he'd also given each of them a small capsule. "If you are attacked, take as many Germans with you as you can. But you won't want to fall into their hands. If everything else fails, swallow that. I won't lie to you, you will feel pain, but you'll be dead inside a minute." Zoltan took his capsule from his pocket and looked at Yanek, an eyebrow raised. Yanek nodded. Zoltan handed the capsule to the woman. 'I won't shoot you. But swallowing that will have the same effect. But, please, have the grace to wait until we are out of the room.'

When she took the capsule from him, the woman placed her hand for a moment on top of his. 'You're not really Germans at all. Are you? But God bless you.'

Later, Zoltan said, 'When Shlomo told us what they wanted us to do, he talked about taking back Jewish jewellery and Jewish money from Russians who had stolen it. But those things the woman gave us today... The stuff we got from Majeskyi yesterday... They weren't like that. Those things had been in those people's families for years.'

'Does it matter? If it means more Jews get to Israel? If the new Jewish homeland becomes more able to defend itself and to grow, and if more Jews are able to live with honour and self-respect for the first time in 2,000 years, does it really matter?'

'No. I suppose it doesn't.'

#

The defeat of Germany didn't bring what they were doing to an immediate halt, because it took more than a year before Russia was able to subdue Poland completely. Poland was unusual among European countries in the number of Nazi collaborators it hunted down and jailed when the war was over. A lot of them lost their lives, and not always on the orders of the judge at their trial. Yanek and Zoltan saw a new group of people to target: Poles who had collaborated with the occupying Germans in rounding up Jews and sending them to the death camps. Why not? What better reason could they have for demanding money and jewellery with menaces? How many Jews had been killed by or because of these people?

They developed a sales line – a patter – that meant they didn't usually have to use violence, but when they did they told themselves that the people they hurt deserved it. Perhaps those who handed over precious belongings believed that they were buying themselves protection from the law. Perhaps they believed there was some underground organisation that would get them out of Poland to some safer place. Argentina may have been mentioned. When he was asked about it years later, Yanek would simply smile and say that anyone who ate with the devil needed a long spoon. 'They were all adults. They should have learned long before that promises need to be tested.'

Every extra donation they prised out of Polish hands meant more Jews on their way to Israel. It wasn't something they wanted to stop before they had to. One day in 1947, Zoltan said, 'Do you think someone is watching us?'

'I don't know. Why?'

Zoltan shrugged. 'It's just a thought. Not even a thought, really: more a feeling.'

'A feeling?'

'That I'm looking at a face I've seen before. Just fleetingly, it's in a crowd and it doesn't hang around and maybe I'm imagining it, but then I see it again. Or I don't see that face but I see another and I think, that one, too – I've seen it before. Maybe I'm wrong. Maybe I'm getting nervous.'

'And maybe you're not. Maybe time is running out for us here. Listen, that merchant we have down for tomorrow. Let's do that one and then call it a day. We'll take what we can get from him and give it to Shlomo and then we'll be gone. To Palestine. To a new life.'

Zoltan nodded. Yanek sensed his relief. He felt it himself. The years since they'd first been arrested by the Germans and thrown into a camp had been hard. Not just physically wearing for men who weren't given enough food to survive but also emotionally destructive. They'd held in their hearts for so long the dream of finding themselves Jews in a Jewish homeland, and now the dream was almost within their grasp. One more job for the benefit of other Jews and it would be time to make their own way to Palestine. Staying in Poland any longer would put them at risk of capture by the Russian military or the special units the Russians had set up for privates in the Polish army after they'd shipped the officers to Siberia. Yanek knew what those units were capable of. They acted just as he had acted in the camp – as Kapos, keeping the Polish people in subjection to Russia at whatever the price. Yanek with his experience could only admire their efficiency and it even crossed his mind to join them. But that would have meant staying in Poland and Yanek's determination to help build a Jewish homeland in Palestine was stronger than anything else.

As it turned out, for Zoltan it was one job too many. They arrived as so often before at the merchant's place of business just as he was opening. The way he looked at them should have been a warning. A sign that they were expected. And if the merchant expected them, wouldn't he have prepared? Yanek looked at the half-smile on the man's face. 'I think we should go, Zoltan.'

'Go? What do you mean, go?'

But Yanek was already turning away. 'Come on. Let's get out of here.' Moving at speed he was across the road and turning into a side street when he heard the shots. He looked back and saw Zoltan lying in the road. Yanek had seen death many times. Too many not to know the difference between a body where the soul is still in residence and one where it has left forever. He had no idea whether Zoltan was now in heaven or in hell but there was nothing he could do for him. And he was in no doubt: if he didn't take to his heels right now, wherever Zoltan was, he'd be joining him.

CHAPTER 5

1947 TIME TO LEAVE POLAND

Fifty-six years before the robbery

This visit to Shlomo to deliver jewellery was unlike all the others. In the past, Yanek and Zoltan had shown a certain swagger. A pride in what they were doing and in what they had done. A knowledge they shared with Shlomo of the fruits of their work. The thousands... perhaps tens of thousands? Possibly even more?... of Jews who, because of their efforts, would reach Palestine. Would live with a swagger of their own because they had been victims in countries that refused to believe they were really citizens, however many generations their families might have been there, and now they would be in a country of their own. Now, if they failed, they would have to accept responsibility for the failure. And, if they succeeded, success would be theirs alone. That was worth a little swagger, wasn't it?

But today Yanek approached Shlomo's rented apartment with caution. He paused some distance away and watched. Who was nearby? What were they doing? Did he, as Zoltan had, see a face he had seen before? And was anyone looking at him?

Spies receive training to keep them as safe as they can be kept in a dangerous life. Yanek had to make it up as he went along. He bent down to re-tie a shoelace that hadn't been untied in the first place. While he was down there, he looked behind him. Had anyone stopped walking when he did? He lit a cigarette and leaned against a wall to smoke it. That way, he could look up and down the street and check whether anyone was paying him more than usual interest. He loitered in front of a shop window, looking to see who was reflected in the glass. At last, satisfied that if anyone was watching him they were too good at the game for him to see them, he covered the last quarter mile, gave the agreed coded raps on the door and slipped inside.

Shlomo looked up. 'Zoltan not with you?'

Yanek shook his head. It came as a shock to realise that his eyes were touched by tears. That he, with his past and everything he'd been through, should feel such a sense of loss over one departed comrade. 'He's dead.'

'Dead? How?'

'They were waiting for us. I was lucky to get away myself.'

He handed over the briefcase. Shlomo emptied it and handed it back. 'I'm sorry to hear that. Zoltan was a good man. You will miss him. You will need a new partner.'

Yanek shook his head. 'It's over. Zoltan's death was a sign. My time here is done. I need you to get me to Palestine.'

Shlomo stared at him for so long that Yanek feared he might have to argue, but eventually Shlomo nodded. 'You two were the best collectors we had. But you're right. Everything comes to an end.'

‘And a beginning. A new life.’

‘And a beginning. Yes. Right. We will get you to Palestine. It is no longer as simple as it was.’

‘No? Why? With all the money we raised...’

‘It isn’t getting there, Yanek. It’s being allowed to land. You know, right after the first war, the League of Nations was set up to make sure there wouldn’t be a second war.’

‘Fat chance.’

‘The world knows that now. People are vicious. Tribal. They have been since we came down from the trees. They will kill anyone they think is not one of them. We Jews, of course, have known that forever. Now it’s knowledge shared with the rest of the world. But that’s not the point. The League of Nations gave the British a mandate for Palestine. Palestine was to be divided. Half for the Jews and half for the rest. And we were to get Jerusalem. And by and large the British honoured that. And now we have the United Nations, and they passed a resolution supporting partition and the Jews in Palestine accepted it but the others did not. So now you have a population of nearly two million in Palestine, and more than 600,000 of them are Jews, and they fight each other.’

‘Like a civil war.’

‘It isn’t like a civil war, Yanek. It *is* a civil war. But you know all this. You learned about the League of Nations at school, and you read about the war in the newspapers.’

‘Shlomo. I didn’t go to school.’

‘Not for long, no, I understand that. But...’

‘Not at all, Shlomo. I didn’t go to school at all. So no-one taught me anything there. And when you never went to school, newspapers are a bit of a mystery.’

‘Oh. Right. I hadn’t realised... All right. So now in Palestine we have a civil war, but it isn’t like any war Jews have been involved in for thousands of years, because Jews are fighting back. They are giving at least as good as they get. And the British have to try to hold the line, and sometimes one side kidnaps one of their soldiers and sometimes the other side does, and sometimes one of the soldiers gets killed for doing what the United Nations told them to do, and the British have just had enough. They are getting ready to sail away. Wash their hands of the place. And until then they've stopped the immigration they used to allow. So, yes, we can get you to Palestine. But you'll be going illegally, so you can't just pitch up in a boat and walk down a gangplank and say, "Hello. I'm Yanek, I'm a Jew and I've come home." We have to sneak you in there. I'll be going myself in a month or two because I think you're right, we're all done here, we've got the money out of them that we were going to get and it's time to move on. And I'll have to sneak my way in, too.'

'I don't care how I get there, just as long as I arrive. So what do I do?'

'We have a group of eight people we need to get to Metaponto.'

'Which is where?'

'In Italy. A long way to the south.'

'That's a port?'

'I wouldn't dignify it with the name of port. But it's possible to sail a ship from there. A small ship.'

'And these eight people. Who are they?'

'They were all in the camps. They survived. I don't need to tell you of all people how lucky that makes them. I also don't need to tell you they aren't in the best of health. They can get there, because we have a truck with room for them and a driver prepared to take them there for money. He's Italian and he wants to go home.'

'He isn't Jewish?'

'No, he isn't. Can we trust him? I don't know. We were ready to, because we didn't think we had a choice. But you could go as the group's leader. I can give you enough money to pay for emergencies. It may be difficult to buy food between here and there and especially kosher food, so we'll be loading enough rations onto the truck before it starts to keep them alive all the way to Metaponto. But it would be good to have someone in charge who can share out the rations to make sure they last and take care of the driver if he decides not to do what he's been paid to do. You've still got your revolver?'

Yanek took the gun from his pocket, showed it to Shlomo, and put it back. And I still have the MP3008 submachinegun I brought out of the camp. But that's in hiding. I need to go and get it.'

'Good. And enough ammunition?'

'I should think so. Unless another war breaks out. When we get to Metaponto? What then?'

'You have to be there no later than eight days from now. You will board a ship. The Shabtai Luzinsky. It will sail for Gaza. The British Navy has six ships patrolling the sea off Palestine and they will do everything they can to prevent it landing. If they succeed, everyone on board will be sent to an internment camp in Cyprus. The captain will try to make sure that doesn't happen. You accept?'

'Sure. If I end up in Cyprus, I could swim to Palestine. If I'd ever learned to swim.'

'That's settled. Go and get your submachinegun and come right back with it. You leave the day after tomorrow. You can sleep here until then. Don't leave the building after you get back with the gun. We don't want you to be seen until it's time to go.'

CHAPTER 6

PLANNING THE JOURNEY TO METAPONTO, 1947

Fifty-six years before the robbery

The man who had agreed to drive the truck to Metaponto was called Marcello. He told Yanek, 'My home is in Naples. It's about 300 kilometres to there from Metaponto. Once I get into Italy, my aim is to drive down the east coast to Bari and then head overland to Metaponto. The truck is still good for a lot of miles. Once I've delivered you all, it will be a way to support myself.'

'What were you doing in Poland?' For Yanek, that was the most important question, and he wasn't sure he'd be able to believe whatever answer he was given. Marcello wasn't Jewish. He wasn't a gypsy. Yanek couldn't think of any reason the Germans might have had for transporting him here – so why had he come when a war was raging? But the answer, when he got it, went a long way to convincing him. It was just one more of the millions of stories of how war had disrupted ordinary people's lives.

'What do you think I was doing here? I was following a woman. An Italian actress cast by a film company in propaganda movies. She claimed she loved me. She got me a job as a driver. That's how I came to have the truck. Italy was between a rock and a hard place. If I'd stayed, I'd either have been conscripted or I'd have had to take to the hills. So I came. That was two years ago. When it still looked as though Germany would win, and Poland was peaceful. Well, maybe not peaceful. But calm.'

'And the actress? Where is she now?'

Marcello shrugged. 'Your guess is as good as mine. She took up with a German army officer. I couldn't tell you even now whether that was what she wanted or whether she did it to save her skin. We were halfway through making the third movie when the money ran out. There wasn't going to be any more. We were told to do whatever we needed to get back home. I still had the truck, although it belonged to the film company. What I didn't have was money to buy fuel. Fuel is expensive even when you can get it, which you mostly can't. But then I met Shlomo. He bought enough gasoline to drive all the way to Naples by way of Metaponto. It's on the truck in jerry cans.'

'How far do you think it is from here?'

'If we can go straight there, less than two and a half thousand kilometres. But there are bound to be places we can't drive through. We'll have to go round them. So say three thousand.'

'From the time we set off, we have to be there in six days. Can you do that?'

'If I could drive without needing to stop for sleep, I could be there in a day and a half. That's if...'

'If we could go straight there. You said that.'

'And I do need to sleep, and there will be diversions, but I'll get you there with at least two days to spare. That's a promise.'

And that would have to do, so Yanek said, 'Okay.'

'What do I need to know about you?'

'Me? I'm called Yanek, I'm a Jew and I want to get to Palestine.'

Marcello smiled. 'I'd like a little more than that, if you don't mind. There's a lot of risk to this journey. A lot of danger. And Shlomo seems to think we should be glad to have you along. Why? What does he know about you that I don't?'

'I survived one of the camps.'

'Not many can say that. How did you do it?'

'I was a kapo.'

'Ah.'

'Yes. Ah. I got extra rations and better conditions. But in return, I had to do things that didn't make me a lot of friends.'

'You're armed?'

'I am.'

'Have you killed anyone?'

'Yes. I'm afraid I have. And I'll do it again if anyone looks like stopping me and these other eight people from going where we want to go.'

Marcello nodded. He put out a hand and Yanek shook it. 'Yanek, I'm glad to have you along. It feels like this journey just got a little bit safer.'

#

There was a shock for Yanek when he met the four men and four women he would be leading on their journey to the promised land. The look in the eyes of one of the women was open contempt. He took her to one side. 'Am I going to have trouble with you?'

'Shouldn't it be me asking you that question? I told you the first time we met that you disgusted me. And then when you left the camp… Well. You know what you did. I wouldn't treat an animal the way you treated me. I'll tell you this quite frankly: I made up my mind when you'd finished with me, if you'd made me pregnant I'd have killed myself rather than bear a child to a pig like you.'

Yanek tried to hold her gaze, but he was the first to look away. 'I'm sorry.'

'Sure you are. How many other women have you taken by force?'

'I don't keep count. But I do do the things I say I'm going to do. And I've said I'll get this group onto a ship for Gaza. If you want to back out, say so now.'

'I wouldn't give you the satisfaction. Although I have no idea why you're being trusted to do this.'

'What's your name?'

'That's you in a nutshell. Isn't it? You rape a woman, you don't even know what she's called.'

'What's your name?'

'It's Rachel. Though I'd rather you didn't use it.'

'Well, Rachel, I'll tell you why I'm being trusted to get you all to Palestine. It's because, without me, you wouldn't be going.' When she stared at him without speaking he said, 'These journeys have to be paid for. The Haganah doesn't have that much money, and what it does have it needs to fight the enemies of the Jews. So someone had to collect donations. And that's what I've been doing. I don't know how many Jews have already found their way to Palestine because of the money I raised, but I can tell you it's a hell of a lot more than eight.'

Scorn had not left her face. 'Donations? People gave you money willingly?'

'If they'd been going to give the money willingly, you could have done it. It needed people like me and Zoltan because sometimes force was necessary.'

'And, as I know to my cost, force is something you don't hesitate to use. Who is Zoltan? Is he coming with us? Do I have to watch out for him, too?'

'Zoltan was the best friend I ever had. And he died. Collecting donations so that people like you could move to a Jewish homeland without dirtying your own hands.'

For the first time in the conversation, she backed away just a little. 'I'm sorry for your loss.'

'I'll ask you again. Am I going to have trouble with you?'

She was silent for some time. Then she said, 'If I have none with you, you'll have none with me.'

'I'd be happier if you didn't tell the others what I did to you.'

The silence this time went on even longer. Then she said, 'You get me to Gaza and I'll never speak of it to anyone.' As she turned away she said, 'You can't imagine I want people to know I've had someone like you inside me.'

CHAPTER 7

1947 ESCAPE FROM POLAND

Fifty-six years before the robbery

Before they left, Shlomo talked to Yanek and Marcello together. 'It's as well that you won't have to go through Germany. If you did, you'd need to stay to the south and keep in the American zone because the Americans are doing nothing to prevent Jewish migration to Palestine and a lot to help it. The French don't care, in the British zone they'd do everything they could to prevent you, and if you were stopped in the Russian zone they'd either shoot the lot of you or send you all to Russia. But Austria, too, is occupied and in zones. The first zone you come to from here is Russian, and you don't want to go there. But get out of there into the southern part of Austria after the Russian zone and that's the British zone. You don't want to go there, either. So when you leave here, head south through Czechoslovakia into Hungary. Once you get south of Budapest, turn to the West and drive through Yugoslavia. Aim for Trieste. From there, head for Venice and then go south. And good luck.'

It seemed the whole of Europe was on the move and, indeed, it was. The ten people on the truck were a tiny fraction of the number who were either trying to get back to the homes they'd been taken from or to get away from those who intended to remove the way of life they felt comfortable with. The journey went quietly for about the first hundred miles, and then they reached Rzeszow.

Before the war started, half the population of Rzeszow had been Jewish. Things had not gone well for them. When the Germans occupied the city in September 1939, they changed its name to Reichshof and conducted a census in which they identified all the Jews. The old and infirm were killed; most of the rest were forced into jobs like street cleaning. All were beaten at one time or another, apparently for the entertainment not just of Germans but also of Poles who had realised that safety lay in siding with the Germans. Between them, they vandalised the synagogues and German officers took over the apartments of the rich. Any Jew aged twelve or over had to wear a white armband with a blue Star of David. They were subject to an evening curfew and even outside that time where they could go was strictly controlled. By the end of the year, the Germans had moved thousands of Jews to Reichshof from elsewhere. Everyone over fifty-five was taken into the Rodna Forest, forced to dig trenches that would be their graves, and shot. The same happened to anyone under fifty-five who wasn't fit for manual labour.

Within two years, the Germans had created a ghetto that you could enter and leave through only three gates. By December 1941, every Jew in the city had been moved into the ghetto. There were 12,500 of them in a space suitable, under normal living conditions, for a quarter of that number. They lived three families to a room.

Dysentery and typhus were rife. Bodies piled up in the streets. The residents built a small hospital, but it had no beds and no medicine. More transfers happened and by the middle of 1942 the 12,500 ghetto Jews had increased to 22,000. It clearly couldn't stay that way and the Germans announced that the ghetto would be evacuated. First to go would be anyone unfit to work. The Germans described the evacuation as resettlement, but the fact is that people were being "resettled" into the next world, so there was a touch of humour about the choice of the old Jewish cemetery as the place where they were taken. Some were killed right there, but most were shipped by train to die in the gas chambers at Belzec Death Camp. The Germans were so proud of what they had done that they put up a wooden eagle inscribed with this message:

'This eagle, the German sign of superiority and dignity, was put up to mark the liberation of the town of Reichshof of all Jews in the month of July 1942. It was put up during the service of Sturmbannfuhrer Dr. Heinz Ehaus, first District Headman and first Station Commander for the NSDAP for the district Reichshof.'

Rzeszow had its old name back when the truck reached there, but a place does not recover quickly from the kind of violence this town had suffered. As they approached the city limits, they found the road blocked on the outskirts by two burnt-out German armoured cars. Marcello had just brought the truck to a halt when four men came out of the trees beside the road. They had clubs and heavy staves, but only one of them carried a gun – a German rifle. He stepped forward from the others and said, 'Do what we tell you and there's no reason for anyone to get hurt. Get down from the truck. All of you. Now.'

Before anyone on the bed of the truck could move, Yanek swung open the passenger side door holding his revolver, jumped to the ground and put a bullet into the armed man's head. The other three froze where they were. Yanek reached into the cab, pulled out the submachinegun that lay on the floor, and made a show of moving it from one man to the next and then to the next. He said, 'I'm the one who decides whether anyone gets hurt. And I'll tell you my decision. If those vehicles aren't off the road in one minute, all three of you die. Make up your minds.'

The three men looked at each other. Then they took hold of the first armoured car and manoeuvred it into the ditch. It was heavy and they looked undernourished, but they got it done though it took longer than the minute Yanek had allowed them. While that was going on, Yanek picked up the rifle and cracked it open. 'Ha! No ammunition!' Then he got back into his seat and Marcello drove into the city, leaving the three would-be bandits behind.

That was only the first interruption they faced on the drive towards Budapest. On the other hand, some things went more smoothly than they could have hoped. No-one asked for their papers or where they were going when they crossed the border from Poland into Czechoslovakia, but that was less surprising than it might have been because Czechoslovakia had only just been brought back into existence. There could have been more difficulty when they crossed from there into Hungary, but there wasn't – what guards were on duty had long given up interrupting the movement of refugees. All they wanted to know was that the truck was going to continue all the way to the next border and then leave.

But they would not reach Hungary until the second day. The question of how to find a safe place to spend the night had been exercising both Marcello and Yanek. Marcello said, 'Can you drive?'

'Not a truck,' said Yanek. 'Not at night, when the roads are blocked in some places the way these are and in others they've been bombed to smithereens.'

'Then we have to stop, because I can't drive twenty-four hours without rest. But where? There seem to be bandits and renegades everywhere.'

In the end, they decided on Košice, which for a short time had been named Czechoslovakia's capital. Driving slowly down Rostislavova Street, they came across three cemeteries each running into the other – a Christian cemetery, an Orthodox cemetery, and a Jewish cemetery. Marcello said, 'If I back in here, we'll have the trees and bushes for people to relieve themselves in. Do you think you can defend this position?'

'I'm certainly willing to try.'

When they had got the truck in position and the passengers had been able to walk around both to stretch their legs, aching after so long on a truck's flat bed, and to take advantage of the privacy offered by the trees and bushes Marcello had mentioned, Yanek distributed food and water. As they settled in little knots to eat their meal and enjoy the break from travel, Rachel approached Yanek. 'That man you shot in Rzeszow. He had no bullets. He couldn't have defended himself.'

'I didn't know that.'

'You shot him.'

'Yes.'

'He was unarmed.'

'But pretended otherwise. Suppose he'd had ammunition. And I had spared him. Do you think he'd have spared me? Or you?'

Rachel held his gaze for a while. Then she said, 'He shouldn't have tried to bluff.'

'No. He shouldn't.'

'But the Talmud tells us to avoid violence.'

'Rachel. Perhaps you would like to take over as leader? Do you think we can reach Gaza without violence? The roads being the way they are?'

'I see I've irritated you. I must be more careful. If I don't know the violence you're capable of, who does?'

Yanek bowed his head. 'Perhaps violence is all I have. I certainly can't match you for righteousness.'

CHAPTER 8

1947 CZECHOSLOVAKIA TO HUNGARY

Fifty-six years before the robbery

There was no great love between Czechoslovakia and Hungary. Czechoslovakia had been ravaged by the Germans; Hungary had been German allies. And so Marcello and Yanek had no confidence that they would get across the border without trouble. But the Hungarian border guards had a simple question: 'Where are you going to?'

Marcello said, 'Parli Italiano?'

'Momento,' said a guard, and turned and bellowed something into the guards' hut.

Another guard came out, straightening his uniform hat. 'You are Italian?'

'Si,' said Marcello.

'Where are you going? I mean, your final destination?'

'Bari. In Puglia.'

'You don't plan to stay in Hungary?'

'No, sir, we don't. We want to get back home.'

'And that applies to all of you?'

'Si.'

'Have you got enough fuel to get there?'

'Si.'

'And enough food?'

'Si.'

'Then carry on. Hungary doesn't have enough food for its own people, so we have no interest in arresting strangers who we will have to feed. But be warned. If you stay in our country, you will be dealt with. And I just told you we can't spare any food for you, which we would have to do if we kept you alive. So...'

'We get the message.'

'I'm glad you do. And I strongly recommend you drive without stopping until you have crossed the border with Yugoslavia.' He stepped back, and waved to the guard to lift the barrier. Marcello put the truck in gear and drove on.

#

They found Budapest in a dreadful state. Hungary had been the fourth member of the Axis – the position Russia had expected to take for itself. Hungarian soldiers had fought alongside German soldiers in what had been Czechoslovakia and in Russia with such casual ferocity and such obvious enjoyment in slaughter that even the Germans referred to them as "murder tourists." When America had entered the war and the tide had turned, Hungary had paid the price. In 1941, the German air force had bombed London for fifty-seven nights in a row, destroying huge parts of the city. They'd done the same in Liverpool, in Newcastle, in Coventry and elsewhere. But two years later, the British and Americans had shown German cities how it felt to be bombed without mercy. They had done the same to Budapest. It was like driving through a wasteland. Three times in twenty minutes, small groups looking more like scarecrows than men had attempted to stop the truck. Each time, Yanek had put his submachinegun out of the window and felled the attackers. And then they were out the other side and turning in the direction of Zagreb.

Marcello pulled in to the side of the road. 'I need to fill the tank. Cover me.'

This was the third time they had refuelled and they had the routine to a fine art. Yanek climbed onto the roof of the cab with his submachinegun clearly visible. Another man got onto the roof behind him so that they could cover 360° of their surroundings. Marcello got one of the other men to help him lift enough jerry cans down to the road and then to pour the fuel. Then the empty jerry cans were put back on the truck, Marcello got into the cab and started the engine, the man sitting behind Yanek got back onto the truck bed and, finally, Yanek climbed down and rejoined Marcello. Then the truck set off.

Yanek said, 'It's 5 o'clock. We've got about another three hours of daylight, but our passengers haven't eaten since six this morning.'

'I'm taking that guard's instructions about not staying in Hungary seriously. Unless something holds us up, we'll be in Yugoslavia in ninety minutes. We'll all have to stay hungry till then.'

And that was how it was. Just before seven, they crossed the border. Twenty minutes later, Marcello found a place by the road that Yanek said he could defend. They pulled in and distributed enough food and water to keep everyone alive. It couldn't really be called more than that.

#

The night was anything but peaceful and Yanek had to shoot two intruders who wouldn't accept his advice to leave. He half expected Rachel to seek him out and chastise him for ignoring Jewish law's commands to avoid violence at all costs. If she was going to spend her life in a Jewish homeland surrounded by people who opposed that homeland's existence, she was going to have to come to an accommodation with violence. In any case, he was pretty certain that Jews were allowed to take part in war, as long as the war was just. And, if this wasn't war, what was it? He hadn't up to now felt any regret for his lack of schooling but it did strike him that, if he'd had an education, he might have been more sure about what his religion did and did not condone.

Because of the troubled night, everyone was ready to leave good and early. Yanek supervised the distribution of food and water and then they all climbed aboard and were on their way. They headed for Karlovac, and then Rijeka, and Yanek could feel the lightning in the mood as they all gazed at the sea. On the other side, they could actually see Italy. But they didn't have to wait to get all the way around the northern edge of the Adriatic because, just over an hour after leaving Rijeka, they were in Trieste. Yanek said, 'You're home.'

'I've been home since we were in Rijeka. You do know it used to be in Italy? And Trieste isn't really in Italy any longer. Or not in theory. They call it the Trieste Free State. But it's Italian in all but name. I can promise you, the people who live here think they're Italian. So, yes, I'm as good as home now. I'm in my own country, at any rate.'

'How does that feel?'

Marcello took his time to reply. 'It's difficult to find the words,' he said. 'There's something about the place where you grew up. I never felt at home in Poland, even when I was still with Bianca. It's not that there's anything wrong with the people – they're just different. You never feel you belong.'

'That's why I want to get to Palestine. To be with the people who are like me. Who think what I think and believe what I believe. And who don't want to kill me, of course,' he added. 'But that's a Jewish thing – an Italian wouldn't feel that.' He paused. 'Do you ever wonder what happened to Bianca?'

'Of course I do. But what's the point? Dead or alive, she isn't with me.' He turned from the road for a moment to look at Yanek. 'That's the funny thing. I care about her. I hope she's still alive and somewhere safe.

Somewhere she can be looked after. Get her life back on the rails. But none of that matters as much as the fact that *I* am alive. I've survived. I've made it back to my own country. And for the last three days, I've owed that to you. And so have those people on the back of the truck. They've been rained on and they've been wet and cold and I don't doubt they've been frightened, but they're alive. If you hadn't been with us, I don't believe we'd have got this far. So thank you.'

CHAPTER 9

1947 ANCONA, ITALY

Fifty-six years before the robbery

It wasn't over – and yet it was. It took them two days to drive all the way down the coast as far as Bari, a journey that before the war would have taken half that time, but the delays were caused by damaged roads and not by bandits or hostile officials. When they blew a tyre on the outskirts of Ancona, Marcello found a mechanic able to fix it in return for a jerrycan of petrol that was more than they needed to reach Marcello's eventual destination of Naples. Yanek said, 'If that had happened before we reached Italy, I don't know what we'd have done.'

'But it didn't,' said Marcello. 'My mother would tell you to accept that as evidence that God is watching over you.'

But Yanek had never doubted that.

Marcello said, 'We'll be in Metaponto before midday tomorrow. And then I'll say goodbye.'

There was one more frightening incident and it came after they had found in Bari what they believed would be a safe place to wait until morning. The passengers had spread out, looking for somewhere private to do what they needed to do. Because things now seemed so much quieter and safer, they took fewer precautions. Crucially, Yanek had left his guns in the truck's locked cab when he heard a scream for help. Running as fast as he could, he reached a place where three men had hold of Rachel and were dragging her into the bushes. When he shouted, one of the men let go of Rachel and turned to face Yanek. He was holding a revolver and he pointed it at Yanek's face.

If Yanek had understood Italian, he'd have known that the man was saying, 'If you think she's worth dying for, go ahead and I'll kill you.' He didn't understand a word – but he did understand the obligation he had taken on when he agreed with Shlomo to protect eight people in their journey to Palestine. He'd never had any training of the sort soldiers and police have, but he had smarts learned on the street from a young age. He ducked and hurled himself at the gunman's legs. The last time he'd attacked a man carrying a gun, the gun had not been loaded. This one was, and Yanek was momentarily deafened by the sound of a shot passing close over his head. But now the man was down, Yanek had wrested the revolver from his grasp and smashed the butt into the man's head. His victim lay still. It would be some time before he was ready to stand up again.

Yanek stood and pointed the gun at one of the two men who had been holding Rachel and who now stared at him in something approaching terror. He said, 'Move away from them, Rachel.'

'Don't kill them, Yanek.'

'What? They were going to…'

'They were going to do what you did. They didn't succeed. I want you to let them go.'

'I don't approve.'

'I don't care. Let them go.'

He stared at her for some time. Then he gave a gesture with the gun that told the men to pick up their fallen comrade and get out of there. They didn't need to be told twice.

#

That evening, after Yanek had distributed food, Rachel came to eat hers beside him. 'I've said some nasty things to you. And you deserve them. Face it: you did something to me in that camp that was beyond nasty. If I say I think you're an animal, you can't complain. But you got us here and I think you're going to get us the rest of the way. So I also need to say, thank you. And today you were prepared to be killed to keep me safe. I can't pretend to understand a man like you, but I can tell you how grateful I am.'

Yanek stared at her. What was someone like him supposed to say to someone like Rachel? They came from different worlds, and he knew that despite knowing nothing about her. Well, if there's something you don't know, ask. 'Where are you from?'

'I grew up in Łódź.'

'No... I mean... That was the wrong question.'

'You want to know about my life? Before the Germans?'

'What did you do? Who is your father?'

She smiled. There was no humour in the smile. 'I notice you ask about my father and not my mother. I suppose to you women have no purpose except to cook your meals and wash your clothes and bear your babies.'

'Who is your mother?'

'She's the wife of a rabbi. If she's still alive, which I doubt.'

They'd got there in the end. 'Your father is a rabbi. If he is...'

'If he's still alive. Which, once again, I doubt. They were taken before me. I don't know which camps they went to. I don't even know whether they went to a camp or whether they were shot where they stood.'

'There are going to be a lot of people searching, now that the war is over.'

'Oh, there are. Children looking for their parents. Parents looking for their children. Brothers and sisters looking for sisters and brothers.'

'Do you have any of those?'

She shook her head. 'They had only me. Our faith tells us to go forth and multiply and I'm sure they did their best, but I am all they have. What about you?'

Did he really want to talk about himself? He wasn't sure. Was she entitled to know? He wasn't sure about that, either. But he couldn't help feeling a certain warmth that someone might want to know something about him. It didn't happen often. In fact, he couldn't remember the last time it had happened. He said, 'I don't know.'

'You don't know? Of course you know. Who did you grow up with? What did your mother teach you?'

'Rachel. Do I strike you as someone who had a mother who taught her children things?' When she stayed silent he realised that she had no understanding of the kind of life he had led. What would it be like to have grown up in such a sheltered world? He said, 'There was a woman who said she was my mother, but she didn't behave in the way I think your mother probably behaved. And every so often a man would show up who she said afterwards was my father, but he didn't stick around. And if they had any other children, I never saw them.'

That look on her face. Sympathy? Or pity? Or even condemnation? He couldn't be sure. She said, 'Your mother fed you, at least. She must have done. And she made sure you got up in the morning and went to school.'

'Never. I never went to school. And as for feeding me. Well, yes. From time to time. When she had something. When she'd been with a man and he'd given her some money and she hadn't spent it all on drink. From the age of about five, I probably ate more that I had stolen than anything she gave me. Pies from a butcher's shop. Bread from a baker's shelves.'

'Did no-one catch you? Were you never sent to reform school?'

'They'd have had to catch a bunch of us. I wasn't on my own. I may not have had brothers and sisters, but there were other kids like me. Gangs of us. You didn't just run into a baker's shop, grab something and run out. You got half a dozen other kids to run wild in the shop. The baker's wife would be working so hard to get them out of there she wouldn't even see you till it was too late. And then when I was maybe fourteen, maybe younger, I don't know, I was with one of the gangs all the time. And now we weren't stealing pies and bread. Now we were into more serious stuff.'

'What do you mean, maybe fourteen, maybe younger, you don't know?'

'I bet you know your exact birthday. Don't you? Possibly even the actual time you were born? Well, I don't even know the year. Not for certain.'

He could see from the look on her face that she was struggling to understand the kind of life he was describing. The kind of person she was talking to. Eventually, she gave up. 'Well,' she said, 'I'm sorry your life has been like that. And maybe now it will change, once we get to Palestine. You are going to get us there, aren't you?'

'I am.'

'Thank you. I said that's what I'd come to tell you. And it is. Thank you.'

CHAPTER 10

1947 PALESTINE AT LAST

Fifty-six years before the robbery

Next morning they were, as Marcello had promised, in Metaponto before midday. Metaponto wasn't very big and the place from which even a small ship might sail was fairly obvious. They climbed down from the truck and unloaded the food that remained. The full jerrycans they left for Marcello to take to Naples. Marcello wrapped his arms around Yanek. It was a strange feeling. Zoltan had been Yanek's closest friend, but he and Yanek had never hugged. It would not have occurred to them. That didn't mean Yanek didn't like it. He did. There hadn't been much closeness to other human beings in his life and he realised he'd been missing something. Marcello said, 'I told you yesterday. We wouldn't have made it without you. Thank you. I'll be thinking of you on your journey to Gaza. God bless you all.' And then he was gone, leaving Yanek to realise that, until they were on board at which time the captain would take charge, he was responsible for his eight charges. He'd shared that responsibility, and now it was his alone.

The only ship that looked capable of carrying passengers in any number was called the Susanna. That was not the name of the vessel Shlomo had told him to look out for. But there were people on board, and so Yanek instructed the others to stay where they were and walked up the gangway. It wasn't very long, but well before he reached the ship two men were waiting for him. Both looked more than capable of dealing with anyone they didn't want there. Yanek said, 'Can you tell me where to find the Shabtai Luzinsky?'

'I might be able to,' said one of the men. 'It depends who is asking.'

Yanek gestured towards the eight people waiting on what passed for a dock. Restraining his irritation, he said, 'Those people and I are supposed to sail on the Shabtai Luzinsky.'

'Where to?'

The irritation was becoming too strong to ignore. 'Does that matter? Do you know where the damn ship is or not?'

'Who gave you that name?'

'A man called Shlomo.'

The man looked a little less hostile. 'And where was he?'

'In Lublin.'

And now the hostility was gone. 'Forgive me: we have to be careful. This is the Shabtai Luzinsky.'

'It says...'

'Yes, yes, it says it's the Susanna. Since we bought it we'll be changing the name. Shabtai Luzinsky ran a committee that helped migrants. He was killed. Don't ask me who by, because I don't know, though I have my suspicions. We'll be repainting the name in his honour before we sail. We've had other things to concern ourselves with. You are Yanek?'

'How did you know that?'

The man nodded. 'You are. Good. Shlomo has paid the passage to Gaza for you and your eight friends. I'm the captain. We don't sail until the day after tomorrow, but you may as well all come aboard now. Shlomo said you would be armed.'

'I have a revolver and a submachinegun.'

'You can keep the revolver with you. You will have to leave the submachinegun in my cabin. If we get you to Gaza, you can have it back but I won't have someone walking round my ship with a weapon like that. Now get your people up the gang and Josef here will show you to your quarters. Men and women separate – if you have husbands and wives in that group, I'm afraid they'll spend the nights apart until we land. Is that rations they are standing beside?'

'Yes. It's the food Shlomo gave me to last until we got here.'

'It looks as though you've husbanded it well. Bring it on board – you're not the only passengers and we've only just got enough to go round as long as the British don't delay us.'

The next twenty-four hours felt strange to Yanek. It was the first time he'd been able to spend a whole day in idleness since he'd been a small child. By the time they were ready to sail, he was more restless than he could ever remember being.

#

When the ship sailed, it carried 650 passengers, all seeking a new life in a new homeland. Five days later, the Albertina came alongside carrying another 173 passengers who transferred to the Shabtai Luzinsky, making a total of 823. Eight days after it had sailed, a British vessel attempted to intercept it before it could make landfall. The captain knew all about the would-be migrants who had been stopped from landing and taken to internment camps in places like Cyprus and he wasn't going to let that happen to the people he was responsible for. He ran the Shabtai Luzinsky onto the rocks near the kibbutz of Nitzanim, where a unit of the Haganah's elite Palmach force was waiting to help keep the migrants safe. It took three hours to get all of them ashore and before the landing was complete the British Army had arrived intending to arrest them. The Haganah had thought of that and arranged for several hundred Nitzanim residents to be on the shore mixing with the migrants to make it impossible for the soldiers to determine who had a right to be here and who did not. Two British ships deported 700 people to Cyprus, of whom 240 had to be released straightaway because they were Nitzanim locals and another seventy-five came back to Palestine later. None of the deportees were among Yanek's contingent, because he had anticipated how long it would take to get 823 people off the ship and made certain that his eight were among the first to leave. By the time the British soldiers arrived, they were all being fed and made welcome in the kibbutz.

The day after he'd landed, a man came to the table where he was eating breakfast and sat beside him. 'You are Yanek Hoffman.' It was a statement, not a question. 'You will not be forgotten. If you need help from your friends in Etzel, or simply feel lonely and want to talk to people who know what you went through so that Jews could return at last to their homeland, go to the bookshop on the corner of Curzon Street and ask for Ezra.' Then he walked away, leaving Yanek to think about what he'd said. And what Yanek thought was that the last few years were best forgotten. His job was done. Like Moses before him, he had brought his people home. Now, he needed to find a way to live in his new country. It would almost certainly not be by continuing the sort of work he had been doing.

CHAPTER 11

1947 KIBBUTZ NITZANIM

Fifty-six years before the robbery

He began, naturally enough, in the kibbutz. That was where he was, they had space for him, and they could find him work. The Nitzanim kibbutz is still there today, though three miles from where it was when Yanek landed there. The Jewish National Fund had bought 400 acres of land and most people were involved in farming, but that did not appeal to Yanek. 'So,' said the woman responsible for placing new arrivals in jobs. 'The carpentry shop needs people. Have you done any carpentry?'

The honest answer to that question would have been "No," but that wasn't the answer Yanek gave. He didn't know whether he'd be any good at it, but the idea of being in a workshop appealed more than being out in the fields. He was coming to terms with the difference between the sunshine in Berehove and here. Yes, it was very pleasant to be out in the sun for a while. While you ate breakfast or lunch, for example. But all day, every day, in that heat with the sun beating down on you? You probably needed to be born to that, and Yanek had not been. So he said, 'I've done some.'

'Well, the head carpenter is an experienced man and a good teacher. If you've got the makings of a carpenter, he'll get it out of you.'

And, as it turned out, Yanek was at least as good as any of the other people starting work in the carpentry shop. He was a joiner more than a cabinetmaker, but that was fine. There was no demand in the kibbutz for high class marquetry; they were making frames for houses, doors, windows and long tables at which communal meals were taken. Their customers weren't looking for a Chippendale, Sheraton or Hepplewhite:

they were looking for fast delivery of something that wouldn't collapse within a year of being made. So he settled down to thinking of himself as a carpenter.

Now he had a job, there were two other things he thought were lacking. One was to make contact with the people he thought of as his friends and colleagues in the business of getting Jews to Palestine. Because Yanek saw himself as different from most migrants. Those others had put themselves in the hands of a small number who were capable of getting them here, either because they had the money or because they had established workable routes. Yanek was one of that small number. Hundreds and quite possibly thousands of Jews were in their new homeland because he had raised the money to make it possible. He thought of those he had worked with as a sort of elite in this egalitarian world and he wanted to see them again.

The second thing had to do with women. In the past, women had represented only release to him and he'd set about getting that release in ways that didn't really stand examination. That was no surprise: people form their ideas of family life from the example their own family gives them, and in Yanek's case that example had not been good. And the people around him had been in the same plight. But now he was surrounded by examples of a different way of being. Men and women falling in love with each other and treating each other as equals. Husbands and wives showing each other and their children real affection. Caring about what happened to them, rather than just taking what they wanted when they wanted it.

Yanek decided he wanted that. He wanted a wife. And a man who wants a wife will almost always find one, however undesirable he may seem, because at least half the female population share the belief that, if they marry a man, they can change him. In Yanek's case, the woman who saw that he wasn't the best bet when it came to marriage, but was sure she'd be able to change him, was Ilana.

Marriage was not new to her, after all. But this one was a mistake. Having children made it worse. It wasn't that Yanek wasn't willing to be a good husband and a good father. He simply didn't know how. His only examples of good marriage and good parenthood came too late. The universe already knew who and what Yanek was. And, deep inside, so did Yanek. And having children reminded her that she had others. She loved Arie and Bat-Sheva every bit as much as she had loved Peter and Yudka, but the new love did not take away the pain of the old. Would she ever see them again? Would they even want to know her, little Roman Catholics as they now were? She had been as close to Christina and Imre as it had been possible for a Jew to be close to Catholics in prewar Hungary; she knew they would have done everything possible for her children, but Peter and Yudka belonged to them now. That was easy to say. Believing it deep in her heart was something else again.

One of the first things Ilana did before the children were born and while she still believed that changing Yanek was a possibility was to teach him to read. They sat together when work was over as long as the light made possible and first she introduced him to the shape of letters and then she showed him how they came together to form words and sentences. He was never fluent, but he could read. And it did, as she had intended, change his life – but not in the way she had expected.

The day would come when Ilana would leave Yanek, but Arie and Bat-Sheva were in their teens by then and they had a very clear view of their father's meanness. When they had birthdays, he'd allow them a few days to enjoy their presents and then he'd take them into work and sell them. When his uncle sent a new bicycle for each child on the son's bar mitzvah, he sold those. He did the same with a transistor radio sent two years later by an uncle in America. That transistor radio was the talk of all the children's friends. A technological miracle brought to a country that would one day be a match for anywhere in the world in electronics and software but for now was fighting to build the agricultural and manufacturing basis to sustain a growing population – and Yanek refused to let them keep it.

So that he could spend the money on himself? Far from it. He was as mean in that direction as towards them. He ate bread straight from the freezer with salami and yoghurt so that he never had to throw anything away. Ilana loved to bake, but he wouldn't let her make a cake unless friends were coming to play cards. Friends were the thing – any neighbour or friend in need knew they had only to turn to Yanek and they'd get all the help they could want, though his children were the skinniest in the neighbourhood. And if those children ever protested, or even asked for something he didn't want them to ask for, he beat them with his leather belt. The damage done by the big metal buckle made sure they did everything they could to avoid another occasion for a beating.

The neighbours saw what went on. They assumed that Yanek's children must hate him. But life is not that simple. His daughter, Bat-Sheva, saw the way their mother was treated and she held it against her father but Arie, the son, was more conflicted. No son wants to believe his father has nothing good about him. A great deal can be forgiven in return for not very much. In the case of Yanek and Arie, the not very much – which was actually a great deal – was the stories Yanek had to tell. They weren't a regular thing. He wasn't consistently talking about the past. But occasionally, when Arie and his friends were together, Yanek would talk a little about some of the things he'd done before he came to Israel.

No-one who heard the stories necessarily believed them. Young people become accustomed to the fact that their parents tell them a great deal and some of it isn't really true. But the stories were great on their own account.

Of course, Yanek didn't dwell too much on things he had done that people – even people as young as his son's friends – might not approve of. He mentioned Rachel, for example, but only in connection with the journey from Lublin. His earlier meetings with her in the camp were never mentioned, any more than he admitted to killing fellow prisoners so that the crew of which he was kapo would achieve its targets and he would remain alive. He talked about his work raising money so that Jews could come to Palestine and he did admit, in a jokey kind of way, that not every donor had been a willing giver, but he never said it had been necessary to hurt, much less kill, anyone to get them to part with precious possessions. He talked about Zoltan as a hero who had died so that the parents of the boys he was telling the story to could have a homeland to come to, but he went no further than that.

It was enough. Arie was never going to regard his father as a Prince among men, but the stories meant he could at least have some regard for him. And that was true even though he believed scarcely a word his father said.

Yanek had been a city boy and he was never going to stay long in the kibbutz. As soon as he felt he'd learned enough, and he'd saved enough to buy the tools of his new trade, he and Ilana moved to a small basement flat in Jaffa and set up a carpentry business. It failed – but it established him enough that he could get a new job that would change his life. And something else life-changing happened when he and Ilana went to Tel Aviv for the day and took a walk in the smart shopping area. Not to buy things – he wasn't going to waste his money on expensive frivolity. Just to get a look at how some Jews in Palestine lived. Ilana said, 'Maybe we'll do well enough to live here some day.' But Yanek wasn't listening. In the window of 44 Allenby Street he had seen a piece of jewellery he recognised. An intricate silver necklace set with pink topaz stones. He stood motionless in front of the window as Ilana tugged at his arm. 'Yanek! What is it, Yanek?'

He couldn't answer. The words would not come. And then he saw a man's face through the glass in the shop door. The way he was moving things in a cabinet made it clear that he was the owner of the shop. And, therefore, the owner of the pink topaz necklace. The necklace for which Yanek and Zoltan had risked their lives. The necklace that was supposed to have been sold to fund the movement of Jews to Palestine.

He grabbed Ilana's arm and led her, still demanding to know what was troubling him, away from the shop as fast as he could.

CHAPTER 12

1948 – JAFFA, ISRAEL

Fifty-five years before the robbery

Ilana said, 'Yanek? What are you doing?'

The look he gave her suggested that that was a strange question to ask. And so it was, because what he was doing was obvious. But it was something Ilana had never seen him do before. 'I'm reading this magazine. What do you think I'm doing?'

"But you never read magazines" would have been the obvious reply. "And certainly not the society pages." But Ilana had already learned that it was best not to annoy her husband. Instead of speaking, she looked over his shoulder. He was looking at a picture of a man and woman dressed for the kind of high class gathering she no longer believed she and Yanek would ever attend together. If it hadn't been for what had happened outside the jeweller's shop in Allenby Street, she might never have noticed the necklace the woman was wearing. She said, 'Yanek... Is there something about jewellery that interests you?'

'Of course there is. That's how I got here. It's how a lot of other people got here, too.'

'Here?'

'To Palestine. Which, any day now, will not be Palestine any more. It will be Israel. I played a part in that. And jewellery made it possible. So of course I'm interested in jewellery.'

'Tell me about that.'

So he did. Not the whole story: he didn't mention being a kapo in a death camp, he didn't mention Rachel and he didn't mention having killed anyone, but he told her about Shlomo and about how he and Zoltan had raised "donations" to make it possible for Jews to make their way to the land that God had promised them.

'Why have you never told me about this? You've saved lives. Maybe lots of lives.'

'I was doing my duty as a Jew.'

'And you saved lives. You're a hero. Tell me about Zoltan. You never mention him. Where is he now?'

'He didn't make it here. They killed him.'

'They?'

'They. Them. People who hate Jews. God knows, there are enough of them.'

'How do you know he was killed?'

'I saw it happen.'

'You were there?'

'We were collecting donations. The man we asked for a gift objected to the request. He had friends. They shot Zoltan in the street. They would have shot me if I hadn't been quick on my feet.'

Ilana put her arms round his neck. 'My poor darling. I had no idea.'

Yanek pointed at the necklace around the neck of the woman in the photograph. 'You like that?'

'It's all right. A little... I suppose I'd call it a little primitive.'

'That's the idea. It's a style called cannetille. It's supposed to be like the embroidery on an Indian peasant woman's clothes.'

'I had no idea you knew so much about jewellery.'

'I've seen that necklace before. The newspaper gives the name of the man the woman is married to.'

'Did you ever meet him?'

'No. But I know who he is. While we were collecting donations, that man was the associate of someone called Shlomo. It was Shlomo we used to take the donations to so that they could convert it into cash and use that money to bring Jews here.'

'That was as good a thing to do as you and Zoltan were doing.'

'We certainly thought so at the time. Tell you the truth, I'm a little surprised that his wife owns that particular necklace.'

Then Ilana asked the other question that had been occupying her. 'Yanek. That magazine. Did you buy it?' Because she had never known him spend money on something so frivolous.

'Of course I didn't buy it. It was on a table outside a café. Someone had left it there. And it was open at that page. So I picked it up.'

'Oh. I see. When you're finished with it, can I read it? I mean the whole magazine.'

Yanek searched his head for some reason to say no, but couldn't find one. 'Yes,' he said at last. 'Of course. Take it.'

#

The dark suspicion Yanek had worried over since the visit to Allenby Street had been solidified by that picture in the newspaper. He, Zoltan, and every Jew who wanted to come to Palestine and hadn't been able to get on a boat had been betrayed. Some of the money they had raised had not gone where it was supposed to go. Instead, it had been kept to enrich people Yanek and Zoltan had trusted. People like Shlomo, because it was Shlomo Yanek had seen in the shop with the pink topaz necklace. And now it was clear that the pink topaz was not the only piece that had been held onto instead of being sold, because the one he'd seen in the newspaper was a different necklace. How many more traitors were there? Just how much of the money they had raised had been used for what they thought it would be used for, and how much had been pocketed by people he had thought were patriots like him and now regarded as the lowest of the low? There wasn't a lot of time to think about that, because David Ben Gurion had just announced the creation of the state of Israel and hell was about to break loose. But Yanek was not a man to forget or forgive. Justice would have to be served. The wrongdoers would have to pay. And Shlomo would be the first. The war that was about to break out would give Yanek a chance to strike the first blow against the people who had betrayed him.

Three days later, when the Arab countries surrounding the new Jewish state had launched the attack they meant to be final, Yanek tucked his revolver into his jacket pocket and a kitchen knife into his belt. Ilana didn't see the weapons, but she watched with horror as he prepared to go out. 'Yanek. What are you doing? You're not going out of here? They're dropping bombs. We are in a basement. We have a better chance than most of surviving.'

'I have something I must do.'

'What? What is so important that you'd leave your wife alone while people are trying to kill her with bombs? What is so important that you'd go out into the street while those bombs are falling?'

Yanek had no answer he could give her that she would understand. So he walked out of the door without saying a word.

From Jaffa to Tel Aviv is about five miles. A pleasant enough walk in normal circumstances, as long as you don't mind that it's all in built-up areas. But these circumstances weren't normal. By the time he reached Allenby Street, Yanek was convinced he had God's blessing. Had he not, he would have died on the way. He walked into Number 44, exchanged a few chastising words with Shlomo, and brought his life to an end. And then he started on the journey back. When he walked through the door, Ilana stared at him. 'Yanek. What have you done?'

'I've been for a walk.'

'Don't give me that. I can see just from the look on your face that you've done something terrible. What was it?'

'I have nothing to tell you. Give me something to eat.'

CHAPTER 13

MAY 1953 HAGIVAA, RAMAT GAN, ISRAEL

Fifty years before the robbery

The circumstances on 16 May, 1948 had been very special. They'd allowed Yanek to get to Tel Aviv, shoot Shlomo, and get back home again without anyone having the first idea who'd been responsible for the killing. The general assumption would be that Shlomo had been killed by an Arab in retaliation for what Arabs saw as the theft of their country. But in the weeks following, the new state's nascent armed forces and police had a firmer grip on things and it would have been very difficult for Yanek to continue his search for vengeance. Apart from which, he had no idea where to find the others he might want to deal with. And then there was the need to earn a living.

What is now Rafael Advanced Defence Systems Ltd began life as AMT, a secret government organisation developing weapons for the Israeli armed forces. Yanek's carpentry business had failed but they recognised his skills and gave him a job. The job was to help build rockets, a subject about which Yanek knew nothing, but he learned quickly.

At about the same time, Yanek and Ilana got into the worst row they had yet experienced. During the war, most of the Arab population had fled Jaffa and Yanek and Ilana were offered, free of charge, a large house fully furnished and equipped with everything they could need. For Yanek, this was simply the right thing to happen after a war – one side had lost and the other had won and the spoils went to the winners. Ilana didn't see it that way. She refused to move.

Yanek said, 'How is this any different from what the Germans and the Poles and Hungarians did to the Jews in the war? They took everything we had and gave us nothing in return. Now we are in the position they were in, so we get to take what the Arabs had.'

'It's different because we are Jews. We are a righteous people. We cannot do to the Arabs what was done to us.'

'But that's exactly what we are doing! It's happening all over Israel.'

'Other people can do whatever they want to do. I will not do what I know is wrong.'

Yanek accepted her decision because she gave him no choice, but he never forgave her. He threw himself into his new job and only came home at weekends. As far as his wife and children were concerned, he was a carpenter. They had no idea that he was out in the desert, taking measurements, filming rocket tests, and making adjustments so that the rockets would be more effective.

For him, all this was just a continuation of the work he had done to get himself and others here. Because Israel had never enjoyed anything that might be called peace. In 1949, they had signed Armistice agreements with their Arab neighbours to bring that first war to an end. One of the things agreed to was that there would be no attempt to close the Straits of Tiran to Israeli shipping but, in 1956, Egypt broke the agreement by doing precisely that. Israel invaded Egypt and forced the Straits of Tiran to be reopened. The United Nations sent an emergency force to keep the peace along the border between Israel and Egypt. All of this brought Yanek great satisfaction. Israel was now the country of people who had been kicked around, enslaved, beaten and killed by others. And Egypt had been foremost among those others because it was Egypt all those centuries ago that had been first to take the people of Israel into captivity. Since the fall of the Ottoman Empire, Egypt regarded itself as the leader of the Arab world even though the best way to make an Egyptian angry was to call him an Arab, but – as Yanek said to anyone who would listen – 'We kicked them all the way back to Cairo.'

Things got tense again in 1967 when Egypt's leader, Colonel Nasser, once more closed the Straits of Tiran to Israeli shipping and ordered the United Nations Emergency Force to leave. Israel had warned Nasser that closing the Straits would be an act of war and in June Israel launched air strikes against Egyptian airfields, penetrated the Golan Heights in Syria and entered the Gaza Strip.

The fight stretched its tentacles much further than just Egypt and Israel. Colonel Nasser and King Hussein of Jordan broadcast to the Arab world, though their words were heard further afield. Egypt, they said, was vastly superior to Israel in military strength. These quick victories Israel was claiming could not have happened without outside help. Clearly, the Americans and the British were helping Israel and it was the duty of all Arabs to kill the British and the Americans wherever they found them. This despite the fact that Hussein had been educated at Harrow School in England and then at Sandhurst, Britain's highest military academy, had been supported by Britain, and was shortly to marry an English woman called Toni Avril Gardiner who would change her name to Princess Muna Al Hussein.

Those who sought to apologise for him pointed out that he was in a difficult position. Jordan was a young country, had little in the way of resources, and following the first Arab war was now home to a very large number of Palestinian refugees capable of making his life very difficult. Nevertheless, people did listen to what he said with unfortunate results for a number of British and American citizens finding themselves in the Middle East.

The Arab tradition of hospitality had not died, however. One British man recalled years later that he had been working in Libya in 1967. 'We were known to be a British firm. I was the only person in the office and a huge crowd had gathered outside. They were baying for blood. There were rocks coming through the window. I seriously thought that today was probably going to be my last day on earth. I knew that, just a few hours ago, they'd thrown an expat to his death and he wasn't the only one. Then the door opened and in walked one of our local staff. He said, 'Come on. You can't stay in here.' I said, 'I certainly can't go out there. Those people want to kill me,' and he said, 'And if you stay here they'll come in and kill you is exactly what they will do.' So I walked out with him, very much against my better judgement, and I was met with a lot of abuse from the crowd outside, but it opened up as we walked to my car. The man who'd escorted me said, 'You have an apartment in the Sciara Bandung, don't you?' I agreed that I did and he said, 'You probably shouldn't try to spend the night there. Do you know anyone in Giorgimpopoli?' That was a big estate just outside Tripoli where a lot of expats employed in the oil industry lived in rented villas. I said I had some friends out there and he said 'Drive me to them. You'll be safe, because the army has put a cordon round the place.' So that's what we did and I was safe because he was with me, and then he walked back into town. And a couple of days later it was all over. And so was the war.'

#

If anyone had asked Yanek why he conducted his home life the way he did, he probably couldn't have answered. His wife and his two children lived in fear of him. The children didn't know, and Ilana couldn't be sure, that he had killed in the past but all three sensed that murder was something he was capable of. As he tightened the screw, it got worse. He refused to give Ilana money to buy food, insisting that she would only waste it. Instead, he opened an account with a local food store: they were to allow Ilana to buy a limited amount on credit, and only from the list of cheap things Yanek provided, and Yanek would settle the bill each weekend when he came home. Something he never knew was that the store owner would pad the bill just a little and give the money to Ilana so that she could buy books and other things the children needed.

By 1983, Ilana could stand it no longer. Both children were now grown up and left home, so that barrier to a breakup had gone. Summoning up all the courage she could muster, she told Yanek she wanted a divorce.

'You want to leave me?'

'You give me no choice. I can't bear this life any longer.'

'Then you can go. But you go with nothing. You will sign over your pension to me.'

'You can't make me do that.'

'Perhaps not. But I can kill you if you don't.'

She stared at him. This was not an empty threat. She said, 'You know you're not sane?'

'I'm the same as I've always been ever since you first met me. Here. Paper and pen. Make the pension over to me. Start writing.'

And so she did. When she left, she took with her a handbag and nothing else.

#

Yanek already felt responsible for the fact that so many Jews now lived in Israel – and now he felt additional satisfaction in the knowledge that the rockets he had worked on had been a major part of the Israeli armed force's victory. He had been an important part of the young nation's defence, photographed beside Moshe Dayan in the desert at rocket launch sites. He had turned out to be extremely good at his job and he actually received a medal for his significant contribution to the development of Gavriel, the first ground to air missile developed by Rafael. He was, though, growing older and the hard continuous graft in a desert that could be intimidatingly hot during the day and uncomfortably cold at night was taking its toll. By now, Israel was not only receiving scientific graduates from abroad as migrants but also growing her own. In 1985, with regret on both sides, Yanek was made redundant. He used the redundancy money to buy a small restaurant just outside Be'er Sheva in Southern Israel. He didn't make a lot of money, but that didn't matter because money wasn't important to Yanek. So true was that that, after Ilana left him, he buried all the money he had in the garden.

Although he didn't yet know it, he had learned one traditional skill during his time at Rafael that, one day in the future, would prove very useful. Rafael had a number of very sensitive items that were classified to be used and even handled by very few. Some of these items had locks, and the sensitivity was such that they could not allow third parties to touch them and so they set up their own internal key-cutting department. Yanek was assigned to that department. On his first day, he remarked on the unusual design of some of the keys. 'I've seen keys like that before.'

'Then you probably know someone with a safe-deposit box. Because we modelled those keys on the keys to safe-deposit boxes.'

Yanek had no idea what a safe-deposit box was, but when he thought about it that evening he did remember where he had seen that key design before. Shlomo had had one. And someone else. Rosenbaum. Rosenbaum had been one of Shlomo's colleagues. One of the others who handled the jewellery that Yanek and Zoltan and a handful of people like them collected. Yanek had only met Rosenbaum once, but he'd seen his keyring and he'd seen a key just like Schlomo's attached to it. Why would Shlomo and Rosenbaum have safe-deposit keys? What would they have used them for? He didn't know. It would be a few more years before he found out, and that would involve a meeting with a woman he had never expected to see again.

CHAPTER 14

1954 FAMILY REUNION

Forty-nine years before the robbery

Rachel had been at the kibbutz for six years. As far as she knew, she was alone in the world. Her mother and father had gone to the camps before her and she'd never heard another word about them. She'd tried. A very active information exchange largely run by volunteers attempted to put back together families broken by Nazi Germany. Sixty years later, agencies carrying out DNA analysis for genealogists would find that 40% of their clients were Jewish – this despite the fact that most clients were either in America or Europe and Jews now made up 2.4% of America's population and less than half of 1% of Europe's. The reason was the same – at the end of the 1930s and the first half of the 1940s, sister had been ripped from brother, child from parent, wife from husband on an almost unimaginable scale and now those who were left, and the children of those who were left, wanted to find whether any trace of any lost relative existed.

For the most part, these searches ended in sadness. Most of those being looked for were dead. But there were enough joyful reunions to encourage people to carry on looking. Rachel had made sure her name was out there and she'd listed everyone she could think of: not just her parents but aunts, uncles and cousins. And one day one of the kibbutz's administrators sent word to the nursery in which Rachel was looking after children too young for school that she had a visitor.

When she walked into the administration block, she burst into tears for she recognised immediately the woman she was looking at. The woman stepped forward and hugged her. 'Rachel?'

'Sela? Is it really you? Is it?'

Her cousin laughed through her own tears. 'It is.'

The administrator, a gruff man who wiped angrily at his eyes, said, 'Rachel, I'll send someone to the nursery in your place. Take the rest of the day off.'

When it was over and Sela had returned to her home in Jaffa, Rachel felt it was one of the happiest days she'd ever experienced – and yet, the subject of the conversation for much of the time had been death. The death of those they loved, the death of friends, the death of people hardly known at the time but now remembered as shades, their lives taken from them for no crime except that their existence offended a man who, for a brief period, had dominated the world. Not everyone was gone, and Rachel heard of people she had once known, friends of friends and relatives of friends who were known to have survived.

'And still,' said Sela, 'they want us dead.'

'They?'

'They. Them. I refuse to say Arabs although that seems to be the common currency now. People talk about Israel's enemies and they use the word Arabs.'

'They mean Muslims.'

'That's exactly my point. There are Jewish Arabs, but they seem to be forgotten, just like the world wants all of us forgotten. In fact, at one time Arab Jews were the only kind of Jews there were.'

'There are Christian Arabs, too.'

Sela grunted. 'Yes. There are. And the Christian Arabs are not determined to sweep Israeli Jews into the sea and Israel off the map. But most Christians aren't Arabs and most Christians have spent two thousand years hating us. The pogroms weren't conducted by Arabs. Have you ever been into a Christian church? Seen the images they have of Christ? Would anything about those pictures with their immaculate white skin and sparkling blue eyes even hint that Christ was a Jew? Or from the Levant? We are getting support from America now, but American country clubs still have a no Jews policy. In any case, what I say is true. Israel is going to have to defend itself because half the rest of the world wants us gone and the other half doesn't care enough to stop them.'

'I'd hoped so much that it was all over now and we could live in peace.'

'And we can. But it's a peace we'll have to keep ourselves. Look, never mind all that. This kibbutz. What are you doing here? I mean, do you like it? Is this how you want to spend the rest of your life?'

It came as a shock to Rachel to realise that she had never asked herself that question. 'I don't know. I mean, I just haven't thought about it.'

'You are a rabbi's daughter. An educated woman. You have something real to offer the world. And here you are with a bunch of farmers.'

Rachel laughed. 'Israel needs farmers, Sela. And I like a lot of them. Their enthusiasm for what they do. Making the desert bloom.'

'Really. You haven't liked any of them enough to marry one?'

The laughter came again. 'Some of the most attractive men are married already.'

'You work in the nursery?'

'Not for all the six years I've been here. I spent some time in the kitchens. As a cook, I was disastrous but there was no-one to touch me for cleaning pots. But now, yes, I work in the nursery.'

'Looking after other people's children.'

Rachel's smile faded. 'Yes. That's what I do. I look after other people's children. It's a worthwhile occupation.'

'So is looking after children of your own, Rachel. I'll say it again: you're a rabbi's daughter. Have you never heard the instruction, go forth and multiply?'

'God sends what God sends, Sela.'

'Yes. And now God has sent me. And perhaps my duty is to get you out of here so that you can meet the right kind of man.'

#

When the 1980s started, Israel had existed for just over thirty years. Israelis had become used to the idea that the world was hostile to their existence and that they must always be ready to defend themselves. It wasn't all war and confrontation, though. There were some straws in the wind. When you've been there for three decades, when you have citizens born and raised to adulthood right where they now live, you can expect signs that at least some people have begun to recognise that you're there and you're not going away.

Egypt had been Israel's most vociferous opponent yet, in 1980, Egypt appointed an ambassador to Israel. Israel responded by opening an embassy in Cairo. Commercial air links were established between the two countries and they signed a tourism agreement. Egypt agreed to sell oil to Israel.

All of that suggested a more peaceful coexistence might be possible – but, at the very time these arrangements were being made, the United Nations Security Council adopted a resolution saying Israel must remove existing settlements and promise not to create new ones. America voted in favour of the resolution, though President Carter later said that had not been meant to happen. A month or two later, terrorists in Hebron killed seven Jewish students and wounded sixteen others.

Prince Fahd of Saudi Arabia told the *Washington Post* that, if Israel would declare its intention to withdraw from areas occupied in 1967, Saudi Arabia would do everything it could to get other Arab states to cooperate and try to reach a settlement. President Begin invited Fahd to Jerusalem to address the Knesset.

So far so good. But then Morocco hosted a conference of Islamic foreign ministers who agreed to try to force Israel's expulsion from the United Nations and to begin "a holy war" against Israel. Peace was not here yet.

Iran and its puppet state, Syria, decided that Lebanon – poor, beautiful, divided Lebanon – was a perfect base for anti-Israeli terrorists. Very few of them were Lebanese, but Lebanon lacked the power to eject them. Israel could sympathise with that weakness but, as W H Auden observed, History to the defeated may say "Alas," but cannot help or pardon. When rockets were fired and fighter bomber sorties flown from inside Lebanon, Israeli planes shot down two Syrian aircraft and struck the terrorist bases in Lebanon.

The following year, Israel shot down two Syrian helicopters in Lebanon. When Syria introduced ground to air missiles into Lebanon's Bekka Valley, Israeli planes attacked the sites.

Five years earlier, Iraq had bought a nuclear reactor from France. Iraq and France both said that the reactor was for peaceful scientific research only, but Israel didn't believe that. They were concerned that the reactor could be used to produce nuclear weapons and they were in no doubt who those weapons would be used against. They launched Operation Babylon, a surprise airstrike which destroyed the reactor. Oddly enough, this incident also pleased the government of Iran which was constantly at loggerheads with Iraq and had no desire to see a nuclear reactor operating there.

In 1982, terrorists assassinated an Israeli diplomat in Paris. The Palestine Liberation Organisation shelled Galilee, killing a number of Israelis. Israel shot down two Syrian MIGs over Lebanon and bombed terrorist bases in Sidon. The Israeli Defence Force removed PLO terrorists from Lebanon and clashed with the Syrian army. Israel carried out air raids on Beirut and the PLO's withdrawal from Lebanon was completed, but the Lebanese president refused to sign a peace treaty with Israel. Eight Israelis soldiers were kidnapped in Lebanon and Israeli jets attacked PLO and Syrian positions in the Bekaa Valley. Syria moved SAM-9 surface-to-air missiles to Lebanon and Israeli jets destroyed them on the ground.

And so the 1980s went on, though not everything was about war and diplomacy. In 1983, the rabbinical college decided that women could now become rabbis. The following year, they added gay and lesbian candidates to that list. Palestinian gunmen hijacked a bus travelling from Tel Aviv to Ashkelon; when the Israeli security services killed two of the gunmen, their actions received more international condemnation than the original hijacking. International approval for Israel's existence was still far from wholehearted. The Israeli response was to increase their determination to continue to be able to defend themselves.

#

And, whatever else was going on in his own life and in the life of the new country he had helped bring into being, Yanek began a search that would occupy him for the next twenty years. Shlomo had betrayed Yanek and his like, and Shlomo had paid the price. But betrayal had not been unique to Shlomo. Others had done the same, and Yanek had not abandoned hope of dealing with them as he had dealt with Shlomo. But first he had to know who they were.

They were in no hurry to help, those betrayers. They knew what had happened to Shlomo. Yes, that could have been pure chance – the random slaughter of one person on a day when so many had been killed, done for no reason except that he happened to be there. A classic case of wrong place, wrong time. Perhaps. But that did not remove the possibility that his killing had been an act of revenge for the same thing that they knew they had done. If someone was out there who would take revenge on Shlomo, why not also on them? It was a chance not worth taking. They didn't want to follow in Shlomo's footsteps, and so they began to flee. One went to South America, most who left chose to go to Britain.

But Yanek never forgot about them. As long as he had breath in him, he could hope that his day would come. He got on with his life – but he went on searching.

For Yanek it was time to go to work, whatever time it takes!

Chapter 15

June 1984 Be'er Sheva

Nineteen years before the robbery

If you want to succeed in the restaurant business, you need to give people food they enjoy eating and create an atmosphere that makes them feel welcome and want to come back. Not the most obvious career choice for a loner who had eaten bread straight from the freezer with cheap salami to make sure nothing was wasted. Anyone who knew Yanek would have expected him to be bankrupt in six months. In fact, he took to it like a natural. He amazed not only others but also himself.

What the restaurant gave him was something he hadn't known he needed: the opportunity to be surrounded by friends. Zoltan had been his closest friend, and Zoltan was dead, but when Marcello had hugged him at the end of their journey from Poland to Italy he'd had a sense of how friendship could feel. He began to understand what Ilana could certainly have told him if they ever spoke: he was a man's man, who enjoyed spending time talking to other men about the things men talk to each other about. What also became clear was that, in the right company, he had a wicked sense of humour. That helped attract customers to the restaurant, and when they got there they found good food made by a competent local chef without any penny-pinching portion control. It wasn't *cordon bleu*. The restaurant was not spoken of as a new Ritz or George V. But that was okay, because the clientele had never been to either of those bastions of great cooking and would probably have found them unbearably fussy and patronising if they had. They liked what Yanek offered them.

And then he met Amos, and Amos filled the gap left by Zoltan.

Human nature is a series of continuums. Of lines between two extremes. Great meanness and boundless generosity. An absolute lack of humour and the need to be constantly laughing. Sanity and craziness. There are many others, but everyone can be placed somewhere on each line and those three will serve to introduce Amos because he was on the right hand end of all of them.

When he walked into Yanek's restaurant, he created an explosion of ideas that would lead Yanek to the most exciting and dangerous trip of his life. Most importantly, that meeting would give Yanek the chance to take the revenge he had longed for for nearly 30 years. Because

Yanek had never forgotten or forgiven those who had kept for themselves some of the jewellery he and Zoltan had obtained to fund the movement of Jews to Palestine.

Yanek and Amos became good friends. And then, early in 2000, Amos told Yanek he was leaving.

'Leaving? Why? To go where?'

'I'm getting married, Yanek. My new wife is English. And England is where we are going. Come and see us sometime. And you must be a guest at the wedding.'

Yanek did go to the wedding. He wasn't hugely impressed by Amos's choice of bride and he knew he would never visit them in England, but he saw no need to say so. He was softening.

Then, two years later, Yanek walked into his restaurant and found Amos at a table on his own, eating a rum baba and drinking his favourite drink. Yanek said, 'What the hell are you doing here? I haven't seen you in almost 2 years, and by the way the Savarina is on me.'

'Thank you for the rum baba. Look. What can I tell you? It didn't work out. She was a right Jewish cow so I just packed up and left. Luckily we hadn't had any kids. I tried to get on with her father but that didn't work out, either. Anyway, I'm back here and this is where I can be happy. I am still a true Israeli.'

Yanek moved around the restaurant and checked in the kitchen, making sure that all was going well and his customers were happy. Then he came back to Amos's table carrying a refill for Amos and a drink for himself. He sat down to chat. And that was when he saw, on the bunch of keys Amos continually played with, something he knew he had seen before. He said, 'Amos. That little thing on your keyring. What is it?'

'Oh, that? We used to have a small deposit box in Hatton Garden in London. I forgot to give my key back so I decided to keep it as a lucky charm.'

Yanek could hardly concentrate. He went back to the kitchen and brought back another Savarina. He knew where he'd seen that key before. Shlomo had had one on his keyring. And someone else – someone associated with Shlomo – who had that been? He racked his brain. He said, 'Amos. Tell me about deposit boxes. What do you use them for?'

Amos grinned. 'Why? Have you got money, or something precious, that you want to keep safe and out of sight and away from the tax people?'

'That's their purpose?'

'Yanek. A safe-deposit box's purpose is whatever the person renting it wants it to be. Some people store photographs there. Personal things of sentimental value. Useless to anyone else, but the owners would hate to lose them. Then there's documents – a will, details of a Swiss bank account, the deeds to a house, a map showing where treasure is buried on an island in the Caribbean. That last one was a joke, by the way. At least, I think it was. And then you go right to the other extreme and the safe-deposit box is a place to store something you don't want anyone to know you've got. Anyone in this case usually meaning the tax authorities.'

'Or the people you stole it from?'

'Or that, I suppose. What you want to use it for will help you decide who to rent a box from.'

'There's more than one place?'

'In London, where ours was, there are hundreds. There are probably quite a lot here in Israel, too. Banks have them. But banks tend to be a bit nosy, and they get you to sign an agreement that they can open the box without your permission if, say, the police or the tax people ask them to. That could be a bit difficult if you do have one of those Swiss accounts. Or even if you've been salting away money you haven't declared, or things you've bought with money you didn't tell the tax people you'd earned. I'm using the word earned loosely here.'

'So where was yours?'

'Hatton Garden.'

'Which is where?'

'It's London's jewellery quarter. My wife has jewellery. So has her father. I didn't ask too closely where it came from because I could see he didn't want to tell me. People with jewellery like to keep it near diamond traders, and Hatton Garden is where the diamond traders are. And diamond traders themselves have boxes there, of course.'

'Do they have to sign one of those agreements the banks ask for?'

'Not on your life. Those boxes are secret. The only people who know what's in them are the people who rent them.'

Yanek found that sleep impossible that night. He'd never given up thoughts of revenge against those who had tricked him and Zoltan, but it had seemed a hopeless dream. He'd ended Shlomo's life, of course, but that seemed a long time ago now. He'd known where some of the others were, but the police and the IDF between them had given Israel a level of security unknown in any other country in the region. That was great for everyday life, of course, but not if you wanted to carry out personally motivated executions. But now Amos had offered him the hint of a different form of revenge.

And then Rachel reappeared in his life. Rachel, who had rejected him in the camp. Rachel, who he had taken by force when he left there. Rachel, who he had brought from Poland to the Italian coast and then to Palestine against all the odds. Rachel, who he had risked his own life to save from three men who were abducting her. Rachel, who had made clear the disgust she felt for some of what he did but had thanked him for the good things and with whom he had reached some kind of understanding. She walked into his restaurant the day after Amos had returned.

CHAPTER 16

1986 OSTEND, BELGIUM

Seventeen years before the robbery

Arie was working in London. He hadn't seen his father in years and didn't particularly want to. He still had his memories of his father's stories about Europe in wartime, though stories is how he thought of them. He knew, because everyone knew, that people had done remarkable things during the war and he also knew that not all of the things people said they'd done were actually true. The bond with his mother, on the other hand, remained strong and when he got her call asking him to come to Ostend his first reaction was shock. What the devil was she doing in Belgium? Only one way to find out: the ferry from Ramsgate took four hours to reach Ostend, and Arie was on it.

Ilana was waiting for him where she had said she would be. Beside her was a woman about ten years older than Arie. The look of excitement on both faces was something Arie had never seen before. He looked at his mother for an explanation. 'Arie,' she said. 'This is Yudka. Yudka is your sister. Your half-sister, I suppose I should say.'

But Arie didn't need to be told that, because his mother had told him many times the story of Peter and Yudka, Christiana and Imre. He held out a hand and Yudka shook it. He said, 'You came here from Hungary?' When she smiled and nodded, he said, 'You work for the government?' Because Hungary was still held tight in the grip of Russia and ordinary people were not free to leave the country the way his mother had come here from Israel and he had arrived from England. But she smiled and shook her head. 'Then how...?'

'My husband is a tour guide. He is trusted to leave the country as long as his wife and son stay behind. As hostages, you might say. He brought me here in the luggage compartment of his bus.'

Arie nodded, impressed by the courage they had shown. If they'd been caught, the Soviets would have shown them no mercy. 'Your son, too?'

She shook her head once again. 'He is at home. My husband will smuggle me back there, just as he smuggled me out. I was not leaving Hungary: I came to meet my mother. It's been so long.'

'Forty-six years,' said Ilana.

'And your brother?' asked Arie. 'Is he with you?'

A look of discomfort crossed Yudka's face. 'I haven't seen Peter for many years. We were brought up by different parents. You know your mother found him?'

'No. I didn't know that.' He turned to face his mother. 'Why didn't you tell me?'

'It was a long time ago. In fact, in 1953. I found Peter, and I wanted him back. But Christina and Imre, they had looked after him for eleven years and they didn't want to give him up. They had no other children, remember, and they'd risked their lives to look after Peter and they didn't feel like guardians – they felt like parents.'

'You seem very understanding.'

'I am. Of course I am. I know how it feels to have your children ripped from you. I knew it then. But they were still mine and I wanted them and I talked to a lawyer and he said the law was on my side. So I used all the money I could get my hands on to ask the Hungarian courts to give me back my child. It took for ever. But eventually the court decided in my favour. They said Peter should come to Israel and live with me as my son. But someone gave Christina and Imre advance warning that that was going to be the decision. And they vanished. Simply disappeared, taking Peter with them. For years, every time there was a knock on the door I'd think "Is this him? Has my son come home to me?" But, of course, it never happened. Where is he now? Only God knows, and He has not shared the information with me.' Her look of despair turned in a moment to one of joy. 'But at last and at least I have my daughter back. I don't believe I would be safe in returning to Hungary as long as it remains under communist control. So Yudka and I decided to meet here.'

Yudka said, 'The people your mother gave me to were good to me. They treated me like their own and they loved me as though that's who I was.' She smiled at Ilana. 'But they always told me what had happened, and that I had a birth mother somewhere. Of course, I thought she was probably dead. But when someone knocked on my door and told me that a woman called Ilana was looking for someone who sounded a lot like me, I knew straight away. And straight away I knew I had to do whatever was necessary to meet her.' Now the sadness was replaced by a huge smile. 'And now I know I have a brother and sister I didn't know existed.'

1987 Be'er Sheva

Seventeen years before the robbery

Yanek didn't recognise her when she came into the restaurant. He could be forgiven: he hadn't seen her for forty-one years. But she knew him. 'Hello, Yanek. It's been a while. How are you?' He stared at her, knowing he'd seen her somewhere before but not quite sure where. He looked at the bracelet she wore and knew he'd seen that before, too. In the case of the bracelet, he had no difficulty remembering where. She said, 'It's Rachel.'

'Rachel? Rachel from the camp? Rachel from the Shabtai Luzinsky? That Rachel?'

She smiled, though Yanek saw no humour in the smile just as he had not when he asked her what her father did but didn't mention her mother. 'As you say. That Rachel.'

He waited for her to say more. When it became clear that wasn't going to happen, he said, 'Did you come in here by accident?'

'Hardly. Do you get many women without men coming into a place like this? I didn't think so. No, Yanek, I heard about a man called Yanek Hoffman who was running a restaurant. I knew it couldn't be you, of course. You're the last person I could imagine in a job that demanded skills with people. But I had to check, because I have information that might interest the Yanek Hoffman I once knew. And it *is* you.'

'Information?'

'I need half an hour of knowing that you are listening only to me.'

'That can't be now. The morning rush will begin soon and I need to talk to the chef and the waiters. I must be sure we aren't short of anything. Give me twenty minutes.' He led her to a table in the corner and, pulled out a chair. 'Take a seat. I'll make sure no-one troubles you. Some of our regulars can be a bit... boisterous. And, as you said, they're not used to seeing women on their own here. You'll have a coffee, at least?'

'Coffee will be fine.'

'I promise it will be better than fine. I spent a lot of money on a big Italian machine.'

Yanek did the things he needed to do and then he brought his own coffee to Rachel's table. 'Now. You have all my attention.'

The expression on Rachel's face told him that this conversation came, for her, at an emotional cost. She said, 'I stayed at the kibbutz for a few years after you left.'

Yanek shrugged. 'I wasn't cut out for the kibbutzim life.'

'I'm not sure I am, either. But I felt I owed such a debt for being brought here, being able to live an upstanding life as a Jew, knowing I had nothing to fear from the people around me just because I was one... I suppose I felt the need to give something back. And I learned some things while I was there about the debt I owed, and who I owed it to.' Her eyes came up to meet his for the first time. 'I know I thanked you once before, but now I need to say thank you again. Without you, I might never have been able to come here. And not just me. You did that because you wanted the Jewish people to have their own homeland once again, didn't you?'

'Of course.'

'You're a killer, a rapist and a thief, Yanek. But you're also, God help us, a righteous man. How many people do you think are in Israel because of the money you raised?'

Yanek held his hands out wide. 'How can I know?'

'I suppose you can't. But it could be fewer than you think.'

'Oh?'

Rachel seemed lost in thought. Yanek was not the most sensitive person, but he knew enough to let the silence continue. She had something to tell him and was finding it difficult to say the words. She would get there, or she would not. Eventually, she said, 'I might have stayed at the kibbutz forever. But I was reunited with a cousin. Sela. I had assumed she was dead.'

'Like so many.'

'Yes. But she's alive and she's here, in Israel. She talked me into leaving the kibbutz. She helped me get a job as a teacher. I like teaching. It's me, in a way that nothing I did at the kibbutz could ever be.'

'They have teachers in the kibbutz.'

Rachel waved a hand as if to brush the objection away. 'It was never offered to me and in those days I did the things they asked me to do instead of asking for the things I wanted to do. I can't explain, it was all part of the relief and the pride at being here. And knowing that others more worthy could never be here because those animals killed them.' She paused and let her eyes meet his. 'Including you, Yanek. Including you. Do you ever think about the things you did in the camp?'

'No. I don't. It warms me to know that you think about them for me.'

'I'm sorry. Your sarcasm is well-placed. You did many wonderful things, too, when you had the chance. Something else Sela did, apart from getting me a job, was to introduce me to what she thought were suitable men. 'I'm Rachel Rosenbaum now.'

'You're married.' It wasn't a question – he accepted what she told him, even though he'd already checked her ring finger and seen an area fainter than the skin around it. That could mean she simply wasn't wearing a wedding ring right now. It could also mean she'd taken it off and didn't intend to wear it again. Whichever, there had been a ring there long enough to make that mark on the skin.

She said, 'I was married.'

'To someone called Rosenbaum.' It wasn't, of course, an unusual name. A colleague of Shlomo's had been called Rosenbaum, and he'd been in Yanek's mind only yesterday, but that was surely coincidence. But then Rachel took a keyring out of her purse and on it was the key to a safe-deposit box. Yanek felt himself coming more upright.

Rachel said, 'My husband has gone to England.'

'On holiday?'

'Permanently. He isn't coming back. He suggested I go with him, but I don't think he really meant it. Things haven't been the best between us for a while now. When I said I was going to stay, he put our house in my name only and gave me his car.'

'A generous man.'

'He could afford it. And that, really, is why I'm talking to you.'

'To tell me you married a wealthy man?'

'To tell you how he came by his money.' There was another long silence and then, 'He's a jeweller. He hasn't always been a jeweller and he certainly wasn't a diamond merchant. Not one of those Jewish lapidaries in Amsterdam Hitler's men stole from and enslaved and sent to the camps to die. When war broke out, I believe he had a furniture shop.'

That titbit got Yanek's attention. 'Zoltan and I gave the jewellery we persuaded people to donate to the cause to a man called Shlomo. He had a friend... a colleague... called Rosenbaum. I think Rosenbaum sold furniture before the war.'

Rachel had smiled at the word "persuaded." 'It's the same man. He and Shlomo split the jewellery you "persuaded" people to donate between them.'

'They sold it to raise money to pay for people to migrate to Palestine. I expect that was easier for two men than for Shlomo on his own. It's a dirty business because if you want to sell something you have to find someone prepared to buy it. And people would have known that some of what they were buying hadn't been obtained in a nice, clean, legal way. But they did sell it.'

'They sold some of it, Yanek. And they kept some for themselves.'

'I knew Shlomo had done that. I dealt with him for it.' He reached across and put his hand on her bracelet.

'I wondered if that was you. All Rosenbaum knew was that Shlomo had been shot. But if you were there, you know what day it was and what was going on at the time. I didn't know him then, of course: Rosenbaum only told me the story years later. He assumed it was thieves taking advantage of the chaos. I was less sure. And I see you recognise my bracelet.'

'I remember the man whose wife it belonged to before he so generously donated it to the cause. But why are you telling me this now, Rachel?'

She took the safe-deposit key from the ring and pushed it across the table towards him. 'These are the keys my husband gave me when he left. The important ones – important to me, that is – are the car key and his key to our house. But this one opens a box in Hatton Garden. It isn't the only key – Rosenbaum has one. Obviously, or he wouldn't have left this. What happens now depends on how you feel about it. You extracted jewellery from people to help set up a Jewish homeland in Palestine. If the idea that some of it didn't go for the purpose you extracted it for doesn't trouble you, fine. Forget the whole thing.' She stood up. 'The Yanek I knew wasn't a forgiving person. But then, he wasn't the sort of person to own a successful restaurant, either. So maybe what happened back then doesn't matter to you now. Thank you for the coffee. You're right, it was better than just fine.'

When she walked out of the restaurant, leaving the safe-deposit box key behind her, Yanek stayed in his seat. It was some time before his staff were able to get anything like mean

CHAPTER 17

1987 BE'ER SHEVA

Sixteen years before the robbery

Why now? That was the first question Yanek asked himself. Why is she telling me this now? And the answer was fairly obvious. She is angry with Rosenbaum. Angry enough to want revenge. She knows Rosenbaum did the same thing Shlomo did and she knows, or at least suspects, that I killed Shlomo for it. Now she gives me Rosenbaum's name. Does she want me to kill Rosenbaum?

And then came the second question: How long had she known that Rosenbaum stole some of the jewellery we and others gave him? Has she just found out, and is that what has destroyed their marriage? Or has she known for a while, and done nothing about it, because they were okay together?. Because, if that is the case, he couldn't place much value on her use of the word "righteous." Not if she'd only tried to punish Rosenbaum for the crime he'd committed against the Jewish people after he left her.

These thoughts occupied him for the rest of that day and he was still full of them when he went to bed. He'd come to a partial answer, because Rachel would know that killing someone had been banned from the very beginning. Thou shalt not kill. Whoever sheds the blood of man by man shall his blood be shed; for in His image did God make man. Cain and Abel: "Listen! Your brother's blood cries out to me from the soil. And so, cursed shall you be by the soil that gaped with its mouth to take your brother's blood from your hand. If you till the soil, it will no longer give you strength. A restless wanderer shall you be on the earth." Yanek knew those things as well as Rachel did, but that hadn't stopped him in the past and Rachel knew that. But Rachel was a rabbi's daughter. That had to make a difference, surely?

On balance, then, he had to think that Rachel was not encouraging him to kill Rosenbaum. To take revenge in some other way? A rabbi's daughter would know that Jews weren't supposed to do that, either. The more he thought about it, the more he understood the depth of the anger she must feel for her husband. Because that question, "Why now?" wouldn't go away. And he knew the answer. She was offering him the opportunity for revenge because, if he took it, she would be revenged, too. It was true: heaven has no rage like love to hatred turned, nor hell a fury like a woman scorned. He stopped for a moment to think about the way he had treated Ilana. He was a different person now, to some extent at least. If he and Ilana were still together and she told him today that she wanted to leave him, would he still demand every lira she had in return for her freedom?

Yes. He couldn't be sure but he almost certainly would.

What did that say about him as a person? He didn't like to think about it. When you suspect that even your best friend, if asked, might describe you as a bit of a shit, it's probably best to leave the question unasked. And as for what Arie and Bat-Sheva, his children, must think of him... No. Leave it alone.

#

So what was he going to do? This man who knew he wasn't the nicest person on earth? This one-time killer, one-time rapist and one-time extortionist – was he going to leave this new information alone? Walk away and forget about it? Do nothing to avenge Zoltan, the closest human being ever in his life, not excluding Ilana? Zoltan, who had died while obtaining the goods Shlomo and Rosenbaum had stolen? He didn't think so.

Shlomo and Rosenbaum. And there was question number three: Shlomo, Rosenbaum – and how many others? And who were they?

He couldn't say he'd made a decision when he woke because he hadn't really slept but, when the sun rose and that wonderful east Mediterranean light began to spread over the land promised to his people all those centuries ago, he knew what he was going to do. Nothing happened unless God willed it. When Rachel walked through the door of his restaurant and exposed Rosenbaum's wrongdoing to him, she wasn't acting on her own decision. God had sent her. God wanted him to know what Rosenbaum had done and where he kept his reward for evil. And God does nothing without a reason. God wanted Yanek to be the instrument of His judgement against Rosenbaum and against anyone else he could find. And Yanek might quite possibly be the most unworthy Jew who ever lived, but he was not going to refuse God's command.

#

The restaurant that day ran as smoothly as it ever did, and yet regular customers sensed a change in Yanek. As usual, he checked that everything any staff member needed was present in the restaurant and, if it wasn't, he sent the youngest pot washer to get it. He moved around the kitchen, making sure he never got in the way because the head chef had a head chef's temper and wouldn't stand for interruptions even from the man who paid his wages. He circled the dining area in the same way, looking out for problems before the customer was even aware of them. He used what he knew about regulars to ask after their children, their wives or their parents and to encourage them in their jobs and their businesses. He made customers who hadn't eaten there before feel welcome and made sure they knew what was on offer and got what they ordered in the way they wanted it. He was, in short, the same attentive restaurateur he had been since the day he bought the place. And yet...

He was abstracted. Customers and staff alike could see that he was abstracted. And the reason for his abstraction was that he was forming a plan. As yet, it consisted of only two actions:

1. Find out who else took jewellery for themselves
2. Sell the restaurant to provide funds to go to and live for a while in London.

He wasn't going to rush into the second action because the restaurant would provide his income while he worked on the first action. He needed the names of other people who had worked for Etzel at the same time as Shlomo and Rosenbaum, had taken jewellery and money from people doing the same work as Yanek and Zoltan, and might have kept some of it for themselves. By the time the last customer had left that evening, the waiters had cleared away, the pot washers were washing pots and Yanek, the head waiter and the head chef were enjoying a cigarette and a brandy before heading home, he had understood that the first action needed to be divided in two, so now the plan read:

1. Find out who else accepted money and jewellery from those who had obtained donations.

2. Find out which of those has a safe-deposit box at Hatton Garden.
3. Sell the Restaurant.

And even now he wasn't quite done, because he was almost certainly going to have to visit Hatton Garden and establish some sort of relationship with the people there before he could find out who had a box. And so the plan evolved into its final stage, at least for now:

1. Find out who else accepted money and jewellery from those who had obtained donations.
2. Sell the Restaurant.
3. Find out who among the people accepting money and jewellery from those who had obtained donations has a safe-deposit box at Hatton Garden.

That was it. That was the plan. But how was he going to execute the first action? He had no idea how many people other than him and Zoltan had extorted donations, so how was he going to learn who, apart from Shlomo and Rosenbaum, they had passed the donations to? The answer when it came to him was simple: get acquainted, which in some cases would mean reacquainted, with other people who had served in Etzel and find out what they knew.

CHAPTER 18

1989 BE'ER SHEVA

Fourteen years before the robbery

It probably says something about Israel's perennial lack of peace that 1989 seemed like a relatively quiet year, even though terrorist attacks never really stopped. In February, IDF Sergeant Binyamin Meisner was ambushed and killed in Nablus. A month later, a Palestinian armed with a knife killed two Israelis in Tel Aviv and wounded a third. At the beginning of May, the newly formed Hamas kidnapped and murdered two Israeli soldiers. Sergeant Avi Sasportas who served with Israeli Special Forces got into a vehicle with two Hamas terrorists disguised as Orthodox Jews. They beat him to death and buried his body in a field. Corporal Ilan Saadon was similarly fooled by what appeared to be ultraorthodox Jews but were in fact Hamas, and was shot in the head. His body would not be found for another seven years. Then in July Israel experienced the first suicide attack inside its borders when a Palestinian member of Islamic Jihad seized control of a crowded bus and steered it over a steep cliff into a ravine, killing sixteen passengers.

It went on like that all year. Given his background, Yanek might have been expected to take a strong interest in what the IDF was doing to keep Israelis safe and he did – but, for once, this was not the thing at the centre of his attention. In July, Israeli commandos entered Lebanon and kidnapped Hezbollah chief Sheik Abdel Karim Obeid. While Yanek, his staff and all his customers cheered the commandos' operation just as they had thirteen years earlier when the commandos landed in Entebbe and freed 103 hostages from a hijacked airliner under the nose of Uganda's lunatic president Idi Amin, Yanek had other things on his mind.

His first contact with Etzel alumni had all the mystery one might expect of a meeting between one-time operatives of an always shadowy organisation. Years before, when Yanek had first landed in Palestine, someone he didn't know and had never seen since took a seat beside him at breakfast and said, "If you need help from your friends in Etzel, or simply feel lonely and want to talk to people who know what you went through so that Jews could return at last to their homeland, go to the bookshop on the corner of Curzon Street and ask for Ezra." He had ignored the invitation at the time, feeling no need of it, and his only reaction had been surprise that a bookshop existed so early in his new country's life. Looking back, he realised now that that simply meant he had a great deal to learn when he first arrived. But then, so did everyone. They had built this country one step at a time, not really knowing what they were doing but working it out as they went along.

Forty-two years later, finding the bookshop wasn't easy because Curzon Street now had a different name. One more fitting to its Jewish surroundings. And then the whole area had been redeveloped. But, eventually, he found someone who could tell him where the bookshop that had once been on Curzon Street could now be found. When he got there, a young woman who had not been born in 1947 and who wore a nametag saying her name was Ruth smiled at him. 'Can I help you? Is there a particular book you're interested in? Or an author?'

Yanek had learned to read and write since arriving in Palestine, but he had no great interest in reading a book for its own sake. There was, of course, no need to tell Ruth that. He said, 'I'm looking for Ezra.'

The moment the words were out he could tell that they meant something to the young woman. She paused and then took a notebook from a drawer. 'Ezra was my father. I'm afraid he's no longer with us. He died three years ago.'

'Oh. I'm sorry.'

'Thank you. But perhaps you were looking for something else? An introduction?'

Yannick nodded. 'It's a long time since I was given your father's name. 1947, in fact.'

'That *is* a long time. But there are people still around... They are more careful these days than once they were. I would need to give them your name and tell them where to contact you. Then, if they didn't get in touch with you, I would ask you not to come here again.'

'I understand.' He gave his name and the address of the restaurant and she wrote it in her notebook. 'Thank you, Mr Hoffman. Someone will be in touch.'

'Or not.'

She smiled. 'As you say. Or not.'

#

Divorce had not meant that women had completely disappeared from Yanek's life. He was too young for that, and he had the same needs he had always had. He was never going to marry again, that was not in doubt. Marriage hadn't suited him, and the responsibility of having children was something he didn't want to face a second time. When you've never been parented yourself, parenting someone else doesn't come easy. Yanek saw other parents putting their children's needs ahead of their own. He knew at some level that that was the right thing to do. But it wasn't something the adults in his own life had done, when there had been any, and knowing that he should do something wasn't quite enough.

So no courtship and no marriage. But that wasn't the same as no women. Of course he could have paid for sex, but this was the man who had taken his wife's own pension from her when they parted. Paying went against everything he believed in. And he couldn't behave as he had in the camp. There were no women in Israel so hungry that they'd open their legs for a piece of sausage and the end of a loaf of bread. And they had the rule of law here. If he simply threw someone down and took her, as he had Rachel before he'd walked out of the camp with a stolen machine-gun, he'd end in prison.

He turned to what he thought of as the hand on the hip. Women came to the restaurant. Not customers – as Rachel had told him, this wasn't a place where an unaccompanied woman would choose to eat. And he wasn't interested in the hired help, because they'd be around afterwards and they might want something more permanent than a one night stand. But suppliers: van drivers bringing meat, fish, vegetables and wine were female more often than male. And so were those who delivered cleaning materials and took away table linen, uniforms, towels and the like to bring them back clean. Usually the transaction was straightforward and strictly commercial. They delivered the goods, he signed for them, they went away. But Yanek was a tall, well-built man and not bad looking and occasionally the woman would give him an appraising glance. If the glance lasted more than a moment, she might find Yanek's hand resting, lightly and just for a moment, on her hip. Nine times out of ten, she looked affronted or stepped away and the hand vanished immediately leaving nothing on Yanek's face to suggest any carnal interest.

But the tenth time – the time when, instead of stepping away, the woman turned slightly in his direction. Stepped just a little closer. Those were the ones Yanek looked forward to. A kiss, an embrace, a shuffling out of clothes, and a consummation that would mean a few weeks without that feeling that something was missing from his life.

#

Three days later, he stopped by the table where Simon, one of his regular customers, was eating dinner. With Simon tonight was a man Yanek had never seen before. He had been watching Yanek so closely since the moment they walked in that Yanek was aware that at the very least something was up. When Yanek asked whether they were enjoying their braised chicken, Simon said, 'Please, Yanek. Take a seat.' When he had done so, Simon said, 'Ezra's bookshop.'

So here it was. Contact. And from someone he had never expected it from. He said, 'Yes.'

Even to him it seemed an inadequate response, but Simon didn't seem to mind. The other man said nothing but his eyes didn't leave Yanek's face for a moment. Simon said, 'I've always known you were one of us, of course. That's one of the reasons I come here.' He smiled. 'Apart from the food and the company, of course.'

'One of us?'

He was hoping to hear the word Etzel, but Simon ignored the question. He said, 'You understand, Yanek, things have moved on in more than forty years. To ourselves we are heroes – you are a hero, Zoltan was a hero. But not everyone today sees things that way. If you'd walked into Ezra's shop forty years ago, it would have been very straightforward. Even thirty years. And, of course, we know about your work in the desert with the rockets, so we know you're even more of a hero than you were. But you didn't make contact. You waited four decades. So now we need to know what it is you're looking for.'

Now there was a question. A very simple question in fact, but what answer to offer? "I want to find out who else apart from Shlomo and Rosenbaum received donations obtained by people like me. And then I want to find out which of them took some of the money for themselves, so I can seek revenge." No, it wasn't hard to see the drawbacks in that approach. Starting with Simon's almost certain refusal to do anything for him. Instead, he said, 'When I first came here, I was a young man. A life before me in a new land. Now... Well, life did what life does. It went.'

'You're not an old man yet, Yanek.'

'I'm not a young one, either. I'm divorced, I see my son rarely and my daughter never. The best friend I ever had died years ago. But you know that – you mentioned his name so you know all about it. Those years at the end of the war and right afterwards were the best of my life. I didn't know that then. I know it now. I'd like to spend a bit of time, while I still have it, shooting the breeze with a few other people who know what I went through because they went through it themselves.'

'And that's all?'

'That's all. What else would there be?'

Simon looked at the man beside him, who had still not spoken. Then he said, 'Okay. Thanks for being so open. You will hear something in a day or two.'

CHAPTER 19

1989 BE'ER SHEVA

Fourteen years before the robbery

For the next few days, Yanek was more tense than he would have expected. He barked at waiting staff over minor errors that, before, he would have corrected with a casual word. He was even short with the customers on whom he depended for a living. There was no sign of Simon, who normally didn't let a second day go by without coming in for a meal. Amos sensed that something was troubling Yanek and did what he could to bring him out of his depression, but nothing really worked. And then Simon came in for dinner, this time on his own, and when Yanek came to his table he said, 'Some of your old comrades in arms are having a get-together on Monday night. You're invited.'

Yanek felt the tension leaving him. He still had some way to go to get the information he wanted, but at least the next step was now available. He said, 'Anyone I know?'

'I doubt it. They took care to keep you boys apart, didn't they? If one was captured, he couldn't tell the Germans names he didn't know. But they know who you are.' He smiled. 'You and Zoltan built something of a reputation for yourselves. Did you know you two collected more in donations than any other team?'

Yanek hadn't known that. It gave him a feeling of pride, like an old man who in his youth had been a great athlete and now hears someone in a position to know telling other people about him. 'Where do I go?'

Simon said, 'I'll come here about seven and take you. It has to be someone who knows you, or you wouldn't get in. There'll only be a dozen or so people there. You and Zoltan were younger than many of the others, and some are no longer with us. You left it a long time.

Another few years and there'd have been even fewer people for you to chat with about old times.'

That gave Yanek pause. He'd carried this anger so long, it felt like just yesterday that he realised people he had trusted were in fact thieves. But it hadn't been yesterday, or even last year. It was more than fifty years since Germany had invaded its neighbours in the search for what it called "room to live" and only a few years less than fifty since Etzel launched its fightback. It hurt more than Yanek could say to know that not everyone fighting for the cause had shown the same selflessness or dedication: it hurt even more to realise that death had already placed beyond his reach some of the people from whom he wanted to extract justice. He needed to get into action to make sure no more of them evaded him.

For all that, staff and customers alike saw that whatever had passed between him and Simon had buoyed him up. He was, once again, the patron customers liked talking to and the boss employees enjoyed working for.

#

When Monday came, Yanek showered, shaved with special care, and put on a new shirt and a suit that he had had carefully pressed – an expense he didn't usually put himself to. He thought of this evening as a military reunion. Even though, according to Simon, he had never been in the company of men he was to meet and they had never been in his, he thought of them as what Simon had said they were. His old comrades in arms. They had fought together in times of immense danger to make possible this country they now lived in. Was it childish to want the others to know that he had done all right for himself? Perhaps. But the fact that it's childish to want something doesn't make it wrong.

He had made sure that everyone was in position and aware of what they had to do well before the first dinner servings. His concern was so obvious, the head chef told him to stop. 'I don't know why you're so nervous tonight. Is it just because you're going out somewhere? Do you think we can't be trusted to do the job without you being around to keep us on track? What about that time you had the flu and couldn't come in for four days? Did you get any complaints from customers? No. You didn't. You are not as important as you think you are, so go and do whatever it is you're planning to do and leave the rest of us to get on with our work.'

Yanek knew the danger of irritating the chef, so he poured himself a glass of wine from the Galilee, lit a cigarette and sat down to wait. At exactly 7 o'clock, Simon opened the door and gestured that Yanek should go with him.

#

Simon drove them in a Peugeot saloon. The journey took about twenty minutes, during which Simon chatted about all sorts of things but told Yanek nothing about what was going to happen until they parked outside a bar. Then he said, 'This place is owned by Chaim. He's Hungarian – well, he isn't, he's Israeli, just like you and me but he was born in Hungary – and at the end of the war he did exactly what you did. So that's something you have in common – you both helped to fund the birth of Israel and you both own places of entertainment. You have a restaurant and he has a bar. What else you share, I leave it to you to discover. Chaim has a room upstairs that he makes available for functions of one kind or another. Most of them, he charges for. Old Etzel comrades meetings, he does not. I'll introduce you. You have cab fare home? Don't look at me like that.'

'How else should I look at you? Of course I have the price of a taxi. You're not coming in?'

'Yanek, I'm thirty years younger than you and anyone else in that room tonight. I've attended a couple of meetings. They all go the same way. Old men enjoying a drink and remembering when they were young men defying death. Then they start remembering other young men who didn't defy death quite well enough. It can get a bit maudlin, if you want my opinion. But they're a good bunch of guys and I'm sure you'll enjoy yourself.' Then he opened the bar door and led Yanek upstairs, where he signalled to a man with a large stomach, a red face and no hair. 'Chaim, this is Yanek. Yanek, this is Chaim. I leave you to each other.' Then he walked back downstairs and disappeared.

Chaim shook Yanek's hand. 'Welcome. I used to hear your name from time to time: it's good to meet you at last.' He pointed to a table on which were beer, wine and spirits. 'Help yourself to anything you want. In a while, merguez sausages and various other snacks will be laid out. We ask for a donation of the amount you think you can afford right at the start and that pays for everything. I charge at my cost. Any money left over goes into the funds for events we hold from time to time.' He watched Yanek place some money with what was already there and then said, 'Now let me introduce you to the others.'

#

It was well after midnight when Yanek got home. He'd had a good evening – the best he could remember for a long time and, if he was honest, possibly the best he'd ever had, letting down his hair with a friendly bunch of guys who shared his experiences and his values. And he'd begun the work of collecting the information he needed. There was still a lot he didn't know and he'd realised while he was collecting it that he had to be careful not to let people understand why he wanted it, but he had the start of a list of recipients of donations. What they were doing now, and whether they had been as dishonest as Shlomo and Rosenbaum in the way they dealt with what they received, was something for future meetings – but he had started.

If anything, rather than calming his fever, the fact that he had begun had made it worse. A number of times in his conversations during the evening someone's name had been mentioned and someone else had said, 'Of course, he's gone now. A heart attack.' Or cancer. Or one of the other major killers. The message was clear. He needed to find out who his targets should be and then he needed to hunt them down before death removed them from his grasp.

CHAPTER 20

1989 BE'ER SHEVA

Fourteen years before the robbery

Focusing on the job in hand had never been a problem for Yanek. Why would it? In the early days, it had kept him out of prison; later, it kept him alive. Running with teenage hoodlums in Berehove, making sure his gang got the job done in the camp, prising money out of unwilling donors, getting his charges all the way and against the odds from Poland to Palestine, developing prototypes for the rockets that would keep the young state of Israel safe: he'd done it all and kept his mind 100% on the job. Of course he had. He'd known what the price of failure would be. Imprisonment, being killed himself by the SS, seeing his dreams of a Jewish state fail, allowing Rachel and the others to be picked off along the way, and letting the hostile states that surrounded Israel attack it without meeting an effective response. None of that was acceptable. But now he had two jobs. One was to continue running the restaurant. The other was the first step in the three-step plan he had made: to find out who else had accepted money and jewellery from those who, like him and Zoltan, had obtained donations. But what he had to accept was that those two jobs were not equally important. Once step one in the plan was completed, step two was to sell the restaurant, and step three was to find out more about that list compiled in step one. The conclusion was obvious: the most important task was to get the names of people who'd been in a position to take for themselves some of the money he and people like him had collected. When that was over, he'd be on his way to London for step three, so the task of finding a buyer for the restaurant had to start now but must not displace in importance the job of collecting the names.

He didn't want to make a big issue of finding a buyer because he didn't want people talking about it. He was going to be asking other long ago Etzel members questions about the people they had dealt with and he didn't want any of them hearing that his restaurant was for sale in case it made them suspicious about his true motives. Common sense would have told him that most of those Etzel members were the same sort of age as he was, and so they'd have assumed that he'd made enough money from the restaurant and he was ready to retire, but common sense wasn't very obvious in the way he was thinking right now. So what he did was to mention in the hearing of his younger customers that he was contemplating selling the restaurant and leave it to them to spread the word. He also told the head chef that he was wondering whether this might be a good time to sell, because the chef might know people who could put up the necessary money and was unlikely to want to find himself facing a change of employer without knowing who the new boss would be. He made it clear that he wanted a complete break. Accepting a down payment and keeping a stake in the restaurant would not allow him to do what he wanted to do.

It would work or it would not, and if it didn't, he'd have to find another way, but his life so far had been gilded enough that he could reasonably expect that a likely restaurant buyer would get the message and come to see him.

That left collecting his list of names as his most important task and he went about it energetically. He attended every meeting in Chaim's bar. He told Chaim that he had a room for private functions in his own restaurant and that, any time Chaim wanted to take a break from being the host, he would be happy to make that room available free of charge and to feed and water the guests for no more money than they were used to paying Chaim.

Slowly, the list came together. Three names. Then a fourth. A few weeks without addition and then no fewer than five came in at one single meeting. It seemed that the questions he had asked without making it clear that they were questions had stoked interest that had not been there before. What his new friends really enjoyed talking about was episodes of courage. Risks they had run, capture they had evaded, particularly valuable pieces of jewellery they'd obtained. Running through darkened streets knowing gunmen pursued them. Shinning up drainpipes to get through open windows so that they could hide. Erotic adventures – 'A girl and her panties are soon parted,' said one man to general laughter, inspiring a series of stories, each a little wilder than the last, about young women who'd admired what they were doing and offered themselves as a reward. It was a useful reminder to Yanek that not every story recounted was actually true. "The older I get, the better I was" was as true here as it was in memories of sporting success.

But still the list grew. 'Yes,' someone would say. 'Of course we handed it over. That's why we took the donations: so that we could pass them to people who would use them to benefit the Jewish people.' Who were those people they had given the spoils to? At first, they found it hard to remember. The men who'd received the goods weren't heroes. Those who had collected the stuff, they were the heroes. And they were the men standing here with a drink in their hand, reminiscing. 'But, since you mention it, Yanek, who were they? Let me think now.' And, at the end, he had a list of twenty-five names.

Some of those names were of no use to him because one of the company was able to say straightaway, 'He's dead. Never made it out of Germany. The SS got him, the bastards.' Or, 'Got into a fight with the British when he was trying to land in Palestine. Shot resisting arrest – that's what the Brits said.' Others had made it to Palestine but time had worked its mysteries and, one way or another, they had gone where only God could judge them. Still, Yanek was left with fourteen names on his list. Was that enough? What decided him that it was, was a conversation he had one evening with his head chef.

'I want to buy the restaurant.'

'You have the money? The full price?'

'I can raise it. I have a partner ready to put up what I don't have. We will be 50-50 owners.'

'Make it 51-49. 50-50 doesn't work. You will have arguments. When can you complete?'

'She has a shop to sell.'

'She? Your partner is a woman? Then maybe 50-50 will be okay. As long as... Well. You know.'

'As long as we are also partners outside the business. Yes, I know. She has a buyer. She believes she will have the money within a month. What we ask you is not to sell to someone else until the month is up.'

Yanek clapped him on the back. 'It's a deal. You have your wish. Will you make changes?'

'Does it matter? It will be my restaurant, not yours.'

Yanek smiled. He was still aware of the importance of not upsetting your chef. 'No, my friend. It doesn't matter at all.'

'If you want, you can go on holding your Etzel meetings in the private room.'

'That's all right. Once I've sold, I'll be out of Israel for some time.' And, though he didn't put it into words, Etzel's importance to him would be at an end.

He needed to do one more thing, and someone he met at an Etzel gathering helped him do it. Not a passport – that would have been too much – but the next best thing. There was no way of knowing how far the bad stories about Yanek Hoffman had spread, but he didn't want to find when he launched his Hatton Garden scheme that he was bound to fail because of negative stories about his past. He intended to introduce himself as Moshe Ruben. And now he had a full set of identity papers to back that claim up.

CHAPTER 21

JANUARY 2003, JAFFA

Six months before the robbery

Yossi Shulman the tailor laughed his head off when Yanek walked into his tiny little shop in old Jaffa. 'You haven't bought a suit from me for years, and I doubt you are getting married again, so what is the occasion? And why have you grown that beard? I never saw you with a beard. Unshaven, yes, many times – but looking like a rabbi? Never.'

Not like a rabbi, you damn fool, he wanted to say. I need to look like a successful Jewish businessman. Hence the extra weight. Hence the beard. But all he said was, 'Can't a man want to look his best without people laughing at him?'

'Yanek. If you don't want to tell me, you don't want to tell me. Let's get the tape on you: you've put on a bit of weight since I last measured you.'

Something had begun to worry Yanek. Something that said he might have less time than he hoped. Not just because the people he wanted revenge on might die before he got to their treasure, but also because of the keys. He'd worked in the desert with keys just like that. It was an old-fashioned design, and there must surely be new ideas coming along that would displace it. If he faced his intentions squarely, what he planned to do was to open safe-deposit boxes at Hatton Garden that belonged to other people and remove jewellery that those people should not have had. As long as no-one changed the design of the key, all he had to do was identify which boxes belonged to his targets, and then find a way to empty them while no-one was watching. Just putting it like that was scary enough, because how was he going to get near anyone's box on his own? Wasn't it a standard feature of safe-deposit boxes that you were never on your own? But there would always be two keys, one of which would have to be turned by one of the security guards? That was going to be enough of a problem, without forgetting that his purpose would not be served by robbing anyone who had done the Jewish people no harm. The boxes he opened had to be the right boxes. And he was going to need good luck and a following wind just to find out which boxes the right ones were. If, by the time he knew that, Hatton Garden had issued new keys to a new design, wouldn't that be game over? Before it started? And someone might very well be developing new locks and new keys right now, because the kind of people wealthy enough to have Hatton Garden safe-deposit boxes were likely also the kind to think good security was worth paying for.

Time, in other words, was of the essence. He needed this new suit because he needed to present himself in London looking like the successful businessman he was going to pretend to be. And he needed it now, because he wanted to be on the plane to London as quickly as possible.

Yossi Shulman was a professional who cared about the quality of his work and how his customers looked when they wore his productions around town. He was not a man to be hurried. By the time the suit was finished, the bonds of friendship and humour that had connected Yossi and Yanek had become frayed to the point of disappearance. But finished it was.

He spent that night in a hotel close to Ben Gurion Airport. The size of the task he had taken on came to him as he tried to sleep. He knew there were those who didn't much care for him: his ex-wife and his children first and foremost, but names from his past also came into his mind. Rachel – obviously. Equally obviously, people he had robbed, not just since the war but ever since the childhood he'd never really had. People who'd survived in the camp and knew how he'd behaved as a kapo. But there was another side to that balance sheet – first as a carpenter building prototype rockets for the IDF and then as a restaurateur he'd shown confidence and the ability to charm people who might think themselves immune to charm. Was he guaranteed to succeed in his latest mission? No, he wasn't, and he might very well end up without a cent, living on the street somewhere. But he had a chance. Oh yes, he had a chance. It was up to him.

And with that thought he accepted that daylight would soon be here and, as sleep continued to evade him, he might as well get up and prepare for his journey.

#

JANUARY 2003, LONDON

The flight went well, except that the air hostess spilled coffee on his trousers. Yossi had told him that buying only one pair of trousers with a suit was a false economy because trousers wore out faster than jackets, but Yanek had not wanted to spend the extra money on a second pair. Now he had most of a five-hour flight to regret the decision. It didn't take him long, though, to find a one hour dry cleaner near Paddington station once he was through customs and immigration and had travelled there on the Heathrow Express. The area around Paddington was not where he intended to stay, but when he started looking for digs he wanted to present the right image from the first moment. He needed to look like an authentic Jewish jewellery trader and authentic Jewish jewellery traders were not likely to walk around looking as though they spilled food on themselves.

He'd talked to people who knew London well and he knew roughly where he wanted to be. Hatton Garden was in Holborn, but Holborn wasn't the best place to meet and mix with the kind of people he wanted to meet and mix with. Jewish people. A number of places were likely to make that possible, but some – like Hampstead and Finchley – were likely to cost more than he wanted to pay so he had decided to look for a room in Golders Green.

In the room of a substantial house a short walk from Golders Green tube station, a sign in the window said:

Room To Let

The woman who answered the door bell could have been any age from 30 to 50. Her smile when she saw who had rung her bell said to Yanek, "This is the one. Get in here." And doing so proved easy, abhad guided him here in preference to any other place. He knew that when she was showing him the room and she said, 'Meals are extra, if you want them. Breakfast and dinner: I don't do lunch. And, of course, only cold meals on Shabbat, which I prepare the previous day so you need to book those in advance.' She looked at him as if making sure he understood what he was being told and then, just to be certain, said, 'Everything kosher, of course.'

Yanek nodded. 'How many rooms do you have?'

'To Let? Six. But only one is vacant: my gentlemen tend to stay a long time. They find themselves settled here. Do you plan to be in London for long, Mr Ruben?'

The use of his newly assumed name almost threw him out of his stride. He said, 'I can't say at present. A few months, at least; perhaps longer. Time will tell. In any case, I'd like to take the room. Shall I pay you, say, a month in advance?'

Her smile said that would be splendid. And so, the first stage of his Hatton Garden adventure was completed. The landlady introduced herself as Rosa, and it was clear that she would be eager to gossip when he was in the mood. That was fine – he would be happy to give her, over time, a full account of himself and what he was doing in London. How much of it would be true was another matter entirely.

CHAPTER 22

JANUARY 2003 – LONDON

Six months before the robbery

Yanek spent the weekend getting to know Golders Green and the parts of London he was interested in and establishing his credentials with people around him. He talked to Rosa's other tenants at breakfast, at dinner and in the room Rosa had set aside for them. He asked for advice on the best synagogue to attend, because Golders Green had more than one and London wasn't short of synagogues elsewhere. He actually attended one, for the first time in decades, and introduced himself to the rabbi. He had too much social nous to just reel off the back story he had developed for himself, but he made sure to slip little bits here and there into every conversation. The picture he was developing in the minds of others was one he had worked on with care after deciding that he was going to make this attempt to take back what had been stolen. He was Moshe Ruben, born in Czechoslovakia because if he said he was from somewhere else people would wonder why he couldn't speak that country's language. He'd been raised in a loving Orthodox Jewish family: his mother had stayed home and looked after house, husband and children while his father was a jeweller in Prague. When the Germans had come, Moshe's apprenticeship to his father had been brought to a sudden end but, fortunately, he'd already learned a great deal of what he needed to know about valuing and trading in jewels (especially diamonds) and assembling individual jewels into attractive pieces – a skill at which he had already surpassed his father. He'd gone into hiding after coming home to find that his parents and his sister had been taken away, but a few weeks later his hiding place had been betrayed to the Germans and he found himself in a camp himself. He had no idea what had happened to the rest of his family, though after assiduous efforts to find them he had had to accept that they were dead. Even if they hadn't died in the camps, his parents would by now be well into their nineties. His own life had been spared when Jewish lapidaries had been brought from Amsterdam to the camp he was in and, because of his background, he was assigned to help them instead of being put to backbreaking work outside. Most of the lapidaries were dead; when he talked about his own survival, he simply held out his hands in a gesture accepted universally as meaning "Who can explain it?" 'I survived,' he would say. 'How? Why me? I have no more idea than you have. If the Allies had taken another week to arrive... But they did not. I made my way to Israel, and that is my home now, but business brings me here and I am happy to come because without the British and the Americans I would be dead. And so, in all likelihood, would you.'

This story was easily accepted because it was so similar to the stories of so many to whom he told it. 'And now you are back in the jewellery trade?' people would ask.

'What else can I do? It's what I was raised to. It's all I know.'

And that enabled him to ask, in the most general terms and without appearing to focus on any particular individual, who they knew in London who was or had been jewellery traders. Of course, he already knew the name of Rosenbaum, but he wanted as many of the rest as possible.

#

On Monday, his suit well pressed, he checked into the Hatton Garden safe-deposit company and rented no fewer than four safe-deposit boxes. The fact was that all of them would remain empty, but only he knew that. He needed them to establish a reputation as a dealer in a large way of business. He also needed them to test the keys he was going to make, once he had found out the design of the keys to the boxes rented by his targets.

The cost of four boxes was unavoidable. He had allowed himself a maximum of one year: however carefully he managed his money, he could not see any possibility of stretching the amount he had longer than that. In fact, he gave a great deal of thought to reducing his expenditure. Rent for his room was one obvious possibility: he remembered the remark by one of his new Etzel acquaintances that a girl and her panties are soon parted. It was, of course, a play on the well-known saying about a fool and his money, but it was worth thinking about. If he could persuade Rosa to share her bed with him then sharing her rooms would be an easy next step. And Rosa was far from unappealing. He would set about her seduction. Slowly, though – she was a London woman, a city woman, and persuading her of his good intentions would not be as easy as getting into the knickers of a young Israeli girl of good upbringing who had heard and believed in the command to go forth and multiply in this new land that God had given back to his people after so long in exile.

After making that start, he got into the habit of visiting his safe-deposit boxes every day. They remained empty all the time he rented them, but – once again – there was no need for people to know that. And he made a point of making friends with everyone he met there, especially those who worked for the safe-deposit company. He exuded charm. He took people to lunch, for which he paid, and in the case of those he thought could help him most he even took their whole families out for dinner. People were talking about him. That was a good thing – of course. But it also brought problems.

CHAPTER 23

FEBRUARY 1990 – LONDON

Five months before the robbery

He had been in London for a month. His efforts to make a friend of Rosa had succeeded: Rosa was a warm and affectionate person to whom friendship came naturally. When he tried to push a little beyond the friend relationship, he met the nicest possible brick wall. Rosa had seen it all before. She was attractive to men, and she knew it. A nice face, good figure, outgoing personality, ready smile and she owned that big house free and clear of any mortgage. What was not to like? But she was no young innocent, heart ready to be stolen. Moshe Ruben was not the first man to send the message "I will if you will" and not the first to wonder, when he saw the complete lack of reaction, whether he'd been understood. He might have found it useful to be present at one of Rosa's regular Tuesday lunch meetings with her sister and her female friends.

'This Mr Ruben, Rosa. He sounds like a sweetie.'

'I'm sure he means to.'

'You doubt him?'

Rosa shrugged. 'How can you tell? It's the wrong question. What you should be asking is: Do I need him? Or any man?'

'Oh, well, *need*. Nobody *needs* a man. Do you want one? That's what matters.' When Rosa didn't answer, her friend said, 'That was a question, Rosa. And it was addressed to you.'

Rosa laughed. 'I thought you were just spouting off, as usual. A question? What was it again? Oh – do I want a man? What would I want one for?'

'Well, if you don't know...'

'Oh. That. No, I don't feel any desperate requirement. I mean, it's nice to have someone say nice things to me from time to time. And he does that. But so do others. All the other stuff? Don't you think that's all hormones? And I'm not eighteen anymore. The hormones are still there, but I have them nicely under control, thank you very much.'

Her sister said, 'I haven't met Mr Ruben yet. But he sounds charming. And my sister has never been susceptible to charm.'

'Rosa! Is this about trust?'

'Well, that's a strange conclusion. I'm wary of charm, so I don't trust people who show it. Where'd you get that idea from?'

'You don't, though, do you?' asked her sister.

Rosa sat in silence for a while. What did she really think about her new lodger? 'He seems very genuine. But, if he is, he'll still be genuine a year from now. What's the rush?'

#

Esther lived rent-free in a room on the top floor of Rosa's house in return for keeping the public rooms clean. If

Rosa was in no hurry to respond to Yanek's charm offensive, the opposite was true of her. There were grins from other men in the tenants' sitting room when they saw a startled Yanek turn away from Esther's quite open advance. 'Don't take it personally,' said one of them when the rebuffed Esther had left the room.

'Don't take it personally? How else could I take it?'

'You're not the first. I don't suppose you'll be the last.'

'Responding is a mistake, though,' said another. 'Leonard did that and he had to leave.'

'Leonard?' said Yanek.

'Before your time. He'd been here a couple of years and he seemed settled. Then he had a couple of nights in the sack with Esther. I'm sure he thought she took it as casually as he did, but he was wrong. She never left him alone. In the end, Rosa asked him to leave. It was all becoming a bit too much.'

'Him? She asked him to leave? Why not her, Esther?'

'Ah. You have to understand Esther's position here.'

'And if you do,' said the other man, 'you'll know more than we do.'

'Yes, that's true. But it's clear, Esther isn't just one of the staff. Rosa looks after her. People who were here when she came say there's some kind of family connection. I don't know whether that's true, but Leonard made a mistake when he asked Rosa to choose between him and Esther.'

'You do need to be aware of Esther, though, Moshe.'

'Yes, you do. She's always here. Including times when Rosa is out and so are you. And Esther knows where Rosa keeps the spare keys.'

Yanek said, 'She steals things?'

'I've never heard her accused of that. But she likes to know what's going on. If you've got anything in your room you'd like to keep quiet, lock it away.'

'Thanks for the tip.'

#

His efforts with the Hatton Garden security staff were more successful. That was especially true in the case of a young man called Steve. Yanek got into the habit of inviting Steve to a small kosher café in Granville Street where he bought salmon bagels for both of them. To Steve, their conversations were no more than friendly chat about things that concerned both their lives, and why should he not enjoy friendly chat? Steve had grown up in London, where people placed you in society by your accent. A security guard knew his place and his customers knew theirs, and one was some distance below the other. It was a pleasure to have a customer to deal with who talked to you like an equal. Israel must be a more democratic, egalitarian country than Britain. Steve wondered how easy it would be to move there, and whether he would be accepted. He didn't know much about Judaism, but he wondered whether his possession of a foreskin might be a problem. It certainly wasn't something he could consider having removed. Just thinking about that made him cross his legs and groan.

Yanek saw their conversations differently. He needed to befriend all the security staff, whatever it took, because what he really wanted was to be close to the keys to other people's safe-deposit boxes. He wasn't – obviously – going to ask Steve or anyone else to show other people's keys to him. Nothing so gauche. Nothing so certain to raise suspicion. But he needed to see them. He needed to memorise them. Without that, how could he ever reproduce them on his key-cutting machine?

He wanted Steve and his colleagues in a position where having Mr Ruben around seemed like the normal state of affairs. That was never going to happen if they had any inkling that Mr Ruben was planning to duplicate those keys so that he could open safe-deposit boxes that weren't his. So he was open with Steve about his past. Or part of his past. And not quite as open as Steve thought he was.

'Everyone who went to Israel in the early days had to turn his hand to what the country needed. And it didn't need jewellers. We were a young country surrounded by others that wanted us gone. They were going to sweep us into the sea. Those were the words they used. So I had to forget for a while everything I'd learned about diamonds. I was sent into the desert to help design and build rockets.'

'Why did they want you gone, Mr Ruben?'

'Please, Steve, call me Moshe. Why did they want us gone? That's a long story. You realise Christ was a Jew?'

'Eh? But...'

'I know. It's a shocker, isn't it? You assume Christ was a Christian. But how could that be? Christians worship Christ. Well, they don't, they worship God, but they believe that God was in Christ. But Christ was born a Jew, and it was a Jew – one of his own people – who betrayed him to the Romans. And the result of that betrayal was Christ's death. So the early Christians used to say that Jews had killed Christ. We were Christ killers. Rome is where you'll find the Pope today and people think of it as the centre of the Christian world. But, in fact, it was the Romans who killed Jesus. Still, we were stuck with that Christ killer name. Because it's always the winners who write history, and they write it the way they want people to believe it happened. And there is something in the idea. It isn't completely made up. You've heard of Barabbas?'

'He was a bandit.'

'That's what people say now. It isn't what they said then. The name. Barabbas. It was actually Bar Abbas. And Bar Abbas means son of God in Aramaic, which is the language they spoke there at that time.'

'But I thought Jesus was the son of God.'

'That's where it gets a little bit complicated, Steve. Nobody knows if Barabbas really existed. If it comes to that, Jesus is a bit of a mystery himself. But the idea at the time was that the Jewish people were presented with two sons of God. You have to remember that they had been colonised by the Romans.'

'Like we had in England.'

'Just like you had in England. Yes. The Jewish story was that one son of God – Jesus – taught them that freedom would come peacefully. If they all loved their fellow men at least as much as they loved themselves, God would smile on them. Barabbas was the other son of God and he taught that the road to freedom was through violence. The Jews had to make it too uncomfortable for the Romans to stay there. Only force would get rid of them. The Romans had both sons of God in custody. And then – you understand, this is the story the Christian church has taught for the last 2000 years; it isn't necessarily what happened, and in fact no-one really knows if anything happened at all – Pontius Pilate, who was the Roman governor in Palestine, offered to release one of them. He invited the Jewish people to choose which one should be released and which should be crucified.'

'Mr Ruben… Moshe… This doesn't sound very likely.'

Yanek smiled. Who wouldn't? 'No, it doesn't. But this is the story that has been told for all these years. The Jews asked Pontius Pilate to release Barabbas, the man who wanted them to fight the Romans to the last drop of Jewish blood, and to kill Jesus, the man who wanted them all to live in peace. No, I agree, when you look at it like that it does seem like a made up story. Which, in fact, I don't doubt it was. But it was used to justify the idea that Christ was killed by the Jews. You can understand why a Pope sitting in his palace in Rome wouldn't want the story to get around that it was Romans who killed him?'

'People can be very ignorant.'

'There's no doubt about that, Steve. And as time went on, Jews got the blame for everything. In Europe, when the Black Death was killing half the inhabitants, it killed far fewer Jews than other people. We know now that what caused that plague was disease carried by rats and spread by dirt. And so we can understand that Jews were less likely to be affected because the Jewish religion involves all kinds of rituals centred around cleanness. Whereas the average European from the poorest peasant right up to the richest emperor was, forgive me, filthy. You've heard the story about the first Queen Elizabeth, who had a bath every year whether she needed it or not? Instead of washing, they used to sniff fragrant herbs so that they could ignore the smell. No wonder they got ill and half of them died. But this was happening 600 years ago, and people knew nothing about germs, so when they were told that the Jews had made a pact with the devil, they believed it. And they killed us in huge numbers.

'Steve, we could talk about this for a long time. But where would it get us? You wanted to know why the people surrounding Israel want to get rid of the place. I've given you some of the reasons. If you want what I think is a more convincing one, try this. Israel is a democracy. Like Britain. Every adult has a vote. Like Britain. If we don't like the government we have, we can vote them out and vote in one we do want. Like Britain. We are the only place in the region where that is true. Lebanon, Syria, Iraq, Saudi Arabia, Jordan, Egypt, Iran and all the little island states and emirates have absolute rulers who hate the very idea of people being able to vote for what they want instead of accepting what rulers give them. So if you'd like to know why I really think they want us out, it's because of that. We are a daily example to their people that it isn't necessary to live as serfs. But that's enough history for today. Let's get you back to work before people start asking where you are.'

CHAPTER 24

FEBRUARY 2003 – LONDON

Five months before the robbery

When he went home that evening, Yanek felt something that was so foreign to him he didn't at first recognise it. It was guilt. Steve was a security guard. What his job demanded was not just readiness to physically withstand open attacks on the safe-deposit boxes: he and his colleagues also needed to be constantly aware of what was going on around them. They had to be alert not only to overt attacks but also to people who might be plotting to subvert security and get under the net they were supposed to maintain. And he, Yanek, in his *alter ego* as Moshe Ruben, was setting out by charm and subterfuge to divert their attention. What stage magicians called misdirection. It was a commonplace in the world he lived in in the desert. General Dayan himself had told them, 'We are a small nation with a limited population and we are surrounded by much larger countries who want to destroy us. We will beat them by being stronger. We will beat them because we are more motivated and we know what will happen to our people if we fail. But we will also beat them by making them believe that we have things that we don't actually have and can do things that we can't actually do. Stage magicians call it misdirection. Misdirection will be our friend.'

He was playing so hard on the trusting nature of Steve and Steve's colleagues that without knowing it they would break the most fundamental rule of their employment. Because they would become so used to his presence, they would give Mr Ruben access to what he most needed. And he could tell himself any story he liked, but the fact was that Steve and the others would be suspects when Mr Ruben's lawbreaking became evident. Yanek himself would be long gone, back in Israel where no-one would connect him with the nefarious Mr Ruben – but they would still be here to face the music. They risked being found guilty of knowing involvement in burglary and facing heavy prison sentences for something they'd actually known nothing about. If there was ever going to be a time for Yanek to pull back and accept that collateral damage to others was too high a price to pay to punish those who had done wrong, this was it.

He didn't take it. If he was honest with himself, he didn't really even think about it. It was a pity that innocent men might suffer, but justice was only justice if it was done, and the injustice he was seeking to redress had come first. Yanek had bought a simple key-cutting machine and installed it in the cupboard in his room. Getting hold of blank keys wasn't a problem – the problem was cutting them. And Yanek knew how to do that. When they designed and built rockets in the desert, the documents had been held in boxes locked with precisely this kind of key. Come to that, they probably still were. Yanek had been one of the very small number allowed to be involved with designing and cutting those keys. If he could cut them in the desert, he could cut them here. But only if he knew the design that fitted the boxes he wanted to get into. And that was where Steve and the other guards were going to help him without knowing they were doing it. First, though, there were more names to be accumulated and that meant more meetings to be arranged. It was at one of those meetings that he ran into his first serious concern.

#

He had arranged to have dinner with Desmond Morris, born in Austria with a completely different name and sent to Britain as a child in the 1938 Kindertransport. Desmond had been old enough to remember what his name had originally been and he had brought with him a photograph of his parents. When he grew to adulthood, he spent a lot of money looking for them and he knew with as much certainty as was possible in those circumstances that they had not survived the war. He'd been brought up in a Jewish family in Barnet, north London, and they had formally adopted him to leave his British citizenship in no doubt when it became clear that he was unlikely ever again to hear from those who had brought him into the world. A promising footballer in his younger days, he had been given a trial by Tottenham Hotspur football club: although he didn't make it, he still carried with him the respect and regard the British give to sporting heroes.

He also had good links with a number of people in Israel. Some of them had travelled with him in the Kindertransport and emigrated as soon as they were old enough. Others he had met, through correspondence if not face-to-face, during his fruitless search for his parents. And one of them had mentioned a name to him. As he and Mr Ruben were about to start on their fish, Desmond Morris said, 'In Israel, did you ever come across a guy called Yanek Hoffman?'

It took all the skill Yanek had developed over the years, ever since he'd run with the gang in Berehove even before the Nazis came, to prevent the shock from appearing on his face. He sipped from his glass of water and put a forkful of fish into his mouth. When he had swallowed it he said, 'Hoffman. Yanek Hoffman. No, I don't... Why do you ask?' He felt sure Morris must be able to hear the beating of his heart, so loud was it to him.

'Oh, just something a friend in Israel mentioned. It was the anniversary of the day we both left on the Kindertransport and we were talking on the phone. The conversation got around to food. It always does with him; he had a hard time of it – harder than me – and he was often hungry as a child. So now food is a big thing with him. And he was telling me about his favourite restaurant, which was run by this Hoffman guy. But apparently Hoffman left, and according to my pal, the restaurant is still okay but it isn't as good as it was when Hoffman was there. He says no-one knows where Hoffman went, and he'd really like him to come back and take over his restaurant again. And I just wondered...'

'No. Never heard of him. No reason why I should. I know Israel isn't a big country, but it isn't so small that everyone knows everyone else.'

'Oh, I know that. But my pal lives in Beer Sheba, and I thought... Didn't you tell me that was where you were from?'

Yanek carried on eating his fish. 'I don't think so. I hope not, seeing as how I lived in Jaffa.'

'Oh. Sorry. I really had it in my head... I'm sure someone told me you came here from Beer Sheba.'

Who? Who had told him that? Who was talking about him who knew enough to say where he came from? Was his whole project wrecked before he even started because someone knew who he really was and was spreading the word? If so, who? But he wasn't going to raise Desmond Morris's curiosity by asking that. So all he said was, 'Not me. I don't know who might have told you, but whoever it was got it wrong. If your friend is so keen on food, you should bring him here if he ever comes back to England. This fish is excellent.'

CHAPTER 25

APRIL 2003 – LONDON

Three months before the robbery

That little scare with Desmond Morris was not the last. Yanek was on a bus to Piccadilly Circus. He had sat upstairs and in one of the back rows of seats so that he could smoke, a dispensation that would disappear the following year when it became illegal to smoke anywhere on a bus in the UK. His heart jerked when he recognised the man coming towards him. Sammy Bronstein. Last seen at a Jaffa meeting of Etzel alumni. Sammy took the seat beside Yanek and held out a hand to be shaken. 'Yanek! Yanek Hoffman. How the hell are you? And what the devil are you doing here? I heard you'd sold the restaurant – but London? This is a story I need to hear.'

All the careful planning Yanek had done had never really catered for something like this. Of course he'd known that he might run into someone who knew him. Fate was a bastard, and if you'd lived a life like his and failed to understand that, something was the matter with you. What would he do if it happened? He'd assumed he'd play it by ear. Which was what he now did. 'I'm sorry... I don't know any Yanek Hoffman. And I've never had a restaurant to sell. I deal in diamonds. My name is Moshe Ruben.'

Sammy Bronstein leaned back in his seat and stared at him. His expression was a mixture of disbelief and hilarity. 'If you say so, Yanek. Each to his own, of course. You want to be Moshe Ruben, Moshe Ruben you shall be.' And he slapped Yanek hard on the back and laughed. 'Did you see Jimmy Greaves has a book out?'

'Who? What?'

'Jimmy Greaves. Best forward this country ever produced. Not Jewish himself – his parents were Irish so he was probably Catholic if he was anything at all other than borderline alcoholic in his later years – but he played for Spurs. Spurs is the Jewish club, so we'll give him an honorary circumcision, eh?'

'I'm sorry... What are you...?'

'He's retired now, Greaves. He's just this minute published a book. Well, not this minute, obviously. But this month. He called it "It's a Funny Old Life." Because he once said football was a funny old game and it stuck. I've read it. It isn't bad. Made me laugh a few times.'

'And what has this to do with me?'

'It's a funny old life, Yanek. Sorry, I mean Moshe. And so it is a funny old life, when restaurant owner Yanek Hoffman decides to become diamond merchant Moshe Ruben. But, like I said, each to his own. That's one of the glories of moving to a different country. You can be anyone you want to be. And you can stop being anyone you don't want to be.'

This had gone terribly wrong. He should have given a lot more thought to how he was going to handle something like this when it happened. Right now, he needed to get as far from Sammy Bronstein as he could. The bus was as yet nowhere near Piccadilly Circus, but this conversation had to end. He stood up. 'This is my stop. I'd love to continue our chat, but business waits for no-one.'

'That's all right, Yanek. London is a big city but we Jews tend to move in a very small part of it. I've no doubt we'll meet again. When we do, I'll pretend to believe you really are Moshe Ruben. And in return you can explain why you needed to change your name. Or not, of course – it really isn't my business.'

The knowledge that this part of the bus had fallen silent because everyone around them was listening to their conversation irritated Yanek more than he should have let it. He said, 'No, Sammy. It isn't. Your business is with a psychiatrist because you're obviously not right in the head.'

Sammy Bronstein held up a finger. His face was wreathed in smiles. As he started down the stairs, Yanek realised why. He had called Bronstein Sammy. And Bronstein had not introduced himself.

#

Yanek got off the bus in a state of agitation. He looked around. Where the hell was he? A sign on the bus stop said this was Belsize Park, but that didn't help: Yanek had never been to Belsize Park and didn't know what it was, apart from being a place on the bus route from Golders Green to Piccadilly Circus, or what happened here. He was a little reassured to see that he was unlikely to be mugged, surrounded as he was by what looked like the well-kept buildings of the well-to-do. Georgian and Victorian villas, though he didn't know enough architectural history to place them in their time. He didn't know any British history, either; if he had, he might have known that the name Belsize came from the French bel assis, which meant well situated. And it was. He didn't even know that it was part of Hampstead, once home to intellectuals who were now losing out to people well enough off to afford the rising prices. Karl Marx had once lived here, but so had Agatha Christie.

He needed a rest. He found a bakery that offered in-house service and sat down with a coffee and a pastry. He was shocked to find that his hand when he lifted the cup was shaking a little. Sammy Bronstein could wreck his whole plan. And how many other Sammy Bronsteins were here in London, able to do him just as much damage? He needed a plan. A strategy. A way to deal with recognition by people who had known him before he came here. An explanation that people could believe for his transformation from Yanek Hoffman, restaurant owner to Moshe Ruben, diamond dealer. But what?

And, bit by bit, peace returned. How was this any different from the situation he'd faced right at the end of the war when the murderous state demanded he still wear the yellow Star of David and yet he went about his business pretending to be a representative of that same state? When he carried the briefcase marked with an eagle looking left instead of right and carrying a swastika? How had he dealt with it then? By toughing it out – that's how. By assuming an identity that wasn't his. He'd done it then, when failure could mean instant death, and he could do it now when the worst that could happen was that he'd fail to get the revenge he sought. He needed to find out where Sammy Bronstein was living. Then he would go to see him, admit who he really was, and spin some yarn explaining why he was now pretending to be someone else. What would the yarn be? He didn't know yet. But it would come to him. His imagination had not failed him yet and it would not start failing him now.

CHAPTER 26

MAY, 2003 – LONDON

Thirty days before the robbery

Fifty years earlier, when Jews in Europe faced their biggest threats in centuries, they had known that they might die in what Hitler called the Final Solution. And millions had done so – 6.6 million if you accepted the United States Holocaust Mission's figures and 5.8 million if you believed Yad Vashem. 90% of the Jews living in Poland at the start of the war were dead by the end, but Jews had faced many other killing grounds. No-one at that time imagined the day would come when millions of people denied the Holocaust had ever taken place. And very few can have suspected that, five decades after the Jewish people were finally given back their own land, they would still be fighting to hold onto it, and some would still be dying. But so it was. Attacks had happened every month in 1989, mostly by Hamas.

And then there were the equally murderous counter-attacks by Jewish settlers known as the Daggermen, though it was never clear whether they were a unified group or simply terrorists operating individually. And the settlements didn't help – Jews had spilled over onto land reserved for Palestinians to the point where, by 1990, almost 200,000 were living where they should not have been and exposed to the fury of those they had displaced. It seemed the arguments in Israel itself could go on for ever. The world had always known that no-one on the planet argues as willingly and as loudly as a Jew and that was amply demonstrated. On the one hand were the Jews who said, "We should not be doing this. Palestinians, too, have a right to a home and we should not be taking it from them." And on the other was the counter argument: "This is our land. God gave it to us. And so did the UN. Other Muslim states have masses of room and much of it is empty. Let the Palestinians go there."

Was that racism? Yes, it probably was. Should a people who had been subject to some of the most murderous racism ever seen care? There were those in Israel who said they should. The Daggermen said they shouldn't, and took up arms against anyone who disagreed. What could not be denied was that not every foreign state supported Israel's expansion.

By May 1990, positions were becoming clear. In Israel's early days, right after the war, Russia had been unbending in its support and the West had been more vocal in the interests of the Arab states. That was now changed. Russia refused even to allow commercial flights to Israel, while America lent Israel $400 million it probably never expected to see again to finance the settlement in Israel of Jews from Russia and the former Soviet republics. The month before, Israel's Supreme Court had ordered the removal of 200 Israeli Jews from settlements in Palestinian areas. A rabbi in Hebron shot and killed a Palestinian shopkeeper and was jailed for only five months. An Israeli who had been dishonourably discharged from the Israeli army stole a rifle from his brother, a soldier, and killed seven Palestinian workers.

And so it went on, and it seemed there would be no end to it. Yanek might imagine he'd left all that behind when he flew to London, but he was to find that people there had views and were happy to express them. Yanek had always been told that the British were reticent and unlikely to speak their minds to a stranger, so it came as a surprise when someone sat down opposite him at his table in the Belsize Park coffee shop. 'You are Jewish?'

Yanek studied the questioner. How old was he? Nineteen? Twenty? Thereabouts. Probably a student – his curly hair hadn't been cut or his shaggy beard trimmed for some time and he had with him a battered leather briefcase. His clothes, though, weren't cheap and someone was looking after his laundry. The scent of soap suggested he'd had a bath or a shower before coming out that morning. He wasn't living in a squat, that was clear. 'Yes,' said Yanek. 'I'm Jewish. In fact, I'm an Israeli Jew. You have a problem with that?'

'These settlements. The illegal ones in land that was meant for the Palestinians. Do you think Israel should be doing that?'

The question Yanek really wanted to ask was, "What the hell do you think it has to do with you?" But there was nothing to be gained from getting into a public dispute in London and there could be a lot to lose, so what he said was, 'Israel isn't doing it. It's the action of individuals. The Supreme Court has said the settlements must stop.'

'They don't, though. Do they?'

A smile played at the edges of Yanek's mouth. 'Not so far, no.'

'So I ask you again: is it right that Israelis are occupying land meant for Palestinians?'

Yanek finished his pastry. It had been surprisingly good. He swept up some of the crumbs with his finger and put them in his mouth. 'I'm going to have another coffee. Can I buy one for you?'

'Let me,' said the young man, turning to wave in the waiter's direction.

Yanek said, 'Your question. Is it right that Americans occupy land that the Indians thought was theirs? Is it right that white Australians pursuing a White Australia policy have pushed off their land people who were there for thousands of years before them and subjected them to the white Australians' rule? And isn't it interesting that both of those seizures of other people's land were done by Englishmen? And let's not even think about the way the British and the French behaved in Mesopotamia, breaking all their promises so they could keep control. See how that has come back to haunt them?'

'I think the White Australia policy was abandoned some time ago. So what you're saying is, might is right? They did it, so you can do it. Is that your position?'

Was it? Was that what he thought? He said, 'Well, that's the way the world seems to have operated since time began. And the Jews have suffered from it more than most.'

'Doesn't that mean you should be more sympathetic to the Palestinians?'

Yanek's smile now was open. 'Sympathy? You want me to feel sympathy for them? Well, of course I do. Probably more than you, because I know how it feels and, with the greatest respect, you don't.' He took off his jacket and rolled up his sleeve. 'You see that? You see that number on my arm? Do you know what it means?'

The young man nodded. 'You were in a camp.'

'Yes. I was. I survived. And I know just how many did not. I watched some of them die. Quite a lot of them, actually. It affects you, an experience like that. How you feel. Your capacity to forgive. Most of all, how you view the future. When Jews in Israel say, "Never again," you should assume we mean it. If the world needs to sacrifice more people, they can choose someone else next time.'

The young man leaned across the table. Yanek wasn't sure he'd ever seen that level of earnest intent on anyone's face – not even on the young men and women of the Israeli Defence Force in the desert resisting the attacks of those who wanted to kill them. The young man said, 'But why there? If you were to be given your own homeland, why weren't you given part of Germany? Or Poland, or Czechoslovakia, or any of the other places that joined in your slaughter?'

'It's a matter of history.'

'History? You mean, a collection of books written by no-one knows which men at no-one knows what time that says you were given that land by God?'

'You think if we'd been given Poland or Germany we'd have been left in peace?'

'Of course not. But the Arabs... Why them? Did the Arabs conduct the pogroms? Was it Arabs who sent you to a camp? When you watched people dying there, was it the Arabs who were starving them?'

'You use the word Arabs when you should use the word Muslims. People outside the Middle East think those two words are interchangeable, and they are not. Yes, there are Muslim Arabs: there are also Christian Arabs and Jewish Arabs. Though there are now a hell of a lot fewer Jewish Arabs than there used to be because the Arab countries have got rid of them.'

'They drove them out?'

'Those they didn't kill. And somehow the idea seems to have spread that Muslims were the Middle East's American Indians and Australian aborigines. That they were there first. And they weren't. Islam began 1,300 years ago. The Jews have been there twice as long. Three times as long. And you know how Islam came to dominate the region? They offered people a choice: convert, or we kill you.' Now it was Yanek's turn to lean forward across the table. 'They treated the original Jewish inhabitants the way Jews in Israel now treat them. You ask me if I think the Jews are right to behave that way. You don't seem to have a view on whether Islam was at fault in the first place for removing the Jews from the land they are now re-inhabiting. Why is that?'

#

1991 – HUNGARY

The Hungarian People's Republic had come to an end the previous October. The transition to democracy had been smoother than anywhere else in the Soviet empire. Problems would arise after a few years when Prime Minister Victor Orban decided that sharing power in the Western way might not be the best model for Hungary and, even if it was, it certainly wasn't the best model for Victor Orban – but that was in the future. In May 1989 the barbed wire fence on Hungary's border with Austria had been removed, making inevitable the fall of the Berlin Wall by allowing East Germans to cross into Hungary and make their way from there to the West. Hungary was now free, its citizens could move in and out of the country and people like Ilana could visit without fear of arrest. Arie and his wife conceived a plan to take her for dinner in the Astoria Hotel where she had been the Gestapo's chef but never allowed to sit in the dining room and eat. That would not happen for another five years, but there was nothing to prevent Ilana's own visits.

Yudka's son was on the verge of adulthood now. Like his mother, he had been raised as a Catholic but Yudka's adoptive parents had made sure she grew up insulated from Hungary's prevailing anti-Semitism and Yudka had done the same for her son. It was a happy visit.

CHAPTER 27

JUNE 2003 – LONDON

Twenty-seven days before the robbery

Yanek had enjoyed his interrogation in the Belsize Park coffee shop. Enjoyed it particularly because his final argument was one he had never used before, even to himself, because it had not occurred to him. That would be his position from now on if anyone challenged the right of Israelis to settle in what the student had called land meant for the Palestinians. They weren't taking the land – they were taking it back, after a 1,300 year usurpation. And what the hell did the student mean by "meant for the Palestinians"? Meant by who? Who thought they had the right to tell a monstrously persecuted people where they could live and where they could not? And who could challenge Israel's right to ignore anyone who awarded themselves that right?

But enough of all that. He had come to London with a specific task in mind and it was time to get on with it. He had to meet people, he had to determine which of them were going to be his targets, he had to memorise the exact cut of their safe-deposit box keys which meant he had to get sight of them, and he had to do the same with the master key. Steve had the master key and it was with Steve that Yanek decided to start because, if he didn't have his own copy of the master key, and if he hadn't satisfied himself by testing it that it worked, everything else he might do would be a waste of time.

He became the Hatton Garden company's most regular visitor, turning up every single day to open each of his four boxes. He made sure that Steve or whichever other guard went with him never saw the inside of any box and that was just as well because all four remained empty for the whole of the six months that would elapse before he was done. There were no diamonds in his boxes because he had none, but there was no need for the guards to know that. For them, someone who visited that regularly must be one of the most active diamond traders because why, otherwise, would they spend so much time there? And he even came in on Saturdays when no Orthodox Jew would dream of working. And all the real diamond traders were Orthodox.

One day, alone in the vault with Steve, he made his play for the information he needed. Obviously, he couldn't say he wanted to copy the master key, so he had prepared a little plan that would get Steve to show him his key without becoming suspicious. Even so, and however well he'd thought it out, he felt nervous before putting the plan into action. Taking a deep breath and setting out to look as casual as possible he said, 'Steve. I'll tell you what worries me about this place.'

'What's that, Moshe?'

'Security. I worry that my boxes aren't secure enough.'

'But that's why I'm here. And the other guards. You don't need to worry about your boxes being safe as long as we're here. Don't you trust us?'

'Steve, of course I trust you. All of you, and probably you most of all because you're the one I've come to know the best. No, it isn't the guards – it's the keys.'

'There's no need to concern yourself about the keys. Everybody's key is different. And my key – the master key – is different again.'

'Ah, but are they all different enough, Steve? I worry that someone else may have a key to their box that is too much like mine. So like mine that as well as opening that person's box, it would also open my box. Or their key might be like the master key. Do you see what I mean?'

'I do, Moshe, and I understand why a diamond merchant in as big a way of business as you might worry about that. But I promise you, you're worrying about nothing.' He took from his pocket the ring on which he kept the master key. 'See? That's the master key. Just put yours beside it and compare them. There. You see how different they are?'

Even though he'd planned it, Yanek could hardly believe how well his plan had worked. He took out his own key, held it close to the key Steve was holding, and did his best to commit every shade of difference to memory. He was helped by having worked on this design of key while he was in the desert. Because of that, he knew that each key had seven cuts and that the cuts could have any of five depths with the first being no cut at all and the fifth reaching halfway into the width of the key. So all he had to do was to memorise the depth of each of the seven cuts and the order in which they came. He repeated it inside his head several times in exactly the way that bridge players repeat the number and value of each card played until they remember them. Then he said, 'Thank you, Steve. I don't suppose I'll ever stop worrying entirely, but you've set my mind greatly at ease.' He looked at his watch. 'Good grief, is that the time? I'm going to be late for my appointment.'

In fact, he had no appointment. What he needed was to get out of the vault as fast as possible and, as soon as he was round the corner and out of sight, write in his notebook the master key's seven cuts with their depths in the correct order.

And that's exactly what he did. Then he travelled far enough from Hatton Garden to have lunch where he would not be seen by Steve, who might wonder what had happened to his appointment. And then he went home to attempt to replicate the master key.

Chapter 28

June 2003 – London

Twenty-five days before the robbery

Rosa came out of her ground floor sitting room when she heard Yanek's key in the door. 'Moshe. A man was here for you.'

Yanek's heart beat so loudly he was sure his landlady must hear it. 'A man? For me? You're sure? He actually asked for me by name?'

Who the devil could know that he was here? And calling himself by that name? And then he steadied himself: he hadn't kept it secret. He'd been meeting people around the capital and some had asked where he was living. And, of course, there were Rosa's other tenants. He'd talked to them over breakfast and dinner and, sometimes, after dinner in the room Rosa provided for their use. A room with a television and a radio, easy chairs and occasional tables for when they decided to take advantage of the Cona coffee pot she kept on the sideboard. He was just nervous because of the step forward he'd taken today in his plans. His illicit, illegal, frankly criminal plans. Lots of people might know where to find Moshe Ruben. But his relief was short lived, ending when Rosa answered the question. 'He called you Moshe Ruben, yes. And himself he called Sammy Bronstein.' Bronstein. Who knew that Moshe Ruben was really Yanek Hoffman. What was he up to? What did he want? Rosa handed him a card. 'He left this for you.'

Yanek read the card. Sales agent. So that's what Sammy Bronstein was doing in London. He supposed he should feel proud that Israeli companies had now reached a scale and position where they had things to sell that developed Western countries would want to buy. But pride wasn't his foremost emotion right now. He turned the card over and found that Bronstein had written him a note.

Join me for dinner. Reubens Restaurant, Baker Street. 7 this evening.

That was not phrased like an invitation that could be ignored. Not a single hostile word, and yet "or you'll regret it" hovered over it, unwritten but clearly visible. Yanek said, 'Thank you, Rosa. I won't be in for dinner this evening.'

And nor, he thought as he went to his room, would he be cutting any keys this afternoon. He needed to be calm and in full possession of himself for that job, or he would mess it up. And calm and self-possessed were the last things he felt right now. The question he'd asked himself a few minutes ago was renewed with greater force: What did Bronstein want? Even more important, what did he know?

He'd only been in his room for two minutes when he realised he was too much on edge to stay there. To get to Baker Street by tube would take about thirty minutes, so he didn't need to leave until 6.30. And then he thought he'd make it ten minutes later because he didn't want Bronstein to know how nervous he was, which meant it would be best not to arrive on time. That was still two hours away and if he spent those two hours alone he'd work himself into a state of nervous exhaustion that would be obvious the moment he walked through the restaurant door. He'd heard conversation when he passed the door to the residents' sitting room, so that's where he went. What kind of company he'd make for anyone he didn't want to think, but at least he wouldn't be alone. And, as things turned out, going there at that moment was just the right thing. When he walked in, the man he knew as Alexis Jaffers called to him. 'Moshe! I was talking about you earlier today.'

Dear God, not someone else nosing into his affairs. 'You were?'

'I had lunch with my nephew. It's something I do regularly: I can't say I enjoy his company but my sister asked me to keep an eye on him and you know how it is with sisters.'

Yanek shook his head. 'To the best of my knowledge, I never had one.'

'To the best of your knowledge? Oh, well, disrupted families... The war... Anyway, while we were eating, a woman who knows my nephew because she works with him came in with her husband. The husband is quite a lot older than her: name of Rosenbaum. My nephew introduced them and it turns out Rosenbaum is a diamond trader.'

Rosenbaum. A name that seemed to follow Yanek. And a diamond trader... But the Rosenbaum whose safe-deposit box key Yanek had was married to Rachel, and what Rachel had said suggested that the marriage had not been formally ended. So, if this one had a wife, he couldn't be the same Rosenbaum.

Jaffers said, 'I mentioned your name. I mean, there can't be that many diamond traders in London and I imagine most of you know each other. He said he'd never met you, but he'd heard people speak about you.'

There it was again. People talking about him. Really, there were times when he wished he'd stayed a restaurateur and never got into this shady business. 'I'm in the same position,' he said. 'I've heard of Rosenbaum – as you say, ours is a small world – but I've never met him.'

'He's quite a bit older than you. I mean, he's *a lot* older than the woman he calls his wife, but he's got a few years on you, too. I'd have thought that he might be retired, or at least considering retirement. But no, it seems he'll go on until he dies in harness. I suppose some people are like that. Personally, I'd like to think I can look forward to a few years of comfortable retirement after I stop work, but what would the world be like if we were all the same?' Yanek nodded in a way that suggested he might take one view and might take the other. Then Jaffers said, 'When they'd gone to their own table, which fortunately was out of hearing of ours, my nephew said if she was his wife, he – my nephew, you understand – was the King of Siam.'

'He thinks they're not married?'

'He thinks Rosenbaum has a wife back in Israel. And he thinks the woman he works with is a gold digger. The only thing Rosenbaum has that she wants is money.'

'There's a lot of that around, these days,' said Yanek. 'Still, it's useful information to have about someone else in my line of business. Thank you.'

'If you use that information, you won't tell anyone you got it from me?'

'Of course not.'

So there was every likelihood that this was THE Rosenbaum. The one on Yanek's list. And there was some good news in all of that because, if Rosenbaum wasn't intending to retire any time soon, Yanek probably had time for his plan to unfold. He had the key to Rosenbaum's safe-deposit box, and he would soon cut a copy of the master key, but if he robbed Rosenbaum without yet being in a position to open other people's boxes, the whole thing would go off half cocked. He didn't want that. What he wanted was to get everyone he'd placed on his list.

#

That conversation with Jaffers meant that Yanek was in a better frame of mind when he walked, ten minutes late, into Reubens Restaurant. Sammy Bronstein smiled, stood up and shook his hand. Beside him, a man Yanek was sure he'd never seen before stayed in his seat. Dark, short and stocky, his eyes seemed almost black as they stared, unblinking, at Yanek. Bronstein said, 'I'd just started to think you might not come.' Yanek sat down without commenting. Bronstein went on, 'Have you eaten here?'

'Not here, no.' He picked up the menu and scanned through it. 'But it looks like the usual fare.'

'It is. Just like your mother used to make.' He turned to the hovering waiter. 'I'll have the Reubens chicken soup and then lamb chops with mashed potato and spinach, heavy on the garlic, please.'

There seemed no point in saying Yanek had no recollection of his mother ever cooking him a proper meal. Instead, he said, 'I'll have the same, except I'd like sautéed potatoes and onions.'

'Good choice,' said Bronstein. 'And to drink I suggest a bottle of the Golan Heights Merlot?'

When Yanek had nodded at that suggestion, the man beside Sammy had given his order and the waiter had departed, Bronstein said, 'I get a little frisson from drinking wine from the Golan. It reminds me just how far we yids have come since that German loony tried to wipe us out.'

'I'm glad for you,' said Yanek. 'And now, perhaps you'd be good enough to tell me why I'm here?'

CHAPTER 29

JUNE 2003 – LONDON

Twenty-three days before the robbery

Sammy smiled once more. He half turned towards the man sitting beside him. 'Yanek, I don't think you've met my brother, Monty?'

'I've not had the pleasure.' Monty didn't rise from his chair and nor did he hold out a hand to be shaken, but he looked friendly enough. Yanek said, 'Sammy. Monty. Did your parents have a thing about names ending in Y?'

'I don't think so,' said Sammy. 'Or we wouldn't have a sister called Miriam.'

'I suppose not. But that still doesn't tell me why...'

'Why I invited you for dinner. No, I suppose it doesn't. It was an invitation, by the way: this is my treat. I'll be picking up the bill.' Faced with an apparent unwillingness to address the question he'd asked, Yanek decided to remain silent. Sammy must have got the message because he said, 'Monty and I have some things we want to talk over. A proposal we'd like to make. One that benefits all three of us.' When Yanek still didn't speak, Sammy went on, 'Monty is an investigator.'

So here it came. The subject of Monty's latest investigation was going to be Yanek himself. Well, he'd hear what they had to say. There was a slight pause as the soup arrived. Then he said, 'Investigator?'

'Quite so. I'm surprised you didn't recognise the name, actually: he's been in the press a few times. Not as the lead in the story – some of those accounts of Nazi war criminals being brought back from South America for trial. The war criminal was the star of the show, but Monty often got a mention as the man who tracked him down. We are very proud of him in our family.'

'I'm happy for you.' They needed to get to the point. It was time to say what the investigator Monty had found out about Yanek and what they intended to do about it. But they couldn't expect him to help them out. He finished his soup and he had to say it was pretty good. If he'd had the kind of mother who cooked for her family, this was the kind of soup he'd have liked her to make for him.

Sammy said, 'It was when I met you on the bus and you pretended not to be you. That's when I asked Monty to take an interest.'

'Is that right?'

'Yanek, I get the feeling you think we are hostile. We are not. We are on your side.'

'Yes?'

Sammy sighed. 'Tell him, Monty.'

Another pause as the soup plates were removed and the lamb brought to the table. Yanek said, 'Monty not eating?'

'Monty said, 'I have to eat with my wife later. If I don't clear the plate, there will be questions. Look, Yanek. Sammy and I might have this completely wrong. But I'll tell you what I found out and what it makes us think.'

'Be my guest.'

'A righteous man who committed crimes that could and probably should have seen him jailed for the rest of his life. That's what one person had to say about you.'

He didn't have to think hard. Monty had been speaking to Rachel? Her voice came back to him, unbidden but unforgettable. "You're a killer, a rapist and a thief, Yanek. But you're also, God help us, a righteous man." He said, 'One person?'

'There are others. You have a background that some would say should see you immune from prosecution.'

'Prosecution?'

Monty held up a hand, the palm towards Yanek. 'Please don't misunderstand. We don't want to see you prosecuted.'

'We want to see you rewarded,' said Sammy.

'But we want to make sure you are targeting everyone you should be.'

'I'm targeting people?'

'Oh, we think so, Yanek,' said Sammy. 'Among the things we learned about you is how you collected money for Etzel.'

'Though it wasn't, strictly speaking, money,' said Monty. 'Transforming it into money was other people's job.'

'And some of those people,' said Sammy, 'weren't as diligent as they might have been in making sure that all of the money was used for the purpose it was meant for.'

'The purpose you stole it for, Yanek,' said Monty.

'Some of those people,' said Sammy, 'were a bit like American politicians when they get to be president. They are paid whatever America does pay its presidents. I've no idea how much that is, but I'm sure it's quite enough for their needs. But, somehow, many of them end up a great deal richer when they leave the White House than they were when they arrived. Richer than their salaries could ever explain.'

Monty said, 'That is corruption, Yanek. And what we are talking about was theft. There's no other way to look at it. You and people like you persuaded the generous and the ungenerous donors...'

'And the completely unwilling donors...,' said Sammy.

'Those, too,' said Monty. 'You and people like you persuaded them to donate jewellery and other valuable items to be turned into cash to fund the Jewish people's return to their homeland after all these centuries. You handed the jewellery and the other valuable items to people you trusted to make sure that happened. And you found out later that not all of the money had been used for the purpose you stole it for.'

'I did?' None of this conversation, however startling it might have been, had stopped him eating. The lamb was really good. He'd mark this place down as somewhere to come back to.

'We think so,' said Sammy. 'We think you did. You remember Shlomo?'

'Of course,' said Monty, 'remember him is all anyone can do. We can't talk to him. Ask him if he's proud of his actions. See if he might feel like doing things differently if he had his time over. No-one can ask Shlomo anything anymore. Because Shlomo is dead.'

'Some,' said Sammy,' would say Shlomo had been murdered.'

'But we,' said Monty, 'prefer the word executed. Shlomo was executed. And the interesting thing about that, Yanek, is that whoever did the deed didn't do it for profit. He left everything right there for any passer-by to help themselves.'

'Which suggests,' said Sammy, 'that what motivated that execution was not a desire for enrichment. It was revenge.'

Yanek said, 'Then you should not approve. I'm not going to pretend I ever had a proper Jewish education, but I do know that revenge is prohibited.'

'Of course,' said Sammy. 'King David tells us in the Psalms, "Have I repaid those who have done evil to me? Behold, I have rescued those who hated me without cause." And Jewish law forbids us to bear grudges. But Monty and I believe that there may sometimes be higher causes. Monty is regarded in Israel as a righteous man. A hero. Why? Because he exposes himself to risk to bring those who slaughtered our people to justice. If that is not revenge, then what is?'

'One might, of course,' said Monty, 'ask what kind of revenge Yanek Hoffman could possibly be plotting. And who against.'

'One might indeed,' said Yanek. He pushed his plate, now empty, away. 'That was very good. All I need now is coffee.'

Sammy signalled to the waiter. 'I'll order it right away. A glass of something to go with it?'

Yanek shook his head. 'Just the coffee.'

'So,' said Monty. 'What kind of revenge and against whom? What told me where to look is that Sammy said you called yourself a diamond merchant. And I've uncovered nothing to suggest you possess a single diamond. But you seem to have taken up daytime residence at Hatton Garden safe-deposit company. And when I was digging into your time in Israel, I found out you'd worked on the development of rockets. They use a very particular kind of key to keep their documentation safe there. And the person who told me you were a righteous man despite all the crimes you'd committed also said you'd shown great interest in a key. The same kind of key that the rocket people use. Strangely enough, it's also the kind of key they use at Hatton Garden.'

So he'd been right: it had been Rachel. Monty had stopped speaking and his eyes were fixed on Yanek's. Yanek had been in some tight corners in his time and one thing he'd learned was that sometimes you just had to keep your mouth shut. Speaking, whatever it was you chose to say, would be a bad idea. This, he decided, was one of those times. And his coffee arrived, so he was able to focus on that.

When the silence had lasted long enough for Sammy and Monty to understand that Yanek wasn't going to be the one to end it, Sammy said, 'So now you see what we had to work with when we started putting two and two together. And you're not going to say anything, and I understand that, and I'm sure Monty does, too. So we'll do it. And if we are wrong, there's no harm done and we have had the satisfaction of giving you a meal that you have obviously enjoyed. So here is what we want to say.' He took a piece of paper from his inside jacket pocket and placed it on the table. 'There are three names on that paper. Each one of them rents storage space at Hatton Garden. Each one of them has material goods that they should not have and that they obtained in the same nefarious way as Shlomo obtained his.'

'And I know that... How?'

'You will have to trust Monty's investigative skills.'

'Or not.'

'Of course. Monty and I will leave now. I'll pay the bill on the way out. That way, we won't even know whether you picked the list up. From here on, what you do is entirely up to you.' He stood, and Monty stood with him.' We've offered you information that we know is true and that you may find useful in what you are planning. Or you may not be planning anything. Or, even if you are, you may not find the information useful. From this moment on, if we see you again you will be Moshe Ruben. We will have forgotten all about Yanek Hoffman. And we won't ever refer to this meeting, this conversation or that list.' He held out his hand. 'Good luck, Mr Ruben.'

Yanek looked at the hand for a few moments and then shook it. 'Thank you.'

CHAPTER 30

JUNE, 2003 – LONDON

Twenty days before the robbery

Yanek had come to London with a specific purpose in mind. That didn't mean he was oblivious to what was going on there. On New Year's Day, the Ministry of Defence announced that the death in Afghanistan of a sergeant in the British Army meant the total number of British soldiers who had died there had now reached 137. By the end of the year, that figure would be more than a hundred higher. Those were small numbers by 2009 Israeli standards, but people he met didn't think they were insignificant. 'What are our boys doing out there in the first place? What interest have we got in Afghanistan?'

Yanek would have liked to say that death came looking for your people whether you have an interest in it or not. But was that true if you weren't a Jew? Israelis didn't need to go to foreign lands to find people ready to shoot them, blow them up, immolate them or otherwise bring their lives to an end, but that probably wasn't true of the British. On the other hand, as far as he could tell, the British had been keen for centuries on going out to other people's countries whether the other people wanted them there or not. Yanek Hoffman might have said all of that. But it would not fit the persona adopted by Moshe Ruben. Instead he said, 'I'm afraid I don't know. You'd have to ask Gordon Brown.'

'Brown! Hah! It was Blair who got us into this mess and we don't need to ask what was in it for him. He was currying favour with the Yanks.'

Conversations like that could go on for some time, and Yanek had learned to extricate himself as quickly as possible. Yes, it was a shame that young British men – for the most part, young working-class British men –

were dying thousands of miles from home to burnish the reputation of a former prime minister who had made an art of valuing style above performance, but there was nothing he could do about it. The British would have to learn a lesson that any Israeli hoped the nations surrounding them would learn: If you want to stay out of trouble, stay out of other countries' business. It wasn't just the British: the West as a whole seemed to have difficulty taking that lesson on board.

Today had been a good day in Yanek's own project. A few days earlier, he had used the notes he had taken to cut what he hoped would be a working imitation of the Hatton Garden master key. This morning, he had taken Sammy Bronstein with him and introduced him to Steve. Really, Sammy's brother Monty would have been a better bet because of his experience in subterfuge, but Sammy had told him that Monty was somewhere in South America pursuing a lead he had been given. As it turned out, Sammy had done a perfectly good job on his own.

Yanek had explained to Steve that Sammy had some valuables and might be interested in keeping them safe. Then the three of them had gone into the strongroom where Steve had used his master key and Yanek had used his own key to open one of Yanek's boxes. They'd closed them up again after Yanek had pretended to do something with the contents and then Yanek had given Sammy the signal to get Steve to turn away and engage him in conversation. Yanek had carried out a quick test to see whether the copy he had made of the master key would work with his own key to unlock the box. And it had. Stage I of this project had been collecting as many names of target box holders as possible. Stage II – testing the master key – was now complete. It was time to turn to Stage III. Just thinking about that gave him feelings of intense excitement, which he had to work quite hard to conceal as long as he was in the same room as Steve.

When he and Sammy came out of the building, Sammy said, 'Did it go well?'

'It did. I'm satisfied. I don't want to say any more than that. But let me buy you lunch to celebrate.'

'No. I'll buy. My business is going well and I suspect you may be running a little short of cash by now.'

It was true, but Yanek was not going to say so. He would happily accept lunch at Sammy's expense but Sammy would have to understand that they had not become partners. He was becoming more aware of the risks he ran and the punishment he might receive if he were caught, and those risks were for him alone. In Lublin he had worked with Zoltan and only with him. On the drive to Italy he supposed he had worked a little with Marcello. But working alone was what suited him best. If anything was going to go wrong, let it go wrong just for him. If everything went well and he succeeded, there would be enough conversation about the losses people had suffered for Sammy to hear all about it, though not from him because, if he did make it work, he intended to get out of the country as fast as he could. Whether he'd then go back to being Yanek Hoffman, he hadn't yet decided, but he certainly wouldn't go on being Moshe Ruben.

#

Rosa was once again at lunch with her sister and her friends. There were knowing smiles around the table when her sister said, 'So. Mr Ruben. Any progress there?'

Rosa gave her a look that might have been telling her to mind her own business and might have been encouraging the nosiness. 'Well,' she said. 'What would progress be? And from whose point of view?'

'Rosa, my dear, we have no interest in Mr Ruben's perceptions. We are only interested in how you see things.'

'And even that,' said another woman, 'only because we care for you. We wouldn't want you to think we are prying into your affairs.' This brought a round of laughter from the assembled women.

'If it's affairs you're interested in,' said Rosa, 'I have nothing to report.'

'That is a shame,' said the woman sitting next to her.

'Not in my view,' said Rosa. 'Mr Ruben is the kind of tenant any landlady would like to have. He makes no unreasonable demands, abides by the standards of the house...'

'You mean by your rules,' said her sister.

'I have no rules. I have standards. Guidelines. When someone asks whether I have a room available, I don't simply say yes and I wouldn't even if the whole house was untenanted. I talk to the applicant. I do my best to find out who they are. What kind of person is this who has just come to my door? And at the same time as I'm doing that, I'm also letting whoever it is know in the nicest possible way what I expect from anyone lucky enough to be granted a room. It is my house, after all.'

'And Mr Ruben passes your test?' said another woman. 'He is your idea of the perfect tenant.'

'Well,' said Rosa. 'The perfect tenant? Is that entirely true? Do you know, I'm not sure it is. He is an acceptable tenant. Even a good tenant. But perfect? There I have my reservations.'

'Then tell us about them,' said her sister. 'Describe his imperfections.'

Rosa took her time. This was an opportunity to do what she had not done before and to put into words the vague, almost formless doubts that had entered her mind from time to time. After a pause she said, 'Did you ever have that feeling where you look at someone and you wonder if they're playing a part?'

'Always!' laughed one of the women. 'At least, always with men. I don't know when it happens: I've raised three sons and with each of them all through childhood and into the beginning of adolescence I was sure I knew who they were. What they were. They wore their identity on their faces and everything they did. And then, suddenly, they didn't. Sometime in their teens they started to act. A mask came into place. They were saying to the world, "Here you are. This is me." And it wasn't.

It wasn't them as they really were – it was them as they wanted the world to believe they were.'

'And this is just for the male of the species, is it?' asked another voice.

The woman laughed. 'It's only boys who go through that change. Girls are acting a part from the day they are born.'

'Yes, yes,' said Rosa's sister. 'But Mr Ruben, Rosa. What part do you think he's playing? And why is he playing it? And if he's wearing a mask, what's behind it?'

Rosa paused even longer this time. Then she said, 'I can't be sure. But I'd bet every penny I can raise that he isn't what he seems. You talk to him and you get the feeling, this man is at ease in the world. With himself and with the rest of us. He treats people nicely, he'd walk away from a fight, whatever battles there may have been in his life were over long ago and now he's at peace.'

'And you doubt that?'

'I think he has battles in his past, sure enough. And I think he won them. Possibly with violence. But at peace now? As I said, I think that's the impression he wants to give. I'm less convinced it's true.'

If she'd hoped to reduce interest in her logic, she found she'd had the opposite effect. Every face around the table was agog. One said, 'Rosa. Do you analyse all your lodgers in this depth?'

'Of course she doesn't,' said Rosa's sister. 'Mr Ruben has woken her maternal instincts. And we all know how fast those can change to something else entirely.'

'Oh, we do, do we?' said Rosa.

'Yes, my dear sister, we do. You are analysing this man in depth. And there's always a reason for that.'

'He's an interesting man, that's all. Can we please talk about something else?'

'I put it to you, girls. My sister protests too much. But let's spare her any more embarrassment. At least for now. Who's watching Jonathan Creek?'

CHAPTER 31

JUNE, 2009 – ISRAEL

Eighteen days before the robbery

Rachel had divorced Rosenbaum and was now living with Joseph, a man ten years younger than her who had been born in Israel. There was no talk of marriage but Rachael never wondered what her rabbi father would have said about her situation. His world was gone. The faith he had given her was as strong as it had ever been, but she held onto nothing else from her childhood. The past still held her, though. When Joseph said his brother would be visiting Israel from London, Rachel asked him to pass some questions for the brother to find the answers to before he left.

'Yanek Hoffman? László Rosenbaum? You never mentioned these people. Who are they?'

'I never told you Rosenbaum was the name of the man I was married to? I don't believe you. You've forgotten. Which just shows how important I really am to you.'

'My good woman, you have never discussed your marriage with me beyond saying it was not a success. I have not forgotten Rosenbaum's name because I never knew it.'

'If you say so. In any case, that's who he is and I'd be interested to know what he's up to. Nothing good, I'm sure of that.'

'And the other man?'

'He brought me to Israel. I'd have died trying to get here without him.

'You were in a relationship?'

'My God, NO! Yanek Hoffman? You're kidding me. I can't think of anything worse. He was devoted to the idea of a Jewish homeland, and getting as many Jews there as possible. I was one of a whole truckload he brought, all the way from Lublin. That's in Poland.'

'I know where Lublin is. I'll give these names to Danny and see what he finds out.'

But when Danny arrived a few weeks later, he only had half the answers Rachel had asked for. Rosenbaum was infamous among London's Jews for his relationships with women young enough to be his daughters. No-one Danny had spoken to admitted having heard of Yanek Hoffman.'

Joseph said, 'No-one admitted? That's a strange way to phrase it. They either knew him or they didn't.'

'Yes, indeed. But I spoke to at least one person – a sales agent called Samuel Bronstein – who said he knew nothing of any Yanek Hoffman. His face suggested otherwise.

#

When Yanek met Sammy Bronstein in the street near Hatton Garden, he was immediately sure that what looked like a casual meeting had in fact been engineered. He was confirmed in that idea when Sammy, after the usual "Fancy seeing you heres" and "How are yous?" said, 'By the way. Do you know someone called Danny Levi?'

'Levi? No, I can't say I do.'

'Interesting. He was asking about you.'

'Me?'

'Not you, Moshe Ruben. You, Yanek Hoffman.'

Would he never be free of that cold pit in his stomach when the past came back to haunt him? Yanek took a moment to let his heartbeat return to normal. 'He asked about Yanek Hoffman specifically? What did he want to know? And why?'

Bronstein shook his head. I didn't ask and he didn't say. On the face of it, it was one of those random queries we still get. Someone trying to find out if someone they once knew made it out of the camps. But he was too young for that. And when a journalist asks questions, you wonder just how innocent it might be.'

That word had got Yanek's heartbeat pounding again. 'He's a journalist?'

'He is. He mostly works for Israeli publications but you never know with these guys. They freelance all over the place. And you can't trust them. I'd never tell a journalist anything I wasn't willing to share with the world. They hear a little clue here, another there, and before they know it, they've found a story worth investigating. They have no scruples: they'll invent facts if they need to.

'What did you tell him?'

'I said I'd never heard of you. But you need to know that someone is asking around about the person you used to be.'

'Shit.'

'Exactly.'

Well, it would turn out all right or it wouldn't. He could try to find out more about Danny Levi, but the danger there would be being seen asking questions. And now that Bronstein was here, he could try out the plan he'd been hatching. He needed help and he couldn't think of anyone else who would agree to what he had to ask. The man could only say no. 'While you're here, I wonder if I could get you to do me a favour?'

'Sure, if it's in my power.'

'Drop by my lodgings sometime when you know I'm out. Leave a message for me with my landlady.'

'I can do that. What's the message?'

'Tell her you need me to contact you as soon as possible because you have the best investment opportunity I'll ever hear about but it needs an immediate response.'

Bronstein stared into Yanek's eyes, his face betraying nothing. Then he said, 'You're thinking of fleecing your landlady? Wow, I didn't see that coming.'

'Not fleecing, no. You have some idea of what my plans here are and I need time to put them into effect. I need every penny I have left to get the job done. When it's over, I'll pay Rosa the overdue rent and probably give her a bonus.'

'Seducing her would be easier.'

'I've tried, believe me. I can lay on all the charm I want, but I'm still not in her bed.'

Another long, searching look into his eyes by Bronstein. Then, 'Yes. All right. I'll do that for you. Don't let me down by leaving debts behind you.'

'I promise that's not my intention.'

'Okay. Tell me when you'll be out and you think she'll be in.'

'Three o'clock tomorrow afternoon would be perfect.'

'Consider it done. And, if you're husbanding the cash, let me buy you dinner tomorrow night. Same place as before.'

'Thank you, Sammy. You're a gentleman.'

'It's a good job one of us is.'

CHAPTER 32

JUNE , 2003 LONDON

A week before the robbery

When Yanek arrived for dinner with Sammy the next evening, he said, 'Thanks for seeing my landlady.'

'She gave you the message? Any talk?

'No. Just, "Mr Bronstein was looking for you. He says it's urgent: the best investment opportunity you'll ever hear about, but it won't wait. And he says have dinner with him tonight – you know where." That's all. Your message, word for word, with no additions

'Hmm.'

'You look surprised. You expected something else?'

'She wouldn't be a woman if she didn't want to know more than I told her. And she's all woman, all right.'

'Isn't she?'

'Apart from which, she has an interest in you that isn't just a landlady and a tenant.'

'What are you talking about?'

'Come on, now. She hears your name and her expression changes.'

'Changes?'

'Softens. Melts. I'm hungry. Pick up the menu and let's order.'

And they did, and they ate well, and Rosa was not mentioned again until Sammy had paid the bill and they were standing up, ready to leave. Then Sammy said, 'I want to hear the end of the story. What's your plan for your landlady?'

I''ll wait for her to ask if I saw you. If she doesn't ask, the plan stops there. If she does, I'll do the rueful look and say, yes, it was a fabulous opportunity but I just can't spare the cash right now. Then I'll just see what happens. If she bites, she bites. If she doesn't, she doesn't.'

Tell me the outcome. And, Yanek. That woman has got a thing for you. Make sure she doesn't end up being hurt.'

'You're seeing things that aren't there. I'm her lodger. Nothing more. Thank you for dinner.'

#

But Bronstein wasn't imagining things. Whatever she'd told her sister and the other women, Yanek had got through Rosa's defences. All the lodgers she had now and most of those she'd had in the past were men. She was used to the idea that from time to time they'd put out feelers. Rosa had no false modesty: she knew men found her attractive. She'd developed a way of brushing off advances she didn't want without giving offence. She'd brushed off Mr Ruben's advances, too. But not, in his case, because she didn't want them.

When she'd talked to the other women about the vibes he gave off, she'd been telling the truth. He did seem like someone who'd known struggle. Who'd responded with violence. Who hid ongoing turmoil behind a mask. There were probably women who could see all of that in a man and not want to know more. But Rosa wasn't one of them. What had so far prevented her from succumbing to the invitations he only partly hid was a habit of caution learned long ago. Attraction to a man was no stranger to Rosa. She'd experienced it before. And she'd been hurt.

That was a long time ago. She hadn't been out of her teens the first time and she'd been only twenty when it happened again. She made up her mind then: there wouldn't be a third time. So far, she'd prevented Mr Ruben from slipping behind those defences. She wasn't sure how determined she was to go on keeping him at a distance. Certainly, it couldn't hurt to talk. So, when he came home that evening she just happened to step out of her room as he opened the front door. 'Mr Ruben. Did you enjoy your dinner with Mr Bronstein?'

'I did. Thank you.'

'And did he ensnare you with his investment opportunity? Was it as good as he said?'

'Better, if anything. If I had the liquidity, I'd join him like a shot. But I have another project, a work project, and completing that and meeting my other obligations will take all the cash I have.'

'Other obligations?'

'Of course. My rent, for example. Laundry. Eating. Paying my way when I'm with others. Three months from now, that work project I mentioned will pay off and I'll have more than enough to invest with Sammy Bronstein. Unfortunately, Sammy can't wait three months.' He shrugged his shoulders. 'What can you do? Life is full of opportunities. None of us gets to take advantage of them all. That isn't how the world works.' He shrugged again and turned towards the stairs. 'In any case, I have correspondence to deal with. I'll bid you good night.'

Back in her room, Rosa thought about the conversation they'd just had. If rent and laundry and meals held him back from something he wanted to do, she could help. But did she want to?

#

As for Yanek, he'd achieved his aim. He'd put into Rosa's head the knowledge that money was tight, that he was determined to meet his obligations, but there was room for her to help if she chose to – and only three months from now the rewards would be handsome. What she did with that knowledge was up to her. And by saying he had correspondence to see to, he'd got himself out of her company. Staying there might have made it seem he wanted to discuss his financial needs further. With someone as astute as Rosa, that could only be a mistake. But he didn't have any correspondence waiting in his room. What he had was the need to plan. And a nagging worry about someone called Danny Levi. Who was he? And why was he interested in Yanek Hoffman?

Sitting in his bedroom's only armchair, he faced up to his shortage of friends. He knew people, of course he did, he'd run a restaurant. But the kind of relationships restaurant owners have are casual. Slap on the back, hail fellow well met, ships that pass in the night. They came to eat at his place, they greeted him, sometimes they told jokes and tales about other people, but they came because the food was good and the prices right. Not because he was their buddy. Desmond Morris had told him that someone who had known Yanek the restaurateur wanted him to go back and run the place again because it wasn't as good now as it had been when he was there. But that didn't help him find out about the journalist. He'd been married, but that hadn't ended well. He had a son and a daughter, but he couldn't remember when he'd last spoken to either of them. There was no-one in Israel he could call and say, "I need everything you can find out about Danny Levi." And no-one here in London, either, because Sammy Bronstein was his best informed contact in England and Sammy hadn't been able to tell him much.

Danny Levi was, of course, only doing what Rachel had asked, so Yanek had no reason to fret. Rachel just wanted to know how Yanek's life was going. But Yanek didn't know that. And sometimes it's the things we don't know that lead us to do things we shouldn't do.

CHAPTER 33

JUNE, 2003 LONDON

Six days before the robbery

Sammy and Monty Bronstein had given Yanek a list of three names. Two were already on his list, but one was new. After months of daily visits, he knew that nine of the people had a safe-deposit box in Hatton Garden. And he knew who they were.

None of those nine visited their boxes anything like as often as Yanek visited his. Two were there almost every week. Three put in an appearance roughly once a month. Yanek had only seen two of them once since he arrived in London, and the other two he hadn't seen at all.

He had got to know the seven who had visited Hatton Garden. It had taken time, and if he hadn't known before then that time was money, he knew now. His objective was to become acquainted with their keys, but he couldn't make that obvious. Anyone would be alarmed by someone saying, "Show me your safe-deposit box key." His first plan had been to be in the storage box room at the same time as the others so that he could sneak a look at their key, but that was a nonstarter. Getting Sammy into the room to distract Steve's attention at the critical moment had been one thing: Sammy had been there as Yanek's guest and not to look at a box of his own. The Hatton Garden rules allowed that. They did not allow two people in the room at the same time, each opening their own box.

He'd worked on that by socialising. Making friends with the seven and suggesting coffee, a drink, sometimes a meal. They'd usually split the bill, but it still ended with Yanek spending more money than he had wanted to. He was burning through his restaurant sale reserves faster than expected. That was why he was hoping to get Rosa to wait for his rent. And the job was never done in one visit, because what he needed was to find a way to get the other person to take his keys out of his pocket and keep them out long enough for Yanek to register the size and order of the cuts on the only one that interested him out of what was sometimes a large collection. Bit by bit, he'd collected what he needed and now he had cut seven keys on the machine in his room. That left two. There was an obvious possibility, of course: he could decide that seven out of nine wasn't bad and settle for that. If neither of the remaining two had been a big player in diverting money intended to fund settlement in Palestine, he might have made that choice. But one of the two was among the worst offenders. Quite possibly the worst of all.

Yanek had first heard about Noah Absalom at the meetings with ex- Etzel members. The name always got the same reaction from anyone who had met the man or knew his reputation. "He was a crook from the start." "It was all fake with Absalom. I don't believe he gave a toss about a Jewish homeland." "He handed over just enough to stop people talking. Most of what he was given, he kept." "There's a special place in hell for selling out your own people. And Absalom's name is on it." "They say he changed his name. What to? I couldn't tell you. But he never came to Israel. From what I heard, he made enough out of other people's sacrifice to buy himself a nice little place in England. Lives there like a lord of the manor. And this for a man brought up in a Polish shtetel without a pot to piss in."

There was so little hard information about where Noah Absalom was living and what he was calling himself that Yanek would have decided to forget about him – but one of the Etzel survivors had a photograph of the man. 'He didn't know I was taking it. I couldn't tell you why I did, except that I had my doubts about him even then. I don't suppose there are many others: Absalom shunned the light.'

'Can I copy that?'

'Sure you can. Why not? Show it to anyone you like. Bring the bastard to justice before he dies.'

That might have been the end of it. But Yanek showed Steve the photograph one day. Steve stared at it squint-eyed for minutes. 'I don't know, Moshe. It isn't the clearest picture, is it? And it was obviously taken a long time ago. But...'

'You think you might know him?'

Another long pause before Steve said, 'I don't know. I can't be sure. The man I'm thinking of is getting on in years. He's ten or more years older than you.' His face turned pink. 'I'm sorry, I didn't mean...'

'That's all right, Steve. I'm not as young as I once was. I know that. But the man in the picture?'

'I can't be sure. You understand that? But it could be... It *could* be Norman Arkwright.'

Norman Arkwright. Initials N A. The same as Noah Absalom. And isn't that what people said? When you change your name, keep the same initials? But all Yanek said was, 'Oh, well. Not my man, then. Close, though – I wonder whether they might be related.'

'Will you get in touch and ask him?'

Yanek let it seem he was thinking about it. 'No,' he said in the end. 'It's too long a shot. There's probably no connection. If he's local, though, I might drop in.'

'Oh, he isn't. I think he lives somewhere near Cambridge. I could find out for you?'

'Cambridge? Well, I won't be going there just on the off chance. But, yes – let me know for certain. There's no hurry,' he went on, mentally crossing his fingers at the lie.

When he went to check his boxes next day, Steve said, 'I looked Norman Arkwright up for you, Moshe. I was right: he lives a place called Fen Ditton. That's near Cambridge, like I said.'

'Thanks, Steve. That's that, then. I'm not going all the way out there just to confirm that he isn't who I vaguely thought he might be.' But that afternoon, he took a different line with the Bronstein brothers.

'Arkwright?' said Sammy. 'You can't be serious. Or he can't. That's... I don't know what it is, but I know there's never been a Jew called Arkwright.'

'It's Yorkshire,' said Monty, back in England after his latest Nazi hunt in South America. 'Or Lancashire. I can never tell the difference.'

'It's not his real name,' said Yanek. 'He's really Noah Absalom, a Polish Jew and the worst offender on my list.'

Monty said, 'So what do you want to do about it?'

'I want sight of his Hatton Garden safe-deposit key.'

'That won't be easy.'

'Thanks, Monty. I hadn't already worked that out.'

Sammy put up a hand. 'There's no need for sarcasm. Monty, you know more than either of us about getting information out of people who don't want to give it. Any suggestions?'

Monty said, 'Oh, look. There's always a lot of luck involved. And sometimes the luck doesn't go with you. Men and women are alive in Argentina today who I know without any doubt were responsible for multiple deaths during the war. I KNOW it. And in some cases they know I know it. But I can't produce the proof to satisfy a court. And so they go on with their lives. I hate it, but I can't do anything about it. So, Moshe, you need luck on your side. But one thing I've found useful in the past has been giving the target a bit of a scare. When someone thinks they've got away with it and then something happens to say maybe they haven't, they sometimes do stupid things.'

'So I need to find a way to scare him. Any suggestions?'

'Well, maybe I can help. You know most of the time Clark Kent was a mild-mannered newspaper reporter at the Daily Planet?'

'You're Superman now, are you?' said his brother.

'Some people think so.' He took a card from his wallet and placed it on the table. 'I'm also a reporter. Freelance, nothing to do with the Daily Planet. But that's a genuine press card.'

Yanek said, 'What's your thinking?'

'When people have something to hide, the idea that a reporter is checking them out can put the fear of God into them. I think I might take a little trip to Fen Ditton. Give me a hand here – tell me someone Absalom swindled.'

CHAPTER 34

JUNE, 2003 LONDON

Five days before the robbery

Rosa was in the entrance hall when Yanek got home. He'd begun to see a pattern. He'd be out, he'd come home, and more often than not Rosa would be there. Not waiting for him: nothing that obvious. But she'd be there and she'd speak to him. He noticed because it had happened only rarely when he first came to live in the house and now it was unusual for it not to happen. 'Mr Ruben. Have you got a moment?'

He followed her into her sitting room. She closed the door behind him. 'I wondered... That meeting with Mr Bronstein... The investment he mentioned...'

When Steve had given him Norman Arkwright's name and he'd realised the initials were the same as Noah Absalom's, Yanek had felt a surge of optimism. He felt it again now. Things were working out for him. Monty Bronstein had said you needed luck, and perhaps he was getting it. Events in his life had never suggested that God was taking any interest in his affairs, but maybe what he was doing now had God's support. Assuming there was a God, of course. He said, 'I told him he needed to find another investor. It was a great opportunity, but sometimes you just have to accept that things are the way they are. The time just wasn't right.'

She'd moved a little closer to him. 'Would you have put your money in? If it hadn't been tied up?'

'Yes. I would. It was a good deal.'

Her head was angled away, but her eyes were looking at him. He felt just a hint of revulsion at what he was doing. This was a decent woman, a good woman, and she liked him. Maybe it was more than just liking. Perhaps the hand on the hip approach would tell him more. She said, 'Suppose I didn't charge you for rent and meals? You could owe it to me until your other deal is complete. Would that help?'

She stepped even closer. And then, when he rested his hand for just a moment on her hip, she turned towards him. Her face was looking down but she was so close. She had to be asking him to hold her. And he did, and she pressed against him, and he felt even more of a shit than he had a little earlier, but it didn't stop him. He wrapped his arms around her. 'Yes,' he said. 'Of course it would. But I wouldn't ask...'

'I know you wouldn't. So I'm offering. Okay?' She extricated herself from his arms, stepped back and looked him in the eyes. Whatever she was searching for, it seemed she found it because she took his hand and led him towards her bedroom. Once inside, she pressed against him again and whispered, 'Manners, Mr Ruben. My needs first. Then we'll see about yours.'

#

Monty Bronstein didn't spend enough time in England to keep a car there. In any case, when he was in England he almost never left London and so taxis and public transport met his needs. There was a good train service to Cambridge, from the centre of which Fen Ditton was no distance at all, but trains might be restricting if he wanted to get away in a hurry so he hired a car.

When he arrived, he ate lunch in the Plough, a pub that may have had its roots in the rustic past but was now upmarket even by the standards of someone used to London eateries. Whatever concerns he might once have had about kosher meals had been killed by his constant travels. He drank sparkling water because he would be driving again in he afternoon, and finished with coffee. Then, feeling rather pleased with life, he drove past Norman Arkwright's house. He drove out of that street, navigated his way around three or four more, and then passed the Arkwright house again in the other direction. The only vehicle outside was a Range

Rover with startlingly red bodywork. Better still, there was a phone box just round the corner. Give it another decade and these would have completed their disappearance from residential areas. He parked and dialled the number he had for Norman Arkwright. A man's voice answered, and Monty said, 'Noah! How the hell are you? My word, it's been a while.'

The sudden intake of breath and the spluttering were enough. By the time Absalom got around to saying, 'I'm sorry? I think you must have the wrong number,' Monty knew he hadn't. He put a smile into his voice. 'Come on, Noah. It's me.' And he gave the name Yanek had given him. The name of a man Noah Absalom would know to be dead.

Sure enough, the man claiming to be Norman Arkwright said, 'But you're...' Then he caught himself. 'I'm sorry, my name is not Noah and I never heard your name before.'

But Monty was an old hand at this game. Those war criminals he'd brought in for trial had taught him a great deal about putting on a convincing performance. He said, 'Dead? Was that what you were going to say? A lot of people think I'm dead, Noah. I found that convenient at the time. It still is, if you want to know the truth. But you robbed the people I was working for, Noah.'

'I don't know what you're talking about.'

'I'm talking about the jewellery I gave to you to pay for Jewish settlers to reach Palestine.' The fish was on the hook. If Absalom was going to hang up, he'd have done it already. 'A lot of people put their hands into that till, Noah. Kept back some of the proceeds to enrich themselves. Shlomo, for example. Did you ever meet Shlomo?'

There was a long pause before Absalom said, 'He's dead.'

'Yes, Noah. He's dead. And he only took some of the jewellery he was given. You took all of it.'

Another long pause and then Absalom said, 'What do you want?'

'Now you're being sensible. One week from today, you are going to meet one of my colleagues in London. When you're there, you're going to give my colleague 60% of what you stole instead of handing it over to Etzel. We'll let you keep the rest. Can't have a fellow Jew starving. Even one who did what you did. I'll be in touch with the details of the meeting and the handover, so stay close to your phone.' He hung up and called his brother. 'We need to see Yanek without delay. Please set it up.' And then he began the drive back to London in a buoyant frame of mind.

#

Yanek didn't get Sammy's call right away, because he'd still been with Rosa. For a woman who had taken so long to succumb, she seemed to have cast away all inhibitions. Yanek should have been jubilant that his plans had succeeded. Instead, he felt like a heel. As they lay together in Rosa's bed, her arms round him and her face nestling against his chest, he thought about other women he'd known and how he'd treated them. The women in the camp whose favours he had bought with food. Rachel, where the transaction hadn't even been that two-sided. Ilana, who he had married in the hope that he could somehow share in what she saw about him. A hope that was doomed to failure: perhaps what you needed to be able to have a loving relationship was to have been brought up by two people who shared one. And Yanek had never known that.

Was he being offered a second chance? A chance to settle down with Rosa and be to her what he had never been to Ilana? It was a nice dream, a lovely dream. But he knew, deep down, a dream was all it was. If he tried for that new life, what was he going to live on? Rosa thought he was a diamond merchant with a thriving business and the spare cash to invest in projects like Sammy Bronstein's. In fact, he had never owned a single diamond. And there were no projects, and no investment. Most of the money from selling the restaurant had already gone.

And was he to give up the plan he had come to London to fulfil? He couldn't do that. Yes, he could see how Rosa felt about him. But the memories of what had passed had never gone and never would. Zoltan, dead in the road, never to see the homeland he had worked so hard for. And once Yanek thought of Zoltan, how could he not think of so many others? Those feral kids he had run with in Berehove. How many of them had survived the war? He'd never know, but he was certain it wasn't many. And people in the camps: however he had treated them, he knew that many had had gifts denied to him and could have made a mark on the world. Dead, almost all of them; killed by evil.

No, he wasn't going to make a life with Rosa. The idea was lovely but the reality could never be. It had probably been impossible as early as the day he was conceived.

A fist rapped sharply three times on the door. Then Esther's voice, harsh in the stillness. 'Rosa. Do you know where Mr Ruben is? There's a message for him from Mr Bronstein.'

Yanek was about to speak but Rosa silenced him with a finger to his lips. 'She knows exactly where you are, or she wouldn't be asking me.' In a louder voice she said, 'Give me the message, Esther. I'll see that he gets it.'

'Mr Bronstein says, could Mr Ruben have dinner with him and his brother this evening. They have information for him.'

They waited until they heard the door from Rosa's sitting room into the entrance hall close. Then Rosa said, 'You'd better go. You need to see him anyway, to tell him you're going ahead with the investment. But before you go, kiss me. And remember: when your meeting with the Bronsteins is done, I'll be here waiting for you.'

#

Before leaving to meet Sammy Bronstein, Yanek went to his room to tidy up. He knew the moment he entered that someone had been in here. When he left the house it was Esther and not Rosa who lurked, waiting for him. The look on her face was pure hatred. She stood close to him and in little more than a whisper she said, 'Who is Yanek Hoffman?'

And then she turned and disappeared up the stairs.

CHAPTER 35

JUNE, 2003 LONDON

Four days before the robbery

Yanek was in turmoil. He'd known someone had been in his room, and now he knew who it was. But what could she have found in his room that would have given him away? He hadn't left Israel until he did so with his new identity as Moshe Ruben. So where had she got the name from? And how much did she know?

When the most obvious thought struck him, he shivered. To the best of his knowledge, the only people in England who knew who he really was were the Bronsteins. And that's who he was on his way to meet right now. His life had become entangled with theirs. But what reason did he have to think they were on his side? Everything they had done so far had tended that way – but were they hiding something? Monty had spent his adult life in pursuit of the law. And Sammy had seemed taken aback when Yanek asked for his help in misleading Rosa.

Rosa. Another reason for his mental distress. All he'd wanted was a break from paying rent to eke out his remaining funds until he'd completed what he came to England to do. And he'd got that. But Rosa was offering so much more. Yanek wasn't often honest with himself any more than with anyone else. He could look back on his life all the way to the death camps and even before that and see very little that was good. He'd been a hero on the journey from Lublin to Palestine, even Rachel had admitted that, but otherwise it was not a good picture. If he tried now for honesty with himself, could he say that he had ever been in love? With Ilana or anyone else? Had he really loved his children? He knew the answer and it did not flatter him. Was he now capable of loving Rosa the way it seemed she must love him? He wanted to, and it was probably the first time in his life that he'd ever wanted that. Really wanted it. But could he?

Those thoughts were still churning their way through his mind when he arrived at the restaurant. Sammy welcomed him and called for a drink to be placed in front of him. 'Monty's on his way back from Fen Ditton. He should be here in about half an hour.'

'He went there today? Is that what you want to talk about?'

'I'm assuming so. Monty phoned before he left there and said we needed to meet. He didn't say what about.'

'Okay.' Yanek drank. There was something he could raise... a suspicion he needed to address... before Monty got back here. He said, 'There's a maid at the place where I lodge. Esther. Have you ever met her?'

'Esther... Esther... It's a common enough name. I could probably think of three or four Esthers if I put my mind to it. I don't think any of them is a maid. Not in the sense you mean, anyway. Why are you looking at me like that, Yanek?'

'I don't know, Sammy. How am I looking at you?'

'As though you distrust me. What's happened?'

Was he convinced? Not really. Sammy might be telling the truth and he might not. He said, 'Nothing's happened. It's just the way I look at people, I suppose. I'm sorry if it bothers you.'

'How are things with Rosa?'

'If you meet her again, be aware that I have invested in your scheme.'

'So it worked. Well done.'

However hard he tried, Yanek could not quite keep doubt out of the way he looked at Sammy. Well done, the man said. But did he mean it? He stood up. 'I'll be right back.' He didn't actually need to go to the men's room, but it would give him a chance to give himself a talking to. Paranoia might be inevitable when you'd been through the kind of life Yanek and Zoltan had lived where every man's hand seemed to be against you, largely because it almost always was, but you needed the strength of mind to know when it was misplaced. A gambling man would say the odds were that Sammy and Monty were on his side, without reservation and no questions asked. But a gambling man would also know that the odds were sometimes wrong. He shook himself. He was going to act in the belief that the Bronstein brothers were with him and not against him. If that was a mistake, tough. He hadn't walked away from trouble in the past and he wouldn't now.

When he returned to the table, Monty had arrived. 'Thank God you're back,' said Sammy. 'Monty has refused to say a damn thing about where he's been until you got here.'

'What's the point of saying everything twice?' asked Monty. And then he told them about his conversation with Noah Absalom.

'I was right, then,' said Yanek. 'It is him. Do you think he'll turn up in a week's time with the loot?'

'I'd say that's very unlikely. I think there's a very good chance he'll visit Hatton Garden to make sure whatever he has there is safe. So maybe you need to be watching out for him there. But I think you'll need more pressure than I've put on him so far.'

#

JUNE 2003, ISRAEL

It's a fact of life that people visit their parents – or, at least, the parents they care about who they believe also cared for them – more often as they grow older. It isn't hard to see why: there are so many other things you have to do when you're young, and the feeling that your parents have been there all through your life and always will be is strong. But time goes by, you see other people mourning a father or mother, and you have to accept it. No-one lives forever. It's the same feeling you have when you've been married to the same person for a long time: one of you is going to be left. And so, Arie made a trip to Israel that was partly pleasure and partly a duty visit to see Ilana. And, even though he'd accepted that one day he would be orphaned, it still saddened him to see the physical signs that his mother was ageing. Mentally, she seemed as bright as ever. Physically, simple things were more of an effort now.

They went out to dinner. Arie's business was doing well and he could afford to take her somewhere that Yanek would not have dreamed of paying for when they were together. With a sad smile, Ilana said so. 'Will you visit him while you're here?'

'I don't think so.'

'Think? You don't think so? Arie, you will or you won't.'

'All right, I won't. The memories aren't good.'

'No. And they aren't good for me, either. Marrying him was a mistake. But how can I regret it? Without him, I wouldn't have you and I wouldn't have Bat-Sheva. I'd have only Yudka and the memory of Peter.'

'How is Yudka?'

'Thriving. And so is Fanni. She's at university now, and Yudka tells me she's doing well. Yudka is your half-sister and Fanni is your great-niece, Arie. You should visit them. And you should visit your father. He may not have been very good at being a father, but that's still what he was to you.'

'Not very good? That's putting it mildly.'

'Did he ever talk to you about when he was a child?'

'No, I don't think so. He used to tell us all kinds of far-fetched stories about things he claimed to have done in the war, but I don't think he ever mentioned any time before that.'

'Not to me, either. Or not very much. I used to ask him, when we were first together. I'd say, "Tell me about your mother. Tell me about your father." But he brushed it all off. He didn't want to talk about it.'

'So, really, you know nothing about him before he turned up here. In Israel.'

'Very little. He'd let things slip from time to time but I could tell he always regretted it. I don't think he ever knew his father. Didn't even know who he was, probably. And his mother... Well, I don't think she took being a mother very seriously. You know, when he arrived here, he couldn't write his name? Couldn't read? I don't think he spent much time in school. What I'm trying to say, Arie, is: your parents teach you a lot of things without you or them realising. And one of the things they teach you is how to be a parent yourself. It's taken humans thousands of years to learn how to treat their children. How to treat the person they had the children with, if it comes to that. In some places – Iran, Afghanistan – they still haven't learned. And nor has your father. But he *is* your father. You should see him.'

Arie sighed. 'All right. I'm flying home three days from now. I'll go see him in the morning. Then you and I can have dinner again tomorrow and I'll tell you all about it.'

But when they met again the following evening and Ilana asked whether he had visited Yanek, Arie said, 'He's not there.'

'Not there? What do you mean, not there? Where is he?'

'No-one knows. He sold the restaurant to his chef and left. Maybe the chef knew where he was going. But the chef had a heart attack and died and now the place has a new owner. The new owner never met my father and doesn't much care if you want to know the truth. None of the staff who are there now were there then. It's a mystery.'

'Well. Israel is a small country. I'm sure he'll turn up some time. And in the meantime there may be news. I had a call from a woman called Rachel. Rachel what, she didn't make clear. She said she'd known your father and she wants to talk to me.'

'She knew him? In what way?'

'That's something else she didn't make clear.'

'Another mystery.'

'She may clear up the mystery tomorrow. Because that's when she's coming. Could you be here?'

'Do you want me to be?'

'Yes. Yes, I do.'

'Then I will. How about Bat-Sheva? Should she be here, too?'

'I'll ask her.'

CHAPTER 36

JUNE, 2003 LONDON

Three days before the robbery

It was late when Yanek returned home, and what he really wanted was to track down Esther and question her, but Rosa made it clear that in her bed was where he belonged. When they'd been there long enough for her immediate demands to be satisfied, he tried to push the conversation in that direction. Rosa was woozy from lovemaking, but she could still be spiky. 'Esther? Why are you asking about Esther?'

'She brought the message from Sammy Bronstein. The message was for me but she knocked on your door. Did she know I'd be here?'

Rosa raised herself on one elbow to see him more clearly. 'Does it matter if she did? Does it matter if she does? Do you want to keep it secret? Are you planning to slip out of here in the morning with no-one seeing? Are you ashamed of what we just did? Am I not worthy of Mr Ruben's attentions?'

Alarmed at what he might have stirred up, Yanek said, 'No, Rosa.'

'NO?'

'I mean, no, I'm not ashamed. I'm honoured, delighted, overcome with…'

'Yes, yes, I should damn well hope you are. So why do you care about Esther?'

'She works for you.'

'Yes, she does.'

'But I think she's more than just a maid. I don't want to cause friction between you and someone you care about.'

'She *is* more than just a maid to me. She's family. Distant, but family all the same. And like so many, she lost everyone else in the war. So now she only has me. But why should there be friction between us? I hope you're not going to tell me... Have you... Has she... Moshe. Have you and Esther...'

'No. No, I swear. Nothing like that.'

'Then I don't see that there's anything to worry about. I'm glad you want to talk after making love because in my experience men usually fall asleep. But would you mind finding a different subject for conversation?'

#

Next morning, Yanek was determined not to leave the house until he had spoken to Esther. It seemed she was bent on making that as difficult as possible, and he didn't want Rosa to see what was going on, but eventually he tracked her down on an upper landing. 'Esther. I need to talk to you.' The look she gave him was cold to the point of malevolence. 'Have you been in my room?'

'I clean your room. You know that. It's part of your deal with Rosa.'

'Yes, but...' That line of questioning was going to get him nowhere. 'Esther. Who is this man you asked me about? This... What did you call him? Yanek Hoffman. Who is he? And what has he to do with me?'

She glared and pushed past him. 'What indeed?' And then she was almost running down the stairs, and fear of what Rosa might think prevented him following her. He went to his own room, collected his briefcase, found Rosa, kissed her with a promise to see her later, and set off for Hatton Garden.

He went through his usual routine of opening all of his boxes, writing in the notebook he carried for the purpose, and then locking up again. When he and Steve walked back into the reception area, Steve brightened at the sight of a man Yanek had not seen before. 'Mr Arkwright! A happy coincidence! This is Mr Ruben, another of our customers. Mr Ruben was asking about you just the other day.'

If Yanek had found Esther's expression that morning to be hostile, a whole new word would be needed to describe the look Noah Absalom now gave him. 'Has he? Has he indeed? Well, Mr Ruben, what have you and I to do with each other?'

#

JUNE, 2003 ISRAEL

Arie knew how nervous Ilana had been at the idea of this visit from the woman called Rachel. Nervousness was not something he'd been used to in his mother, even in the worst days of her marriage to Yanek, and so he made a point of being with her some time before the visitor was due to arrive. Bat-Sheva had responded to her mother's call by saying that she had no interest in hearing anything about her father, good or bad, but she was here all the same. When Rachel arrived, it was clear that she was every bit as nervous as Ilana.

Since no-one else seemed to know how to get the conversation started, Arie thought he had better take charge. He said, 'Rachel, you want to talk about our father. Can we ask why? And how do you know him?'

'I'll tell you how I know him in a minute. Why I'm here is more important. I came here because Joseph said I should.'

'Joseph? Your husband? Boyfriend? Something else?'

A smile came and went on Rachel's lips. 'I'm a bit old for boyfriends, don't you think? He is my man. What the English would call my chap. I had a husband, but I don't have him any longer. It took me a long time to tell Joseph my story. When I did, he started digging around the way men do, not leaving well enough alone, and then he told me he'd found out Yanek had a family. And then, once again like a man he wouldn't stop until I said I'd make contact. Which is what I'm doing now. Really, to stop him talking about it.'

'How did you know my father?'

'We met in a camp in Poland. He was a kapo.'

Arie said, 'A kapo? I never knew that.' He looked at his mother. 'Did you know that?'

Ilana shook her head. 'He kept it to himself. You would, wouldn't you? I suppose that's how he survived.' She turned to Rachel. 'How did he treat you? Was he a good kapo?'

Rachel paused before answering. Yanek had been a husband to this woman. A father to Arie and Bat-Sheva, adults now but once his children. How much did they know about him? How much did they want to know? How much could they bear knowing? She shook herself. She'd come here for a reason. She said, 'The worst kind. Yes, I'm sure it helped him survive, and he made doubly sure by ending the lives of others. If anyone threatened the targets he had to meet, that was the end of them. And his treatment of women was despicable. As a kapo, he had extra food. He'd use some of it to get women in the camp to open their legs for him.'

'You?' asked Ilana.

'No. Not me. Though he tried. Offered me bread and a piece of sausage. I hadn't been there long at that time – a few more weeks and who knows what hunger might have made me do? But those weeks didn't happen because the war was almost over. When they realised what the future held, the guards ran away. Before he followed them, Yanek caught me. I suppose my rejection of his advances still rankled. This time, he didn't bother with bread and sausage.'

Bat-Sheva said, 'He raped you?'

'He couldn't have had me any other way.' She sighed. 'It was a dark period. A bad time. Lots of women went through what I did. For many, it was far worse. Later, it almost was far worse for me and this time it was Yanek who saved me.'

Ilana said, 'He saved you? You were together?'

'Not in the way you mean. Let me tell you my story, and then you'll understand. At least, you'll understand as well as I do.' She paused. She'd thought hard about this part. Joseph had offered to come to this meeting with her and she'd said no. Not because she wouldn't find his presence helpful, but because he would realise she wasn't telling everything she knew. Yanek had done heroic things and his ex-wife and children were entitled to know about them. He'd also robbed and killed and she would spare them that. She knew what he would say. She knew, too, that many Israelis would agree with him. He'd only killed in the course of robbery and his robberies had been for the Jewish people. They'd made the return to Palestine possible. Yes, that was true. But they'd also been gross breaches of the sixth and eighth commandments: forgiveness could be granted only by God and God had not spoken yet. So whatever Yanek had been doing before he took charge of the refugee truck in Lublin, she would keep to herself. To gain time she drank the coffee she'd been offered on arrival and ate one of the sweet cakes Ilana had set out on the table. Bat-Sheva immediately refilled her cup. Rachel said, 'After he did what he did to me and left the camp, I never expected to see him again.'

'But you did?' asked Arie.

'Etzel was active at that time. I couldn't tell you how many Jews are alive today thanks only to them, but it's a lot. I'm one of them. You'll hear bad things about Etzel from many people and I don't doubt a lot of them were true, but... Well. You know this, Ilana, without me having to tell you, but Arie and Bat-Sheva are from the next generation. They are free Israelis, they've never known anything else, and memories fade. Perhaps it's for people like us to keep them alive.' That was what Joseph had told her. "Look at what we have here now. A people who walk tall and take orders from no-one. Look at what we had. Slavery, throughout the world. It wasn't called that, but slavery is what it was. Humiliation. Extortion. Murder. And it wasn't peaceful acceptance that made the change. It was the resistance of people like Yanek. Our enemies are still out there. There are still people who would drive this young nation into the sea. We must never forget what happened before because if we do it will happen again. You must play your part. Go and tell these people what it took to create this nation." And that was why she was here. To tell the story of Yanek not as murderous thief and rapist but as a hero.

'I heard stories about someone in Lublin who could help Jews with no money and no friends get to Israel. The stories were true and I found myself with seven other people waiting to board a truck that would get us all the way to Metaponto in Italy where a ship would take us the rest of the way. All paid for by Etzel. Since I reached this country, I've met countless other people who made the same sort of journey. And I've heard of at least as many who started on the way but didn't get here. Europe was a cauldron of hate. There were people everywhere who would kill you for the bread and vegetables you carried to keep you alive on the way. We had an Italian driver for the truck, but he could not have got us to the Italian coast: we came across a number of armed gangs and Marcello would have been no match for them. What got us here was our guard. And our guard was Yanek.'

'That must have been a shock,' said Ilana.

'It was a huge shock. I'd put this man out of my mind. I would have hoped never to see him again. And there he was. I'll tell you frankly, my first thought was to refuse to go. I'd wait for the next one. But there was no way of knowing when that would happen. So, in the end, I went.'

Bat-Sheva said, 'Did you talk to him?'

'Of course I did. I thought at the very least an apology for what he'd done to me might be nice. I didn't get one. But I did get a promise that he'd make sure I reached Palestine. And he kept that promise.'

'You mentioned earlier...'

'Another attempted rape. Yes. And this time, I don't doubt they'd have killed me afterwards. We were in Bari. Yanek had already had to kill people who attacked us, but Bari is in Italy and by then we thought the worst problems were over. Three men, one of them armed, decided I was going with them. That was the first time on the whole journey Yanek left the truck without taking his gun with him. I shouldn't be here now, talking to you. But I am because Yanek, unarmed as she was, took the three men on. They fired at him but he got the gun away from them. If I hadn't stopped him, he'd have killed them all.'

Arie said, 'You stopped him? Why?'

'I've often asked myself that question in the days since it happened. The only answer I can offer is that I'm a rabbi's daughter.'

'And where is your father now?' asked Ilana.

'Dead. Of course. In a camp. Killed by Poles working for Germans but happy to do the job themselves.' She looked up and smiled. Drank more coffee and ate another sweet cake. 'I could go on. I could tell you a lot more stories about that journey and the things Yanek did to keep us safe. But I think I've given you the story you needed to hear. Whatever else he may have been, your husband – your father – was a man of his word. He said he'd get all eight of us to Palestine or die trying. And he did put his life on the line and he did get us all there. Thank you for the coffee and cakes. Without people like Yanek, I wouldn't be here. And nor would you.' She stood up.

'Before you go,' said Ilana, 'did you learn anything about his life before the war? Because I could never get a word out of him.'

'Well, maybe I can help,' said Rachel. 'We did talk once or twice on the way to Metaponto. In the evening, when we'd eaten. Yanek would sit there with a rifle in one hand and a submachine gun in the other, keeping watch. I think he must have slept while we were on the road, because he didn't seem to do it at night. That's when the threats were most severe, of course. He asked about my life and I asked about his. He didn't say much, but I do know he didn't have a father. And for practical purposes he didn't have a mother, either. He never went to school. He was in a gang from the earliest time he could remember. If war hadn't come, he'd probably have spent most of his life in prison. He certainly wouldn't have been a hero. But that's what he was. And that's how you should remember him. Flawed, amoral, a bastard in all the senses of that word. But a hero.'

When Rachel had gone, Arie reflected on what she'd said. So some of his father's stories had been true. Not all the Robin Hood stuff about donations – that was obviously nonsense – but fighting off bandits on the journey through Europe to Palestine. That had really happened. He'd built the rest of the unlikely tale on the back of it. And, yes, he was a bastard. Arie had always known that. But, as now he knew, a bastard who could also be a hero.

CHAPTER 37

JUNE 2003, LONDON

Two days before the Robbery

Yanek had known that his conversation with Norman Arkwright could not take place in Steve's presence, so he'd suggested they have coffee together. 'There's a good place just down the road.'

'Thank you. And, yes, I'll have coffee with you. But first I need to open my box. So, if you'll excuse me...'

And now they were sitting in the coffee shop and Arkwright's glare might have unnerved someone more sensitive than Yanek. He said, 'So, Mr Ruben. Exactly what led you to talk about me to an employee of Hatton Garden?'

Yanek had had time while waiting for Arkwright to conclude his business at the safe-deposit company to call Sammy Bronstein to say that Absalom was there and then to think about the best way to play this meeting. He'd decided that only a direct approach would do. 'Asher Humphreys told me about you.'

Arkwright stared at him. 'When?'

'A few weeks ago.'

'A man telephoned me yesterday. He mentioned the same name. Unless either he was disguising his voice and accent or you are doing it now, you and he are two different people.'

'I didn't call you yesterday.'

'No. But I think you probably know who did.' When Yanek did not reply, Arkwright said, 'Let's get this on the table, shall we? You did not speak to Asher Humphreys a few weeks ago, because Asher

Humphreys has been dead for some years. And he did not know me as Norman Arkwright. There. I think I've told you everything I want to, and more than you're entitled to. You've intruded into my life for a reason. Why don't you tell me what it is?'

Yanek allowed the silence to run. There were a number of ways this could go, and only two of them would be in any way satisfactory. One would end in Arkwright's death at Yanek's hand and that was very high risk. Steve could identify him as the last person to see Arkwright alive: instead of the huge payoff Yanek had planned, his reward would be the life sentence that was mandatory in this country for anyone found guilty of murder. He needed to pursue the other. He said, 'You are Noah Absalom.'

'My name is Norman Arkwright.'

'Yes, yes, but there are men still alive who can identify you as Noah Absalom.' He took the photograph from his inside pocket and placed it on the table. 'One of those men gave me this picture. It was taken a long time ago, but they have tricks now they can pull with technology that would show how the Noah Absalom in that photograph would look today. We both know he would look just like you. The man who gave me that photograph was not Asher Humphreys because, as you have said, Asher Humphreys is dead. Do you remember how he died?'

Arkwright went on staring at Yanek in silence.

'He died the way a friend of mine died. My friend was a collector for Etzel. He collected donations to fund the journeys of Jewish people to what was then Palestine. Some of the donations were in cash, but most of them were jewellery. Collecting that stuff was dangerous. My friend died doing it. So did Asher Humphreys. I survived. I've sometimes wished it had been me who died and not my friend, because being the one who is left fills you with guilt. Why you? Why did you survive when others did not? We gave what we collected to the people we were told to give it to. In the case of me and my friend, that was a man called Shlomo. I understand that that name is not unknown to you. And Asher Humphreys gave what he collected to you. As did a number of other people, at least one of them still alive – the one who gave me your name and that photograph. Some of the people we gave the donations to were men of integrity. Good Jews. Everything they received, they passed on to be used for its intended purpose. Some – a few – were less honest. They kept back some of what they had received. Shlomo was one of those. And one man had no integrity at all. He passed on nothing. Instead, he vanished. His name was Noah Absalom. It has taken years to find you, Noah. But we are seekers after justice, and we did not stop looking.'

'So now you think you've found this man Absalom. And what do you think you can do about it? Of course I deny your ridiculous suggestion that I am him.'

'What can I do about it? Really, that's up to you. As I said, I believe in justice. Shlomo did not hand over everything we gave him, and Shlomo is dead. I killed him, Noah. I can kill you, too. Or you can buy your survival.'

'So there we have it. You're a common criminal, here to put the arm on me. Assuming I had any intention of cooperating, how much do you want? What's your price?'

'For myself, I want nothing.' He watched surprise dawn on Absalom's face. 'My sources tell me what you got away with will now be worth more than half a million British pounds. That's a lot of money, Noah. Much more than a man your age needs to see him through to the natural end of his life. But of course you had to buy the house in Cambridge. So I will be generous. I will see you here three days from now at the same time. You will bring with you clear evidence that you have donated £250,000 to Yad Vashem. Do that, and you can keep the rest. Fail, and I will do to you what I did to Shlomo.'

#

After Sammy got Yanek's call, he and Monty had spent time discussing how the interception would be done. Sammy said, 'Birchanger Green Services would be the best place, because it's chaos there. He gets out, heads for the gents or Starbucks, you stick the gun in his ribs and he gives you the keys.'

'As long as he does stop there,' said Monty. 'But he lives in Cambridge: if you know Birchanger Green is chaotic, do you think he doesn't?'

'Yanek is going to buy him coffee. Absalom is an old man now. Probably gets up three times every night to take a leak. He's going to need to relieve himself before he gets home. And that's the only service station there is.'

'It's a risk.'

'Monty, you take risks all the time.'

'Yes. For Israel.'

'What do you think this is for? Yanek doesn't want money for himself. Everything goes to Yad Vashem. And we need them. Time is passing. The people who were alive in Hitler's day are dying. Yad Vashem keep the memory of what he and his followers did. You think kids are taught in school about attempts to kill the Jews? Not outside Israel, they aren't. You think they understand how close we came to seeing every last Jew slaughtered? They don't. There are still people who won't give up until they've destroyed Israel and everyone in it. And the number of people who don't understand why Israel defends itself is growing. The risks are worth taking. And what's the worst that can happen?'

'I suppose you're right. If he doesn't stop at the service station, there'll be other opportunities. I'll just have to keep watch.'

'You wouldn't break into the house?'

'Not likely. He might have CCTV. Even if he doesn't, it might be in the street. It's all over the place these days. I don't want my face in police records.'

'That's right. You don't. And as you say, CCTV is all over the place. Including at Birchanger Green. So if he does stop there, take care. So, are we on?'

'We are on.'

'I'll drive.'

In fact, it went more smoothly than they could have hoped. Sammy drove, and they picked up Absalom's Range Rover as it left the car park. On Monty's instructions, Sammy kept two cars between them. Monty said, 'It wouldn't fool someone trained to look out for watchers, but Absalom won't suspect anything.' They picked their way through the crowded roads to join the M11 at South Woodford. Thirty minutes later, the tension rose as they approached Birchanger Green service station. Would he stop, or wouldn't he? It was only when his left indicator light signalled he was about to leave the motorway that Monty realised how long he'd been holding his breath. He let it out with a sigh of relief. 'He's stopping.'

The traffic was as difficult as they'd expected and the cause was obvious: inadequate access to the exit roundabout fed all the way back to cause delays. That gave Monty an idea. He'd been planning to get Absalom walking across the car park and he was carrying a hat and a breathing mask to cover the lower half of his face and throw CCTV off the scent. But if he could get into Absalom's car before it was parked, cameras would not be a problem. And Absalom's car, like the one he was in, was moving forward so slowly it might as well have been stationary. He said, 'Follow us.' Then he slipped on a pair of nitrile gloves, palmed his pistol, jumped out of the car, ran past the two cars in front, opened the Range Rover's passenger door and slipped in beside Absalom. 'Hello, Noah.'

A startled gasp and then Absalom said, 'Who are you?'

'Oh, Noah. Have you forgotten so quickly? We spoke only yesterday.'

'I don't know what you're talking about. My name isn't Noah. I'm Norman Arkwright. Get out of my car, please.'

'Noah. What you feel in your ribs is the working end of a Glock 19 semiautomatic pistol. It's standard issue for the Israeli Defence Force, and that's how I came by it. I don't want to press the trigger because that would make a mess from which I'd have to extricate myself. But, if you make it necessary, press it I will. Now drive into the car park. Don't try to attract anyone's attention because, if you do, you will die. And they will die too, and although your past record tells me that won't trouble you much, I don't have your alleycat morals and I'd prefer to avoid any deaths. Including yours.'

Absalom drove the car. Once into the car park, Monty said, 'Right over there, please. Where you'll have the longest walk to relieve yourself. Though I imagine you're in danger of doing that right here and now.'

When the Range Rover was parked, Absalom said, 'What are you going to do?'

'Do? I'm going to talk to you, Noah. I'm going to say the things you really should have heard a long time ago. And then I'm going to let you go.'

'Can it wait? I need to go to the gents.'

'Just hear this, Noah. You met someone today who told you to make a donation to Yad Vashem. Do it, Noah. Or face the consequences. Now go and have your piss. And don't call anyone while you're away, or ask for help. I'll still be here when you get back. And so will the Glock.' When Absalom reached for the keys, Monty said, 'Leave them. I may decide to drive your nice car away. Just so you'll know I mean what I say.'

He watched Absalom walk away. Taking the keys from the ignition, he spread them out on the seat beside him and used his phone to take a picture of the safe-deposit key. Then he put the keys back where they had been, left the car and walked to where Sammy was waiting for him. Sammy's nervousness didn't end until they had passed the exit roundabout and were back on the M11 heading for London, but Monty was at ease. He'd been through far worse adventures than this in his time.

CHAPTER 38

JUNE 2003, LONDON

The day before the Robbery

After all these years, Peter was still never far from Ilana's mind. She did not regret giving him up because it had saved his life. If he'd stayed with her the Germans would almost certainly have killed him. They'd have killed Yudka, too. She'd heard and read about people – women – in fact, most often young women or girls – who had had a child they should not have had, or a child they could not raise, or one their families would not accept, and they had given the child up for adoption. That, really, was what she had done with Peter and with Yudka. And what she knew from what she'd read and heard was that those mothers who had given up a child for adoption lived the rest of their lives wondering how things had gone. The tiny scrap of humanity that could not feed or dress itself or keep itself clean would now be an adult. Had it been loved as she would have loved it? Was it loved now?

She could accept that she would never now know the life Peter had led after she gave him away but to accept it was not to be reconciled to it. There were times even now when she could not hold back the tears.

But Yudka had been given back to her, and through her she had also been given Fanni, a granddaughter she might never have known. She could not put into words the joy she felt when Fanni visited her in Israel. 'The last I heard from your mother was that you were at the university.'

'I graduated! With distinction!'

'And you came here!'

'You know, after the war, Granny never hid from my mother how she came to have her.' She looked solemn for a moment. 'I call her Granny, but I suppose you...'

'She is your grandmother, Fanni. She brought up Yudka, and I have no doubt she helped Yudka raise you. She was a real grandmother to you. That's what you should call her. She deserves it. But there's no reason why you should not have more than one grandmother. And I...'

'I can call you Granny, too?'

'Nothing would delight me more. You were telling me why you came to Israel.'

'Yes. As I said, my mother grew up knowing where she came from. I mean that she was Jewish. And she passed that on to me. So I came here to look for my roots.' She laughed. 'And I found them because you: you are my roots!'

Ilana joined in the laughter. 'I suppose I am. Me and all those generations of Jews going all the way back to Abraham. How long do you think you'll stay?'

Suddenly, Fanni looked just a little shy. 'Well, that's a question. Originally, I meant to stay for only a few months. But... You know what they say. Life is what happens while you're making other plans.'

Ilana looked at the girl's face. There were things that could cause that level of happiness. But there weren't many. She said, 'You've met someone here.'

'His name is Saar.'

'A nice name. Does your mother know? And will I meet him?'

And now the laughter was back. 'Yes, my mother knows. Of course she knows. And yes, I'd love you to meet him.'

'Bring him to dinner. On Friday – bring him on Friday. I'll ask Bat-Sheva to join us with her family. It will be a celebration to start Shabbat.'

'It's a date... Grandma.' And she giggled.

#

When Yanek got home, Esther was waiting for him. 'Rosa is out shopping.' She spat the words out and turned away.

'Esther, I need to talk to you.'

She whirled back to face him. 'But I have no wish to talk to you.'

'What have I done to upset you like this?'

'Upset? Me? I'm not upset. But I will be, if you don't leave me alone.'

He went to his room. Esther's hostility told him he might have very little time left to complete his plan. He wanted a rehearsal: a run-through to make sure all the keys were working but to take nothing. It needed to be on a Saturday because all the people he was targeting were Orthodox Jews and they would not even consider working on a Saturday. He had better make it this coming Saturday before he ran out of time. Then the actual heist could take place the following Saturday. There were plans he needed to make.

At five, Esther knocked on his door. 'Rosa wants you to know she is home.'

There wasn't much doubt that that was a summons. Rosa wanted to see him. But for what? As her lover? Or as someone who had just been sold out by Esther?

The open smile with which Rosa greeted him set his mind at ease. He hadn't been shopped – at least for now. Rosa crossed the room, wrapped her arms round him and raised her face to be kissed. 'Did you miss me?'

'Always.'

She poured coffee for both of them. 'Sit down. Talk to me. Tell me all there is to know about Moshe Ruben. I want to know who you are, who you've been, who you intend to be.' She lowered her eyes for a moment. 'I want to know whether your plans include me.'

Later, when they had talked, and eaten dinner, and talked again and then taken off their clothes and pleasured each other, Yanek lay beside a sleeping Rosa and struggled to get to sleep himself. He had told her so many things about his life, and almost none of them were true. Of facts, he had given her none. His ability to invent had amazed him as it had so often amazed him in the past. But this time, amazement was overshadowed by sadness.

This relationship must come to an end. He must be the one to end it, and he must do so without warning. Until then, he had to continue in this life of deception. What might his life have been if it had followed a different course? Could he have been happy, growing old side-by-side with Rosa or someone like her? And what was the point of even thinking those thoughts? The life we have is the life we have. To change his, he'd have had to go back to a time before he was born. He'd have needed to prevent his conception in the womb of that woman with the aid of whatever man it had been. If fate decreed that he, Yanek, must exist, he would have had to be created by a different man and a different woman. Two people who were together, who loved each other, who wanted a child as he had never been wanted, and who were prepared to do whatever was necessary to raise him as someone they could be proud of.

None of that was possible. He was who he was, he had the life he had, and he would have to see it through to the end. So many things he had done of which the memory alone could make him wish he had never been born. So much he had gloried in at the time that now filled him with horrified guilt. Was there anything he could be proud of? Just the one thing, but a huge one: he had been a faithful servant of Judaism. Many people were in Israel living lives they could be proud of and raising children who were a credit to the Jewish nation who would not have been there without him.

And then his thoughts took another turn. Suppose he had been the loved son of a man and woman who also loved each other? Would he have achieved those things for Israel that he had achieved? Almost certainly not. He'd have been herded into the gas chambers like so many other upright men. He thought about the collectors he had met in his Etzel meetings. None of them had lived his exact life, but all of them had lived on the fringes of legality if not on the wrong side of it. God had needed people like them to do His work. God had needed him – Yanek. And that was why he had been born. And if God had created him for a purpose, God would now want him to finish the job.

And as that thought filled him, he slipped into a deep and peaceful sleep.

CHAPTER 39

26 JUNE 2003, LONDON

The day before the Robbery

It's Friday. Yanek doesn't know it, but this is the day when Fanni is bringing Saar to have dinner with Ilana, Joseph and Bat-Sheva. Yanek will be eating dinner with Rosa, but before that he has to finish all the preparations for the Hatton Garden rehearsal he plans for tomorrow. Thanks to Esther, he is doing this before he is really ready and so – including Noah Absalom's key of which Monty had texted him the picture – he has been able to cut only six keys. He would have liked more, but six will have to be enough.

In his room, he lays out all six keys and the master key and looks at them. If only they could talk, he could ask them: Are you going to work for me? Are you going to make it possible? Are you going to allow the Jewish people finally to have justice? He checks the tiny notation he has made on each key against the list he has written that shows which key unlocks which box. Everything seems to be in order. It's time to go downstairs to join Rosa.

#

Rosa says the blessing and lights two candles. Dinner starts with blessings over a cup of wine before she hands Yanek a piece of challah, takes one for herself and then slices the rest of the loaf. There's hummus to dip the challah into. The first course is a clear chicken soup with matzo balls, lokshen and thin slices of carrot. After that, roast chicken with potato kugel and steamed broccoli, green beans and peas. It is, in fact, a traditional Jewish Friday night dinner but however traditional it may be it's food that Yanek never ate until he reached the kibbutz. Ilana, of course, had always served meals like this on Fridays, however short of money he'd kept her, and she seemed unable to understand that he knew nothing of what to her was at Judaism's core. After the chicken came a fruit salad. Yanek had developed a love for Rosa's cheesecake, but under kosher rules, no dairy product could be eaten as part of a meal that included meat.

The meal over, they sat together and Yanek allowed a sense of peace to come over him, knowing that it could be the last he would experience for a long time – if, indeed, it ever returned to him. Washing the dishes was for Esther to do, and Rosa had made sure that everything that would be eaten next day was already prepared, because no work could be done on a Saturday. And that was behind her question. 'Will you be here all day tomorrow?'

The reference to the next day shook Yanek, who was only too aware of what he planned to do. 'Tomorrow? Oh. No, I don't suppose so.'

'No. You never seem to spend Saturdays here. Unlike my other boarders. Which synagogue do you go to?'

That shook him even more. Of course Rosa would expect him to spend part of the sabbath in the synagogue. He should have had an answer prepared, but their relationship had built so fast he'd never had time to make it a priority. He said, 'It depends where my wanderings take me.'

'Wanderings?'

'Yes. You know. I like to wander around. Get to know the city. For me, it's a good use of Saturdays. So many people are working, and I get pleasure from watching them. Sometimes if the weather is good I sit in one of the parks and people-watch. In the winter I went up to White Hart Lane to watch Tottenham Hotspur a few times but of course there's no football right now.' Improvising furiously, he lied, 'I did try going to The Oval, but cricket is a mystery to me. I hadn't a clue what was going on. So really, I'm just filling the time.'

'Perhaps I could come and fill it with you?'

Why had he not been prepared for this? He knew the answer to that: even though he'd been married to Ilana, he had no real understanding of how life between a man and a woman who loved each other should be conducted. Of course Rosa would want to spend more time with him. But tomorrow it would not be possible. It would not be possible the following Saturday, either. Tomorrow he must carry out his practice run at Hatton Garden and next Saturday he must do it for real. And after that the question would not arise because he would no longer be here. He couldn't tell Rosa any of that, but he needed an answer. And, as though God looked into his heart and saw the worry there, the answer came. 'That would be wonderful. Not first thing, because that's my exercise time. But I could be back here by twelve and we could go out and spend the afternoon together. If the weather stays good, it could be a great time.'

She looked amused. 'Exercise time? What on earth is your exercise time?'

He pasted onto his face a look that said, "I didn't want to tell you, but you've caught me." He said, 'Doctor's orders. I have to walk an hour a day. And one day a week I have to walk not less than two hours, though I try to make it three. And I don't mean the kind of happy walking you and I might do together, holding hands and talking to each other. I mean hard, fast walking. It's for my heart.'

Amusement was gone. 'You have a problem with your heart? Why have you never said?'

'I don't like to make a thing of it. It isn't serious, I'm not going to drop dead today or tomorrow. The doctor said there's no reason I shouldn't make old bones. As long as I do the walking.' Really, the lies he could tell sometimes amazed him.

'I had no idea. Well, my love, I want you to make old bones because I want us to make them together. So, all right – tomorrow afternoon. But will you still want to go out in the afternoon if you've done three hours hard walking in the morning?'

'I certainly will. Recent experience suggests being outside with you might involve a lot less exercise than being together in here.'

Rosa slapped his arm. 'Don't be filthy.' She leaned close and kissed him. 'On the other hand... Why don't we go and be filthy together right now?'

And Yanek couldn't think of a single reason not to.

#

When he woke next morning, he felt strangely calm. Today was a day that could go spectacularly wrong. If he aroused suspicion and the security guards called the police, everything would unravel and the months he had spent here would be wasted. He'd very likely be deported at the very least: he might even go to jail. Well, he'd faced worse threats. If anything had gone wrong when he and Zoltan had carried that briefcase around, dressed like Germans and with no sign of the yellow Star of David, they wouldn't have been threatened with deportation. They'd have been killed. And Zoltan had been killed, and so might he have been. Even if they jailed him, so what? He could handle it.

He ate breakfast, went to his room, collected all the safe-deposit box keys and said goodbye to Rosa. She said, 'Walk hard, my love. Keep yourself well. I'll see you at midday.' And she kissed him.

He had two things on his side when he arrived at Hatton Garden. The first was that there was no camera inside the safe-deposit box room and the second was that the guards did not stay in the room after turning the master key. After the actual robbery the following week there would be a good deal of fuss about that, but when management had wanted to install a camera, customers had threatened to take their business elsewhere. Too many safe-deposit boxes contained things the people renting the boxes could not explain and they weren't happy about the thought that they'd be seen on a security screen, much less recorded for future reference. That was also why guards were required to leave the room before the box was opened. Customers didn't want anyone watching them when they handled what was in the boxes. There were those who said that Britain's entire national debt could be repaid from the taxes on what was hidden in Hatton Garden.

Walking through the door, he felt exactly as he had all those years ago collecting donations for Etzel. Keyed up and on edge, but ready for anything. A fatalistic acceptance that, good or bad, what was going to happen was going to happen. Steve was not on duty that morning, but the guard who took him into the room was welcoming. He'd seen Yanek many times before, and enjoyed coffee and doughnuts at his expense more than once. 'Good morning, Mr Ruben. Are you well?'

'Never better, Malcolm. And you?'

'Mustn't grumble, Mr Ruben.' He turned the master key on the box Yanek indicated. 'I'll see you when you're done.' And he left Yanek alone in the room. Ignoring his own boxes, Yanek went to Noah Absalom's box, turned the master key and then the key he had cut when Monty Bronstein had sent him the photograph. It was only when both keys had turned and the box had swung open that he realised he'd been holding his breath. It had worked. It had worked! He had been confident, but even so the relief that surged through him almost made him shout out. That wouldn't do – he didn't want to bring Malcolm back in here to find out what was happening. He closed Absalom's box and turned his attention to Rosenbaum's. For all kinds of reasons he felt a particular hostility towards Rosenbaum. The master key clicked, his own copy of the other key clicked, and Rosenbaum's box opened. Two out of two. Nothing was going to stop him. And nothing date, because the next four boxes all opened as easily as Absalom's and Rosenbaum's. In each case, he slid the box out, glanced inside, and then pushed it back and locked it once more into position. When he walked back into the reception area, he smiled at Malcolm. 'Thank you. I probably won't be back until next Saturday.'

'Going on holiday, Mr Ruben?'

'Not exactly, Malcolm. But, you know. Things to do. Life moves along.' And then he was out on the street and heading back to Golders Green, a smile on his face that Rosa would interpret as meaning that he was pleased to see her.

CHAPTER 40

27 JUNE 2003, LONDON

The day of the Robbery

The sense of calm continued. Yanek spent so much time at home that Rosa commented on it. 'Don't take this the wrong way, my love, but you used to spend most of every day out. And now you go out much less. I'm not complaining, quite the reverse, it's lovely to have you around, it makes me feel we really are an item. I just hope you're not neglecting things that should not be neglected.'

'I don't think I am. And I do go out most days. But I'd rather be here with you. I've never... It's a new experience for me.'

'Yes. That's the impression I get. Listen, I've never pried and I don't want to now, but there's so much I don't know about your past.'

'There is, isn't there?'

When he didn't go on, Rosa said, 'As I said, I don't want to pry. But I would like to know... I think I'm entitled to know... Have you been married? Are you married now?'

'I was married. It was a long time ago and it was not a success. I think we both had reasons for marrying that weren't good reasons. In my case, I was looking for something I'd never had before. I knew it had to be out there somewhere and I was right, because I have it now. With you.'

She hugged him tightly and kissed him. 'That's a lovely thing to say. It's just what I wanted to hear. But it's all over – you aren't still married?'

'No. We divorced.'

'Do you have children?'

'A boy and a girl. They took their mother's side when we split. I can't say I blame them: I wasn't cut out to be a parent. I'm not even sure where they are now, or what they're doing.'

Rosa was silent for a while. Then she said, 'You told me what your reason for marrying was. You didn't tell me hers.'

'Oh, I think she made the mistake I've seen a lot of women make with a lot of men. She wanted to change me. She thought she could. She was wrong.'

Rosa's silence this time was even longer. Then she said, 'I'm going to take that as a warning.'

'I didn't mean...'

She hushed him with a kiss. 'Yes you did. And I think you're right. It's a mistake lots of women make. I'll avoid it.'

Later, Rosa said, 'You spend every night in my bed. You eat your meals down here instead of with the other boarders. Why don't you move all your stuff down?'

'You want to let my room to someone else?'

'That isn't what I had in mind, but it's certainly something I could do.'

Yet again, Yanek found himself thanking God's mysterious ways of solving problems. He needed to move some of his things to Sammy Bronstein's house before Saturday, because after Saturday he would not be coming back here and he didn't want the police to find his key-cutting machine. Also, he wanted to have some clothes there that he could change into before he flew out of the country. He'd worried about Rosa's possible reaction when she saw him taking things out of the house. And now she herself had provided a solution. He said, 'I will. I've got some things up there that I'm keeping for other people. Let me take those to them so they don't just clutter up the place down here. And thank you for trusting me.'

She wrapped her arms around him. 'I want to feel that you're really mine. I know you are, but knowing isn't feeling. If you move in, I'll feel secure.'

He had stopped allowing himself to feel guilt about what he was doing to Rosa. It was in a higher cause and, if she was going to suffer from it, so was he. Even so, he couldn't suppress a feeling of remorse and a wish, that came ever more frequently these days, that his life had gone in a different direction.

#

27 June 2003, Israel

About the time that conversation was taking place, Saar was talking to Fanni. 'You need to stay close to your grandmother.'

'Close? Why?'

'Didn't you see? When we were there on Friday? She puts on a brave face, but she hasn't long to go.'

'She's ill?'

'She's *old*, Fanni. No-one lives forever, and Ilana's time is not far away. Try to be with her as much as you can. Build up the memories.'

'Should I tell my mother?'

But when she did, Yudka said, 'I know, darling. Saar is right: she's getting on in years. The man and woman she gave me to, the ones who raised me as mother and father, the ones you grew up calling grandad and grandma, they are old, too and I don't suppose it will be long before we are mourning them. But they've had nothing like Ilana's hard life. Think about it. Her parents died in the camps. So did her first husband. She had two children, me and Peter, and she had to give us both up. She's never seen Peter again. She stayed out of the camps because she had a job cooking in a hotel taken over by the very army that had killed her family. She made it here to Israel where she married again, and this time to a complete shit. He made her life a misery. Kept her short of food and money. And all the time, the years were passing. Of course she's old. Of course she doesn't have much time left. The world will be a poorer place when she's gone.'

#

Saturday came, and the sense of calm vanished. This was the point of no return. In every sense. Not just the culmination of years of planning. Not just the final revenge for Zoltan's death. Not just punishment for those who deserved to be punished. All of that was justice in the old-fashioned, Adam and Eve, Lot's wife, Korah and his family tradition, and all of it was good.

But there was also Rosa. He'd never dreamed, growing up in Berehove, that he'd ever be in love like this. When he'd married Ilana, there'd been nothing of this. He'd been a man in the prime of life with a man's needs and a woman on hand to satisfy them had been the obvious solution. But the Yanek he'd been then and the Yanek he was now were two different people. Was Rosa herself responsible for the change? Who could say? But he was going to miss her more than he'd ever missed anything. The feeling in his stomach was one he'd never known, even when he and Zoltan had carried out their most daring raids. He'd never been scared. He wasn't scared now: what would be, would be. But he was nervous as hell.

When he arrived at Hatton Garden, he was carrying a very large bag. He had a story prepared to explain it, but the story wasn't needed. Steve, the guard on duty that morning, simply assumed he was going shopping after he left. And it wasn't unusual for Hatton Garden customers to bring bags with them. They kept things here, valuable things, and sometimes they would want to take some of them away. Part of the reason for renting a safe-deposit box was that no-one would ask what you kept there. If Steve had been paying attention, he might have noticed that Yanek was paler than usual. But he seemed tense, and more hurried than he'd been in the past. That his eyes, which had always held Steve's in the past, now looked anywhere but directly at him. But this was just one more routine visit, and who pays attention during routine events?

They went into the room, Steve turned the master key on all four of Yanek's boxes, and left. Yanek took nitrile gloves from the bag and put them on. He would need to be quick: although it was Saturday, and still early, not all Hatton Garden customers were Orthodox Jews and there was no knowing when someone might turn up and want to take their turn in the room. He held his hands in front of him. Not a tremor: they were as steady as if he'd be doing something both law-abiding and boring. For all that, he could feel his heart racing. He'd never allowed himself to think about what would happen if things went wrong, because what would be the point of that? If it all turned to rat shit, well, rats had been defecating on human endeavours since our ancestors first came down from the trees. Look at the Black Death. But he was thinking about it now. Get it right and he'd still be the loser because Rosa would be gone from his life. But get it wrong and the jail time he'd dodged so often when he was younger would come to him now. He didn't think he could stand it.

He started with Rosenbaum's box, and if he'd been worried before, he was petrified now. The box refused to open. Dear God, they knew! They'd let him get this far thinking everything was as it should be and they KNEW. Steve had led him in here and turn the master key for him as though nothing was wrong, and all the time he was playing with him. Yanek's shoulders slumped. It was all over. The restaurant sold, all the money spent, Rosa's love thrown away, and for what? For a plan that had been rumbled from the start.

How? How could they know? And, of course, the moment he asked the question he knew the answer. The Bronsteins. Ever since Sammy had seen him on the bus, he'd known Yanek was up to something. So he'd befriended him, and brought Monty in on the act – Monty, whose whole life was spent in subterfuge and finding out things people didn't want him to know. And they had told the people at Hatton Garden what he was up to. And the police? Had they told the cops, too? Bound to have.

He squared up. Get it over with. There was always the chance he could bluff it out – he'd done that often enough. And what had he done? Nothing. He'd tried to open Rosenbaum's box, but no-one had seen him. He walked through the door back into reception. Steve took one look at his dejected expression and said, 'Oh, no, Yanek. Not you as well?'

Yanek looked at him. 'What?'

'You haven't had one of your boxes jam?'

The innocence in the man's expression – could it possibly be real? It looked real. 'What do you mean?'

'Mr Rosenbaum came in yesterday and the lock on his box jammed. We had to get it replaced and it took ages. Have you...'

Yanek felt so light-hearted he thought he might float into the air. 'No. No, Steve, not at all. I just suddenly felt dizzy and I thought I'd better get out of there for a moment.'

'Oh, dear. I hope you're not coming down with something. Let me get you a glass of water.'

Yanek drank the water and sat in the chair Steve led him to so solicitously. He watched two Hatton Garden customers come into reception, go one at a time into the safe-deposit room with Steve, and come out again. Then he said, 'Thanks, Steve. I think I'm okay again now. Come with me and turn your key.'

When Steve had gone back into reception, Yanek turned quickly to the second box, turned the master key and then the renter's key – and it opened! Whatever had happened to the Rosenbaum box was not affecting the others. Slowly, his heartbeat returned to something closer to normal. There was no time to go through the individual boxes picking out what was valuable and what was not, so he dropped the whole box into the large bag. Then he turned to the next, and then the next, until he had cleared the lot.

The next step was to close all the boxes he had opened and inject superglue into the locks to delay their opening. And then the gloves were back in the bag and he was in reception, shaking Steve's hand and saying goodbye. There was no time today for long chats and an invitation to coffee. And nor was there any need: Yanek's involvement with Hatton Garden was over. He had made use of Steve and the other guards and he no longer needed them.

#

27 JUNE 2003, LONDON

His time with Rosa was over, too, and that was something he didn't even want to think about right now. When he was out of sight of Hatton Garden, he stopped and leaned against the wall. He was breathing heavily. He had done even better than he had hoped – but it wasn't over yet. He had to get rid of the things he had stolen, and then he had to get out of the country. He would not feel at ease until he was back in Israel, and perhaps not even then.

He had to shake himself to get back in motion. There were things to be done and they would not wait. Thirty minutes later, he was in Sammy Bronstein's house. He dropped the bag onto a sofa. 'I'm going to shave this beard off and then I'm going to change my clothes. Empty the boxes and see what we've got.'

Removing the beard took time, but when he looked into the mirror he was satisfied. No-one who didn't know him well would look at him and see Moshe Ruben. He pulled on a checked shirt he'd bought just for this journey and his only pair of jeans, which he had not worn since the day he landed in England. He stepped back from the mirror to see the whole effect. It would do – but time was passing and he needed to be gone.

Downstairs again, he said, 'How did we do?'

Sammy spread his arms to show the spread of jewellery and the piles of dollars and pounds sterling, some in bank wrappers and some in elastic bands. 'It's a fortune.'

'I'll never get it past security. In any case, it will take time to dispose of it all. You'll see that the money gets to Yad Vashem.'

'You can trust us, Yanek.'

'I know that. I haven't the slightest doubt.'

'But take the dollars. You can easily change those once you get to Israel.'

'I didn't do this for me. I want nothing out of it.'

'Yanek. You've spent your own money on this. You had a successful restaurant, but it isn't waiting for you to go back and pick it up again. Yad Vashem and the state of Israel will thank you, but you're entitled to reimburse yourself. What are you going to live on when you get back home?'

'You could give it to Rosa.'

Sammy gave an exasperated sigh. 'There's a lot of British money on that table. Take out the amount you owe Rosa. I'll see she gets it.' When Yanek had done that, Sammy said, 'That's at least twice what she's due. Maybe three times. She was only renting you a room and feeding you, for God's sake.'

'She gave me a lot more than that, Sammy. I want her to have it.'

'Then she will. But only if you take the dollars.'

Yanek hesitated for a moment, but time was pressing. He said, 'You'll see the rest gets to Yad Vashem?'

'Every penny.'

'Okay, then.' And he picked up the dollars, put some in his pocket, and the rest into his bag.

'Monty will drive you to the airport.'

#

London, Heathrow – the getaway

What followed were three of the most anxiety-ridden hours Yanek had ever experienced. Even evading the law as a youth in Berehove; even staying alive in the camp, sometimes by ending the lives of other prisoners whose failure to meet quotas threatened his own existence; he had never known nervousness like this. He had faced armed bandits on the road from Lublin to Metaponto and been fired at when he intervened to prevent Rachel's abduction, and still nothing matched the tension he felt now. Driving to the airport with Monty, every time a police car passed or he saw a man in uniform standing by the roadside or heard a siren, he felt sure the game was up and they were coming for him. Once in the airport and through check-in, he expected at every moment to feel a hand on his shoulder and to hear a voice saying, 'Would you come with us, sir?'

The flight was called and El Al's seemingly endless security procedures racked up the stresses even more. Finally, he was seated on the aircraft, his cabin bag in the locker above him, and the cabin crew was about to go through the safety demonstration. Surely, take-off could not be delayed much longer?

And then it happened. He'd been right to worry: he was not going to make it out of here safely. A stewardess was bending down and speaking quietly to him. 'Mr Hoffman. Would you come with me, please?' She was smiling, but he wasn't fooled. The game was up. He wondered how many years in an English prison he was in line for, and whether he'd live long enough to go home. The stewardess opened the overhead locker. 'Is this your bag, Mr Hoffman? Let me carry it for you.'

He was in a daze as he walked towards the exit. But instead of turning at the door, the stewardess kept walking. Surely there wasn't another door in front of them? And then the stewardess had stopped. She was still smiling. 'Mr Hoffman,' she said. 'I'm afraid we've overbooked in the economy section. We need to upgrade someone. Would you mind?' And she gestured towards a much larger seat than the one he had just left. Yanek sank into it.

The stewardess turned to another member of the cabin crew, who came forward, turned down the tray in front of Yanek's new seat and placed on it a glass of champagne. The stewardess opened the locker above him and stowed his cabin bag. 'Enjoy the flight, Mr Hoffman.'

And then he was alone. And, finally, he began to believe. He'd done it! Zoltan had died for the cause for which he and Yanek had both risked their lives. And not just Zoltan - others, too, had made the ultimate sacrifice so that their fellow Jews could live lives of decency and self-respect. A handful of men had taken advantage of them and diverted the proceeds of their efforts for their own enrichment. And he, Yanek Hoffman, born and raised in squalid poverty, had executed revenge on them on behalf of each of the dead. It was over. He had succeeded.

As he drank the champagne he heard the aircraft's doors closing. Then they began to move, towed backwards away from the stand, ready to taxi out to the runway and climb into the sky for the journey to the country that he had helped found.

He breathed a prayer of thanks to everyone who had helped him. And another, of remembrance for those who were gone. And then one more, for the almost unbearable loss of Rosa. He had had to do what he had done. There hadn't been any choice. And when he embarked on it, he hadn't known what he was letting himself in for. How could he have known? In all the years he'd lived, and sometimes he felt the number was unbearable, he'd never known what it was simply to love and be loved. Until Rosa. He had only one way to deal with this degree of pain. And that was to forbid himself ever to think about her again.

CHAPTER 41

29 JUNE 2003, LONDON

The day after the Robbery

Mr Ruben did not come home at midday as Rosa had expected. Nor did he come home that evening to share her bed. She telephoned every hospital in London with an Accident and Emergency ward to ask whether he'd been admitted, with no success. At 8 o'clock, she called the police to report him missing but they made it clear that they would take no interest in the absence of an adult male in possession of all his faculties who was not married to the person notifying them unless additional information came into their possession. Next morning, her fears that something irretrievably wrong had happened were strengthened when a boy of about twelve on a bicycle knocked on her door and handed her a package. She said, 'Where did you get this?'

'A man gave it to me.'

'A man? What man? Describe him.'

The boy shrugged. 'He was just a man. I've never seen him before. He gave me this and said I could have a pound if I brought it here.' He opened his hand to show the pound.

'Where? Where was he when he did this?'

The boy pointed to the corner of the road. 'Just there.'

'Show me!' And she ran to the corner the boy had pointed to, with him pedalling hard to catch up. But there was no-one there. 'This was the place?'

The boy nodded. 'He's gone.'

Rosa walked slowly back to the house and took the package into her room. It contained a card saying:

For The Rent

and what turned out to be more than £4000 in cash. Rosa collapsed into a chair. It was over. She hadn't until now allowed herself to know how deeply she had fallen for Mr Ruben, or how much hope she had placed in a life with him. She picked up the phone and called her sister. 'Something's happened. I don't really know what yet, but something terrible. Please. I need you here.'

#

Monday. One by one, the robbed men were to discover what had happened to them. First to arrive at Hatton Garden was Steinbeck. He was early because he had a meeting scheduled with a client for whom he had bought a 5 carat diamond to be made into a ring as a sixtieth birthday gift for the client's wife. He had been full of this purchase: only a few days earlier, he had told his very good friend Moshe Ruben all about it. He greeted the security officer and they went together into the safe-deposit room where the guard turned the master key without difficulty – but when Steinbeck tried to insert his own key, it would not go in. Another dealer, one not on Yanek's list, came in, opened his box, took something out and put something else in, and left. Steinbeck was still trying to open his own box when his good friend David Rod arrived. He had no more success than Steinbeck in opening his box and when he peered closely, for he had cataracts and was waiting for an appointment to remove them, he said, 'There's something in there.'

Steinbeck look more closely at his and said, 'I think it's glue!' He went to the door and shouted for a security guard. 'We need the owner here. We need him now.'

It was nearly one o'clock when the owner of the Hatton Garden Safe Deposit company arrived and by that time no fewer than five of his clients had found their boxes impossible to open. By the time the five had been identified, the guards were making anyone else who came wait outside.

There were strict rules around the forcible opening of boxes and replacement of locks. The job had to be done by two independent locksmiths in front of police witnesses and it was four in the afternoon before the work could proceed. By that time, thirty customers were waiting outside.

When the jammed boxes were opened and found to be empty, the police officers who had arrived to witness their opening brought the five box owners together in a separate room and said, 'We're going to need contact details for all of you. CID are going to want to talk to you. I suggest you all draw up a complete list of everything that's been stolen. CID will need that to trace the items when they come up for sale.' They couldn't fail to see the alarm on the faces of the men in front of them.

#

Steve had watched the CCTV film again and again. He revolted heart and soul against the obvious conclusion, but the evidence was clear. When a detective sergeant and detective sat down to talk to him, he pointed it out. 'Mr Ruben. Watch him. He arrives carrying a large bag. I thought nothing of that: perhaps he was going shopping, perhaps he was collecting stuff from his own boxes... But look at him on his way out. See? When I take him into the room, the bag looks empty. When he comes out...'

'It's bulging,' said the sergeant.

'Yes it is,' said Steve. 'Of course he might have emptied all four of his own boxes in there.'

'We'll have to check them,' said the sergeant. 'See if there's anything in them.'

'You need a warrant before we can let you do that,' said Steve.

'Trust me, Steve. I know the law. I don't think getting a warrant will be difficult. Tell me about Mr Ruben.'

'Well, that's just the point. I can't believe he'd do something like this.'

'Do you know him well?'

'He's a customer. But, yes... I think I know him well. He is almost a friend. In fact, he is a friend. And there aren't any other customers I'd say that of.'

'We need to talk to him. Do you have his address?'

But when Steve had given them Mr Ruben's address and they'd gone there, the solution to the case seemed clearer because Mr Ruben's landlady hadn't seen him since Saturday and didn't know where he might be. She handed over the card saying

For The Rent.

'I don't think he's coming back.'

'No. What was with this card? Was it money?'

Rosa looked him right in the eye. 'Yes,' she said. '£500.'

'You still have it?'

'I'm afraid not. I put it in the bank.'

'That was quick.'

She shrugged. 'I was overdrawn. I wanted to cover it.'

'Who else knew Mr Ruben?'

'He was friendly with some of the other boarders here. Friendly, no more than that. But you could try a man called Sammy Bronstein.'

'Do you know where we can find him?'

'No. I'm sorry. But there can't be that many Sammy Bronsteins in London.'

When they'd gone, her sister said, 'You took a chance telling them you'd already got rid of the money.'

'I took a chance telling them it was only £500. But they aren't going to know that. But if they come back and want to take the money away, £500 is what I'll give them. They're British. You know what they'll think. I'm a Jew, so naturally I didn't want to give up any money. Makes you sick sometimes.'

'They're not all like that.'

'No. I know. But I'm not feeling very kind towards the world right now. All right?'

#

Rosa had been right to say that there couldn't be many Sammy Bronsteins in London and it didn't take the police long to find him. Just long enough, in fact, for him to have got the jewellery and what remained of the pounds, together with Yanek's clothes, out of the house and into a safe place. When the police arrived, Sammy expressed surprise that Mr Ruben could have done anything to attract their attention but regretted that he wasn't able to help. 'I know him. In fact, I offered him an investment opportunity but he turned it down. Said he couldn't spare the cash.'

'You know where he is now, sir?'

'Haven't the faintest idea. Sorry. He boards in Golders Green. I've visited him there a couple of times.'

'Yes, sir. That's how we got your name. The landlady gave it to us. But he hasn't been seen there since Saturday morning.'

'How strange. He didn't strike me as the sort to just disappear. If I hear anything, I'll let you know.'

'Thank you, sir. Sir, I'm sure we could get a warrant to search your house...'

'No need for that, officer. You want to look around? Be my guest.'

And so they did, and they were able to report back to Detective Inspector Pete Milner of Holborn CID that Mr Bronstein had been very helpful, there was no sign at his house of either the missing jewellery or the missing Moshe Ruben, and that Bronstein had no idea where the man might be.

That left Milner able to tell reporters what had happened, but not who had done it. 'It would appear that this was a well-planned and sophisticated theft,' he said against a background of CCTV footage showing a man entering and leaving the safety deposit company with an unmarked black holdall. 'He established himself in the community, becoming known, visiting people regularly, so that he'd never look out of the ordinary. Someone knows who he was. We're publicising this footage to give them a chance to come forward and tell us.'

The police could look all they liked for Moshe Ruben: they were never going to find him. The search wasn't helped by the fact that Moshe Ruben had never existed and that the only people who knew that for certain – the

Bronsteins and Rachel – weren't going to share that knowledge. Esther never told anyone how she had come across the name Yanek Hoffman, and never would, because Esther's experiences as a young woman in occupied Europe had left her unwilling to share information with anyone.

In fact, the case has never been solved.

Epilogue

29 June 2007, Israel

Four years after the Robbery

Yanek settled into life in Israel as a retired man with just enough to live on as long as he kept his ambitions low in the matter of accommodation and food. And why wouldn't he? He'd always lived that way, even when he had the money to do better. It seemed to him his life was over. From a childhood starved of both food and affection in Berehove he'd gone through enough for a dozen boys' adventure books. He'd treated a wife and two children abominably and he knew that now, but he believed he had also banked enough credit with God – if there was a God – to be forgiven. And there had to be a God because, if there wasn't, who had chosen the Jews as his people and promised them Palestine?

He made some enquiries and found that Ilana had died two weeks before he had come back to Israel. He hadn't really intended to look her up, and now he couldn't. He wasn't going to look for Arie and Bat-Sheva because he expected no welcome there. He developed a routine, shopping, cooking, and walking and it was enough for him. But it didn't last long: the day was dark and it was raining heavily when Yanek got off the bus, realised he'd left his umbrella on it and was hit by another bus as he attempted to run after the first. He was thrown thirty yards and taken to hospital, where doctors diagnosed head injuries sufficiently serious to change his life forever. The hospital administration set out to find someone who might want to take responsibility for him.

They learned his wife was dead, but that he had a son and a daughter. Reasoning that daughters tend to be more caring than sons, they told Bat-Sheva her father was in hospital. Bat-Sheva said, 'Good. Let him die there in peace. Peace is something he never seemed to know while he lived.' She told Arie about this conversation and Arie thought he had better at least take a look. As Ilana had said, "He is your father." And this is the time for Arie to take over and talk directly to you. Because I am Arie, and I have been telling you this story since the beginning.

It hasn't been easy, because I didn't know a great deal of the story I've told and, in some aspects of it, I still don't. It wasn't until 2009, when my father died, that I went into his attic and found the briefcase I told you about right at the start. That was when I realised that my father's stories weren't "stories" at all. They were things that really happened. I still don't know the whole truth: I've stitched this story together from things people have told me, from what I read in the newspapers about the Hatton Garden robberies, and – I admit it – from my own imagination when all other sources failed.

I was married and living in England when the bus hit Yanek. Yes, he was my father, but I remembered the kind of father he'd been and I could imagine only too clearly what kind of father-in-law he might make. I wasn't going to bring him to England, but I promised to visit regularly.

He had an old girlfriend, Rivka, and after the accident he started sleepwalking to her in the night. When his neighbours contacted me, I flew to Israel to find him in a shocking state. I warned him that if he did not go to a home by the end of the week there was little I could do and I would fly back to the UK, leaving him to die. To my amazement, he caved in.

For the next three years he lived like a king and with five meals a day and social activities organised by the home. But then his health started to decline and he became violent, forcing the staff to tie him to a chair 24 hours a day.

I found it hard to understand how someone of such immense physical strength and power could have ended like this. It's possible he himself might have thought that God was purifying his soul through suffering before welcoming him home – but if he did he couldn't say so because, as well as not being able to walk, he couldn't communicate very well.

One thing he was able to say was that he wanted to see the Yad Vashem Holocaust Remembrance Centre. I took him there. It was as emotional for me as it must be for all Jews, but it clearly had a greater impact on Yanek. That was the only time I ever saw him cry. I wished many times since then that he could have put his emotions into words. What would he have said? Who would he have talked about?

And then the doctors diagnosed dementia. Something I will always remember is taking him from the home one day to eat ice cream and watch Mississippi Burning at the cinema. He was as happy as a child. Shortly after that, he died.

#

But that's what happens. That's the cycle of life. We are born, we do whatever we came to earth to do, and then we die – but others live on to repeat the cycle. In 2017, my wife and I flew to Israel for the wedding of Fanni and Saar. I was sad that my mother never had the opportunity to witness this emotional occasion, but happy to see real love and the continuation of thousands of years of history.

Yanek died a sad and lonely old man. Although my sister Bat-Sheva and I never had a loving relationship with him this book is, in a way, my tribute to him. He was a bastard, and many people said so.

But he was also a hero. I had reservations about sitting Shiva for seven days, but that week of mourning changed the way I saw my father and made this book possible. Old, old men I had never heard of came to give their support. They told me about Etzel and its activities during and after the war. What they said about Yanek seemed to assume that he would have told me all about it – and, of course, he had, but I had treated what he said as just stories. I now knew they were more than that.

Those old men, and my much earlier meeting with Rachel, gave me one of this book's two main strands, the journey to Palestine across a Europe shattered by war. Then I had another visitor who gave me the other main strand: the search for revenge against those who had double-crossed and betrayed men who risked everything for a cause. Men like my father, who survived, and Zoltan, who did not. He told me I could use his story but not his real name. 'Call me Monty. Monty Bronstein. And call my brother Sammy.'

I said, 'Won't the police in London take an interest if I tell this story?'

'Of course they will. There's no statute of limitations in the UK. The Hatton Garden case is still open. But what are they going to do? Your father is dead. You don't know my real name and the Israeli security services would prevent any attempt a foreign police force might make to interview me. You do know that Israeli nationals can only be extradited for offences committed before they became Israeli nationals? So extradition would be out of the question.'

And then, of course, there was the briefcase. Taken altogether, those things made it possible for me to tell my father's story. I hope you've enjoyed it.

This is in a way a tribute to my long suffering mother, in the hands of a monster!

Yanek, 17 years old, 1942

Yanek in the middle – the Kapo, supervising in the labour camp 1944

Yanek, without a cap, privileged as a kapo

Yanek wearing the Star of David patch with Zoltan second on left 1945

Zoltan and Yanek on left with their suits ready to go on their mission

Yanek, a partisan on right, with the briefcase, in action, Vienna 1945

Yanek, centre with Zoltan on the right, Berehove, Ukraine 1946

Yanek and all fellow Jewish migrants escaping the Shabtai Luzinski to Kibbutz Nitzanim, , 4 March 1947

Ilana and Yanek on their wedding day, 1947

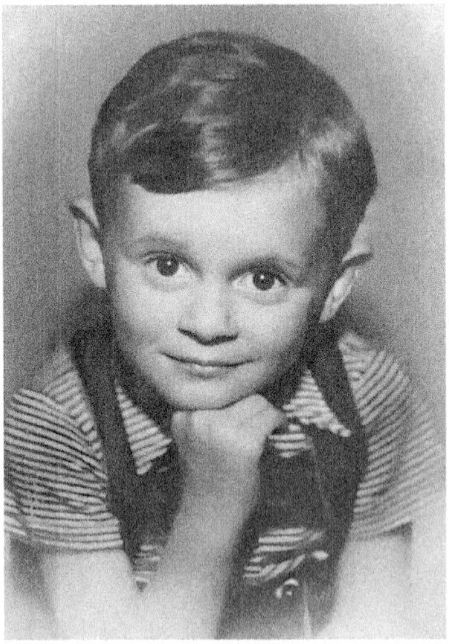

Ilana's only remaining Photo of Peter, the son she never knew after the war

Yanek second left with General Moshe Dayan testing
first air missile, 1965

Ilana and Yanek Hoffman, 1974

Arie and Bat-Sheva with the presents from uncle Mendi from America, Yanek sold both bicycles 3 days after the birthday party!

Arie and Ilana surprise first meeting of his half-sister, Yudka, Belgium 1986

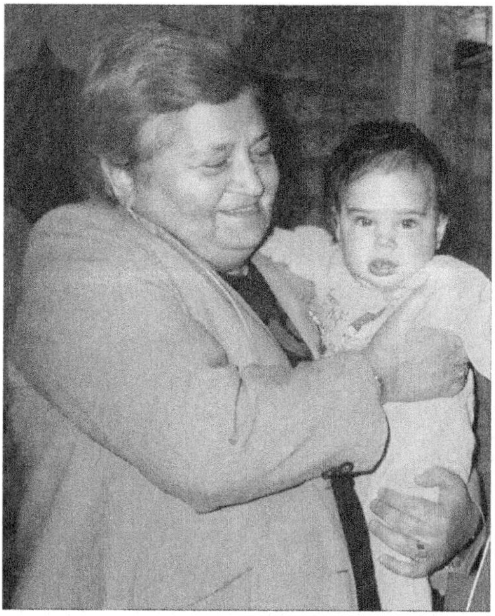

Ilana's only photo with Fanni, her great granddaughter, 1989

Arie, second left and Bat-Sheva, right at a reunion with Fanni's family in Israel 2022

BBC Home | Search | Explore the BBC

Low graphics | Accessibility help

BBC NEWS — BBC NEWS CHANNEL — News services: Your news when you want it

Last Updated: Tuesday, 15 July, 2003, 09:23 GMT 10:23 UK

E-mail this to a friend | Printable version

Hunt for £1.5m safe box raider

Police are trying to trace a man after £1.5m worth of items were stolen from safety deposit boxes in a "well planned and sophisticated theft".

Police believe the theft took place on 28 June at Hatton Gardens Safety Deposit Ltd in central London.

But the theft of the cash and jewellery was not discovered for two days.

The man detectives want to question arrived at the premises with a black holdall on the day of the robbery at 0900 BST.

Police say the theft took place between when the man arrived and noon.

The man opened an account seven months before the theft

The man had opened up a safe deposit facility seven months before under the name of Philip Goldberg and he has been described as a frequent visitor to the place.

A Scotland Yard spokesman said he also uses the name Ruben Luis.

Appealing for information, DI Pete Milner of Holborn CID said: "It would appear that this was a well planned and sophisticated theft targeting security boxes containing large amounts of cash and jewellery."

CCTV image of Yanek Hoffman aka Moshe Ruben in 88 Hatton Garden, 2003

88 Hatton Garden Safe Deposit, the old keys were never upgraded!

Yanek, in Arie's London home, showing off his 'Refael' medal, awarded him for his contribution to his country, 2004

Arie and wife Jean, returning with the grandchildren, Ben and Charlie to the childhood villa in Israel, where the briefcase was found in the attic, with daughter Lisa, husband Tom and sister Shevy, 2022

Mr [redacted]
Hatton Garden Safe Deposit Ltd
99-90 Hatton Garden
London
EC1N 8PN

Tel: 020 7405 9600

Date:21st July 2003

Author: [redacted]
Tel [redacted]

Report

This report is to show how the robbery at Hatton Garden Safe Deposit may have been achieved. The information below will describe the type of Chubb Safety Deposit Lock Key Operating System. This would be a knowledge that most competent Locksmiths would have, and will describe how easy it would be to gain entry by studying the Key System and with a certain amount of manipulation of the people involved.

I will stress at this point that I myself have been a Locksmith since 1985 (18 years). I have also had conversations with Keith White from Chubb Safes with regard to the type of Locking System that is installed. Keith White has been to this site on occasions and has a complete knowledge of the types of Locks used at this establishment.

Lets start by ruling out the possibility of the Locks being manipulated. I have taken one of the locks apart to study the workings and it would not be possible to pick or make a key impression from the lock itself. This was also confirmed by Keith White of Chubb Safes.

So with this knowledge we can understand that the robber must have had access to all of the keys required to open the boxes. So how did he get them with no participation from the people involved. To open the locks requires the use of two keys. One owned by the person renting the box, the other by the manager of the Safety Deposit.

How the keys can be read

The type of key can easily be reproduced with a flat piece of metal cut to shape. There are no complex grooves running along the key to make it more difficult. You would not have to buy ready made key blanks that would normally be available to the trade.

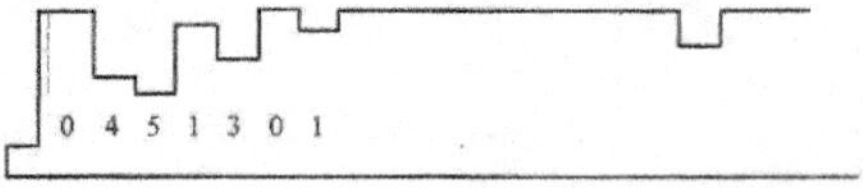

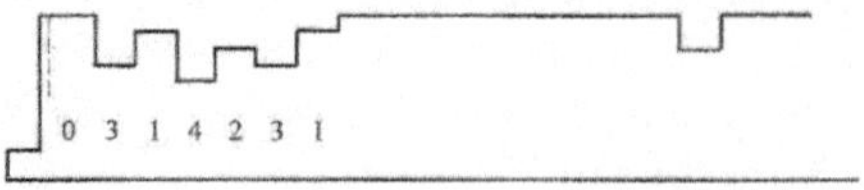

There are a total of 7 cuts in each key. Each key will start with a "0" cut, no cut at all. This is the part of the key that operates the movement of the lock bolt.

There are a total of 5 depths of cut ranging from what would originally be the blank "0" to a cut that measures half of the width of the key "5" This would represent the deepest cut of the key. "1,2,3,4" are simply increments in between. If you look at the pictures, there are 3 different keys. The numbers represent the different cut depths.

By knowing this, you can understand that by looking at a key, you can read it as a code.

The additional notch towards the head of the key is the same on every single key. It is a guide for the turning of the key in the lock.

Expert report on how the keys were easily copied, 2003

THAT'S IT!

Printed in Great Britain
by Amazon

46037520R00136